The Ruby Airship

SHARON GOSLING

Curious
Fox

Contents

One

A New Jewel

It was late, or – depending on your point of view – perhaps very early. Outside the theatre, the streets of Shoreditch were cast in deep shadow. Rémy slipped out of the Albert Saloon's stage door and stopped for a moment, looking up. The moon was curved and yellow, like a hard heel of cheese discarded against the tablecloth of the London sky. From somewhere close by came a rattling clatter, followed by the unholy racket of two alley cats doing battle.

Rémy loved this time of night. She liked it in any town or village, but when she walked the streets of London after midnight it felt as if she were seeing a different world. It was a fairy-tale world: magical, but as cruel as it was enchanting. London by night was a reflection of itself. The people living in it were different, as dark as their surroundings. Rémy enjoyed the danger of walking among them, seen but untouched. She had been one of them once, plotting dark deeds by the light of only a candle and the meagre moon. But that had been before. Now, she was free, as long as she was careful... as long as certain parts of the law didn't find her.

She set off for Limehouse Basin, still energised by her recent performance. Less than twenty minutes ago, Rémy had been on the stage. It was Saturday: payday. The coins jangled in the pocket of Rémy's heavy cloak. She was heading home, back to the Professor's old workshop.

They'd been there three months now, she and J. After all, it seemed a pity to let the old place go to rack and ruin when they were both homeless. Rémy had taken over the Professor's private study as her bedroom, and J – on the rare occasion that the boy slept – had the use of a small anteroom off the main floor. So she hadn't been alone since the circus had left London, even if a certain young policeman's visits had become less frequent than she might have once hoped.

She quickened her step, replacing thoughts of Thaddeus Rec with thoughts of food and hoping that J had left her something on the stove. Ahead of her, a carriage rattled along the narrow road before turning a corner, disappearing through the tame halo of light thrown down by a gas lamp. In her head, Rémy tried to rehearse the new routine she'd been formulating for the past week or so. The problem with being a permanent fixture at a theatre instead of in a touring circus was thinking up enough new tricks to keep the audiences coming back.

A piercing shriek shattered the gloom. There came another and then another. It wasn't cats this time, it was something even more chilling. There were shouts, men's voices overlaid by the whinnying of terrified horses, and a series of sharp bangs that sounded like someone hammering against wood with a fist or foot. Then more screams, echoing through the gaslight, shivering along the road towards her like ghosts.

Rémy ran to the corner of the street. The unlit road beyond was very dark, cast in such blackness that it was almost impossible to see what was happening. Quickly, Rémy reached into a pocket and pulled out the night-glasses she'd borrowed from J and slipped them on. The world immediately took on a faint green tinge, but at least she was no longer blind. The carriage that had passed Rémy a few moments before stood in the middle of the road at a skewed angle. The petrified horses reared between the shafts, screaming as only a scared animal can. Rémy looked for the driver, and spotted a figure lying slumped and still against the kerb. Two men were hammering at the door of the carriage, their voices menacingly loud in the dark.

"Open up, lady!"

"No need to fear us – all we want are those lovely sparklers."

"Tha's right. Hand 'em over, and you'll be right as rain. Make it difficult, and we'll…"

Rémy looked around, but the streets were deserted. More screams came from inside the carriage as the two ruffians began to rock it on its thin wheels. The horses were going crazy, and Rémy couldn't understand why they hadn't bolted. Then she saw the scrawny boy standing bravely between them, holding on to their reins as if his life depended on it, which it probably did. She strained to hear any other male voices, but there were none. The woman – and there was only one, she thought – must be travelling alone. That was unusual, not to mention dangerous, especially at this time and in this part of the city.

Rémy bit her lip. How did she get herself into these situations? She slipped off her cloak. Beneath it, she was dressed in her everyday clothes, which were not the sort the folk of London were used to seeing on a young woman. She wore a black corset with a loose black shirt underneath, open at the neck. Around her waist was a wide leather utility belt that had a place for everything from her lock-picks to her night-glasses. Rémy's agile legs were clad in black breeches, tucked into long black leather boots. Her dark hair was still up from being on the wire, twisted into a coil and pinned neatly against the back of her head. Rémy also hadn't removed her stage mask, the iridescent black bird that she had taken to painting over her eyes, nose and lips to disguise her face. On the wire, it was spellbinding – on the dark streets of night-London, it was fearsome.

She ran out of the shadows and into the street. Surprise was the best tactic – if she could take one of them out before the other realised it, they'd be one-to-one before the fight even began. A few yards before she reached the melee, Rémy pirouetted, launching herself into the air in a quick spin and kicking out at the back of the first man's right leg. He crumpled like a sack of potatoes as her toes connected, his knees hitting the slabs below so hard that he screeched in pain. Rémy was already deep into another turn, yanking herself around so fast that the street became a blur. This blow was aimed higher, and by the time her free foot landed back on solid ground, the man was out cold, sprawled headlong over the filth of the broken cobbles.

The second man had realised what was happening just as his companion lost consciousness. He lunged at her. Rémy sprang sideways and then, in two nimble leaps, was on top of the carriage, eliciting another series of screams from the woman inside. The lumbering brute tried to reach her, but Rémy sidestepped and brought the heel of her boot down on his fingers. He yelled, jerking backwards and almost stumbling over the inert figure of his colleague.

Rémy leapt again, head-height to the scoundrel as she sailed out of the dark, her knee cracking into his chin and then, once she'd landed, her third spin-and-kick levelled at his crotch. He folded in half like a cheap penknife, winded and cursing. She stood in front of him and lifted one foot to push against his shoulder. He slumped to the ground.

The horses bolted, let loose as the boy who'd been holding them scarpered. The animals lurched along the street, no longer in step with each other and completely without regard for the carriage harnessed behind them. The screams from the woman inside grew even more frantic as the two animals tried to escape. The carriage careened erratically down the road and away.

Rémy ran after it, splashing through the stinking, murky puddles to draw level with the gelding in the leftmost shaft. His neck was stretched, his head down and pushed forward, his ears back. She tried to grab at the reins but the horse, its eyes rolling in fear, jerked its head up and away from her hand. Rémy ran on, the muscles of her legs burning as the horses came to a corner. For one terrifying moment she thought the two horses were going to choose different directions, but then the second followed the first and crashed right, almost upturning the carriage as they slewed it against one of the ragged houses lining the street.

There was nothing for it. If she wanted to stop them, Rémy was going to have to take the driver's place. She dropped back slightly, and then leapt at the front of the carriage, her feet hitting the running board as she flung herself across the driver's footrest. The screams from inside the carriage rose again like an orchestra, reaching a crescendo as Rémy scrambled up, first to her knees, then to her feet, grabbing the reins.

Rémy stood on the driver's seat of the carriage. Feeling it tilt and move beneath her, she kept her knees unlocked to help her balance. The horses strained against her as she pulled back on the reins. Then they began to slow, responding first to the bit and then to the familiarity of having a driver. Eventually, they found pace with each other, and then, finally, with her.

Rémy brought them to a stop, pulling the carriage in against the kerb and taking a breath.

"Hey there," she called to the occupant of the carriage. "If you tell me where to go, I will take you home. I can't let go of the horses or they may bolt again."

There was a moment's silence. Rémy pushed her night-glasses up into her hair and spoke to the trembling, exhausted horses in the way she'd learned from the horsemen of the circus – *Breathe through your nose, Rémy, with horses you must always breathe through your nose* – trying to keep them calm. Then there came the sound of wood rubbing against wood as the carriage's window opened. Rémy twisted around to see an elegant woman peering up at her, her hair coiled elaborately atop her head.

"H-hello?"

"Good evening, Mademoiselle," said Rémy. "Are you well?"

"Sh-shaken, but mostly unharmed – thanks to you. I owe you my life. Th-thank you."

"You are welcome, Mademoiselle–"

"I am Lady Sarah Valentine."

"You are welcome, Lady Sarah," Rémy said. "I will take you home, if you will tell me your address?"

"Hanover Square, Miss – it is Miss, isn't it? Who *are* you?"

Rémy smiled, suddenly remembering the greasepaint still covering her face. "Sit back and calm your nerves, my lady. I will have you home quick smart." She turned back to the horses and, a second later, heard the window grind shut again.

"Hey – you!" Rémy called, as a shoeless little boy in tattered trousers slunk out of an alleyway beside them. "Want to earn your breakfast?"

He nodded eagerly and came closer. His expression changed as she came into better view – the black bird on her face cast a pall of fear over him. Rémy dug a coin from her pocket and dropped it into his outstretched hand. "The driver of this carriage is injured. He's lying against the kerb in Worship Street. See that he's taken care of. And see this?" She pointed to her face and the mask painted there. "Cheat me and this will come looking for you. *D'accord?*"

The boy nodded and then, in the space of a shattered second, was gone into the night.

The rest of the journey was uneventful as Rémy drove the carriage from the murk of the East End into the richer, though hardly cleaner, parts of London. As soon as she'd turned into Hanover Square, a group of men started towards the carriage. They'd obviously been waiting for the return of Lady Sarah.

"Who the devil are you?" asked one, as Rémy drew to a halt before the grand house.

"Lady Sarah met with some… misfortune on her journey this evening," Rémy explained. "I was able to assist her."

"Were you, by Jove," said the man, as a liveried footman darted past him to open the carriage door, "and what the blazes have you done with Evans, my driver?"

Lady Sarah appeared, helped down from the carriage by the servant, and for the first time Rémy saw her full finery. She wore a dress of sky blue, edged and embroidered in fine gold thread. At her throat was a sapphire of a matching hue, large enough to take Rémy's breath away. It was Lady Sarah's fingers, though, that truly made Rémy's heart thump. Each was adorned with a ring bearing an enormous precious stone, and none spoke louder to the former jewel thief than the huge ruby on her index finger. She realised that Lady Sarah was looking at her intently as she spoke to the man, who appeared to be her husband.

"Charles, do show this young lady some manners. She single-handedly saw off a bunch of ruffians who accosted me, and then tamed the horses before the carriage could fall to pieces. I owe her my life or, if not my life, then at the very least my jewels."

Charles peered over her shoulder. "Where's your feckless brother? Weren't you under his protection?"

Lady Sarah glanced down at her hands. "He left me during the interval. He's probably at the gaming tables as we speak."

Charles made a disgusted sound, and then glanced angrily up at Rémy. "Well, I am in your debt, whoever you are… if you were indeed Lady Sarah's saviour, and not part of the plot."

"Charles!"

Rémy jumped from the driver's seat to the ground in one fluid movement to stand before them both.

"I am sorry, my dear," began Lady Sarah, "for my husband's rudeness. I know I am greatly indebted to you. How can I repay your efforts?"

Rémy shook her head. "I need nothing, Lady Sarah. I will leave you now. Good night."

She began to walk away, but Lady Sarah stopped her with a hand on her arm. When Rémy turned back, she saw that the woman was pulling the ruby ring from her slender finger.

"Here," said Lady Sarah, "please, take it. I saw how your gaze was drawn to it."

Rémy stared at the glittering jewel in the palm of Lady Sarah's hand. "No, my lady, really—"

"Take it," the woman ordered. "As you see, I have many jewels. And how many does one woman need? Besides, I heard you pay the boy to help poor Evans, and so you are out of pocket, too. Take it – as a token of my thanks."

Rémy did as she was told. The ruby was warm, as if the jewel contained a miniature glowing fire. Lady Sarah smiled once more, and then turned to join her husband, sweeping up the steps of her fine home and into the comfort beyond.

* * *

By the time Rémy finally made it back to Limehouse Basin and the Professor's workshop, it was so late that the sky over the river was beginning to take on the pink tinge of dawn. Weary and starving, she pushed open the door to find the cluttered space empty and still, save for the flickering of embers in the fireplace grate. Rémy sighed, trying not to feel the disappointment that weighed upon her heart. She had half hoped that Thaddeus would be here, waiting for her to get home, as he used to in the weeks after she and J had first moved in. She wondered where he was, and whether he was thinking of her at all.

Two

Unpleasant Duties

"You realise, of course," said Lord Falconer, from over the candelabra at the other end of the table, "that the situation in India is not merely one of economics, but of ideology, too."

There was a general murmuring of assent. Or perhaps it was dissent – Thaddeus Rec couldn't be sure. He stared down at the shallow dish of soup that had appeared before him. It was green and had the aroma of peas. The policeman – Detective Inspector now, no less – had been dreading the soup course ever since he had learned that he would have to attend this dinner. Soup generally landed down his front instead of in his mouth. And this one was green, for goodness' sake! Thaddeus blinked, imagining the horror of tipping food down his only good white shirt in front of the assorted gentry around Sir Henry Strong's elegant dinner table. The thought made him feel faintly sick.

The conversation about the state of the Empire rumbled on around him. Thaddeus wondered again, for the millionth time, just how he had ended up in such eminent company. He'd be happier down by the docks, clearing out the opium dens or chasing cutpurses through Whitechapel. But ever since the affair of the Shah of Persia's diamond, Thaddeus had been no ordinary

London policeman. He had been held up as a shining example of good policing by Queen Victoria herself, which is how the boy from the East End had ended up as the youngest Detective Inspector in Her Majesty's constabulary. At the time, Thaddeus hadn't realised that his promotion would mean less actual police work and more fiddling about at evenings such as this.

Everyone else was beginning to eat. Thaddeus glanced down at his enemy the spoon, and noticed that the cuff of his shirt was poking out from his black jacket's sleeve. It was frayed, betraying its age. He'd borrowed the dinner suit from the Professor's stash of disguises, but he hadn't been able to find a decent white shirt to wear. Buying a new one was out of the question. An inspector's salary, it turned out, wasn't that much more than a constable's.

"Perhaps the young monsieur has an – how you say? – insight into the situation? He must surely come across similar during his duties as one of 'er Majesty's police?"

It took Thaddeus a moment to register that the speaker was addressing him. He looked up to find the eyes of the entire table trained in his direction. Opposite, the man who had spoken – the Comte de Cantal – was watching him with calculating eyes and an unfriendly smile. The ladies present obviously found the Comte handsome, as they had been twittering behind their hands about him all evening. To Thaddeus, the man seemed strangely snake-like. A peculiarly thin, curling scar marked his left cheek, and all his movements were sly and darting. If he'd been dressed in street garb, Thaddeus would have pegged him for a pickpocket.

"Forgive me," the man said, flicking his cool gaze away with a lazy shrug. "I should address you as Lord, no doubt?"

Thaddeus' fingers twitched away from the spoon. "Er – no."

"Ahh," said the stranger, his soft French accent caressing

17

the English words with undue care, as if to make them hang around longer than necessary. "Sir, then. Sir – I'm sorry, what is your name?"

Thaddeus clenched his jaw. Sir Henry had introduced everyone upon their arrival, and there were not so many present that it was difficult to remember who was who. Particularly since Thaddeus was the only guest with no honorific title. The Comte de Cantal knew full well the policeman's name, and that nothing went in front of it. It wasn't the first time that someone had chosen to point out his true station in life among polite company. For Thaddeus, it had become just another tedious aspect of his promotion.

"Neither am I a sir, Comte," Thaddeus said, with a faint smile. "I am merely Thaddeus Rec, born and bred in London town."

"Come now, Rec," spluttered their host, Sir Henry, from his seat at the table's head. "There's no 'merely' about it, my boy. Rec is the very future of the force, Comte, the very future!"

The Comte's handsome, angular face momentarily twisted into a grimace, but was just as quickly forced back into a grin as he looked directly at Thaddeus. "The future, yes," he said, "and how bright the future must be, no? If even one such as yourself may prosper in the glow."

Thaddeus understood. Just a year ago, he would have been nothing to most of these people. Born on the streets of the East End, parentless, homeless, Thaddeus Rec had clawed his way up out of the gutter. There were plenty who wished he had not. For how many other commoners may decide they had the right to follow in his footsteps?

Thaddeus forced a pleasant smile on to his face, and was about to reply when Sir Henry stepped in again.

"Perhaps you did not hear, Comte," Sir Henry began, "about the shocking events surrounding the theft of the Shah of Persia's diamond. It is called the Ocean of Light, you know – quite the biggest in the world, excepting Her Majesty's own stone, the Mountain of Light, of course. Well, if not for Rec here, it would have disappeared into the clutches of a circus brat – one of your countrywomen, in fact. She was rather famous in your parts, I believe… Now, what was her name…? Something flighty, something – well, you know – typically French…"

Thaddeus made no reply, but his stomach churned at the thought of Rémy's stage name being mentioned in connection with the crime. She was still a wanted criminal, still in London – and he knew exactly where she was.

"*Le Petit Moineau*," murmured the Comte de Cantal. "In English, I believe you call her Little Bird." Thaddeus found the Frenchman looking at him with renewed interest, though his gaze was no friendlier. "It is true, she has been wanted in France for some years, but she always seems to slip the net. Well, so this is the man who thwarted the best jewel thief in Europe. Or almost, at least, no? I congratulate you, Monsieur Rec. An achievement indeed."

Thankfully, at that point the conversation moved on, although Thaddeus had not missed the Comte's final jibe. Neither was he ignorant of the Frenchman's inquisitive gaze as the evening continued. Thaddeus survived the soup course, and the fish course, too. They were embarking on the meat course – a huge hunk of beef broiled with onions – when the Comte spoke again. This time, his words were only for Thaddeus' ears.

"Tell me, Rec," he said softly, "the time of the theft of the Darya-ye Noor and your investigation. That was also when Lord Abernathy disappeared so mysteriously from London, yes?"

The Comte's casual mention of Abernathy almost made Thaddeus choke on his food. He forced himself to stay calm, looking at the Frenchman with a deliberately puzzled frown.

"I'm sorry, Comte? Lord who?"

Something unpleasant flickered in the Comte's dark eyes. "You do not remember? Strange, for I believe the lord in question was present when the jewel first disappeared. I thought I heard tell that he had even been the one to help the girl thief into the Tower of London on the night the diamond was stolen."

"Ahh," said Thaddeus, pretending to remember. "Indeed, you are right, of course. I did not know, however, that Lord Abernathy was said to have disappeared. You mean no one has seen him recently? I am afraid I was so busy during that investigation–"

"But of course," the Comte whispered, with a rather mocking nod. "You were... *busy*."

Thaddeus picked up his champagne glass and took a sip. "Lord Abernathy was an elderly gentleman, wasn't he? I am not certain that he disappeared so much as..."

"Died?" The Comte de Cantal supplied the word from a sharp tongue, and shot Thaddeus a piercing look. "It is possible, I suppose. Although for that to happen with no one to hear about it... Strange, do you not think?"

The policeman felt sweat begin to prick at his brow, and cursed himself, hoping that this strange Frenchman could not see his discomfort. Thaddeus had a terrible feeling about this man. Did he know something about the truth of what had happened beneath the streets of London? What Abernathy had sought to bring about through his army of infernal machines? Surely not. Abernathy and his men had died, thanks to Rémy's own willingness to sacrifice herself. Only she, Thaddeus, Desai and J knew the truth about what had happened.

He was trying to come up with an appropriate reply to the Comte's question when a butler entered the room and spoke to his master.

"Comte de Cantal," said Sir Henry, a moment later, "there is a messenger outside for you. He insists on speaking to you in person. Rec, there is a message for you, too – Jackson has it. Go on, Jackson, give it to him, don't delay!"

The Comte stood, dabbing his mouth with his napkin in an elaborate show of delicacy. He bowed to the table. "My apologies, dear friends, for this interruption. Please excuse me for a moment."

Thaddeus watched the Frenchman as he departed the table, but the Comte did not look at him. Jackson appeared at Thaddeus' shoulder, proffering a silver tray that held one small sealed envelope with his name scrawled untidily upon it. The policeman recognised the hand at once – it was from his sergeant, Collins. Tearing open the envelope, Thaddeus read the enclosed note and grimaced.

"A problem, Rec?" Sir Henry asked.

"I am afraid so, Sir Henry," Thaddeus told him, standing. "I am sorry, but I must take my leave. Police business."

"Not another darned burglary, Rec?" Sir Henry demanded. "Lord Theakston is hopping mad, you know. Lost his grandmother's pearls, by Jove."

"I'm not at liberty to say, Sir Henry," said Thaddeus, smoothly, "but my attendance is needed. Can you please excuse me, with thanks for this excellent meal?"

"Of course, Rec. Come, I will walk you out." With effort, the

21

considerable bulk of Sir Henry stood and ushered Rec from the room. Once outside, the kindly old gent placed a hand on the policeman's shoulder. "Now look here, Rec," he said. "You're not to mind that fool Cantal. He may be aristocracy, but he's not got two pennies to rub together, and he's sure as dammit not fit enough to lick your boots. So chin up, young chap. Understand?"

Thaddeus smiled. "Thank you, Sir Henry. And I am truly sorry to break up your party."

"Pish," said the gent, with a wave of his hand. "Enough of that. Bunch of useless windbags, the lot of them. Now be off with you. Save us from the rabble, Rec. Save us from the rabble."

Outside, the night had congealed into a mess of grey clouds tinged a sickly yellow by the weak moon beyond. Thaddeus pulled the collar of his old leather overcoat up around his ears and ran down the steps from Sir Henry's townhouse. There had indeed been another burglary, and Collins had called him to the scene. It wasn't far. Thaddeus began to walk, crossing the square and heading into the streets.

He was passing a shaded alley when a noise caught his attention. He glanced in its direction to see two men standing in the buttery glow of a gas lamp, talking quietly. He recognised one as the Comte de Cantal. The other's face was half hidden in the murky shadows. He was a young man, with a high forehead and a thin nose. He was dressed in a dark tailcoat, a top hat clutched in one hand. The stranger glanced towards him as Thaddeus passed, sharp eyes looking out of a sharp face. Then he turned away into shadow, passing out of the policeman's sight as if he had never been there at all.

Thaddeus walked quickly onwards, shivering slightly in the chill evening. For him, at least, it was going to be a long night.

An Old Friend

At noon the next day, Rémy woke to the familiar sound of tinny hammering coming from J's room. The boy had been hard at work on something for weeks now, but hadn't said a word about it. In fact, Rémy had hardly seen him for days. She wondered what he was doing, but knew better than to ask. The explanation would likely be as confusing as whatever contraption J was trying to cobble together. Since moving into the Professor's workshop, he'd become obsessed with the various mechanical marvels – or, more accurately, bits of mechanical marvels – that were scattered around the building. Still, at least it kept him out of trouble.

She washed and dressed quickly and then stepped out into the chaos of the main workshop. Bits and pieces were piled everywhere – clockwork watch parts here, strange, half-assembled masks there; listening devices; power gauges; odd-looking boxes that held who knew what. The one relatively tidy part of the room was just in front of the great fireplace, where a semicircle of old leather sofas and chairs had been arranged. She picked her way towards it, spying a tray of bread and cheese that J had thoughtfully left out for her after his own breakfast.

As she ate, she looked around, hoping to see a pile of post.

But there was nothing. Anxious, Rémy sat down, drawing her legs up under her.

It was now almost a month since she had heard from her oldest friend, even though they had promised to write to each other every week when Claudette departed for France. Claudette Anjou had once been a talented pickpocket and fortune-teller. She had taken over running the circus that had been Rémy's only home when its canny and criminal owner, Gustave, had finally received his just desserts. Claudette had changed the name from *Le Cirque de la Lune* to *Le Cirque du Secrète* – the Circus of Secrets – and had taken it back to France to begin anew. Rémy, though, had decided to stay behind in London. It had been a difficult decision, but going back to France would have meant never seeing Thaddeus Rec again. At the time, that had seemed unthinkable.

He'd said he loved her.

Rémy shivered slightly as the memory surfaced.

A deep chasm had been between them, and she'd thought she was going to die a watery death, alone. Thaddeus had stood there, shouting over the abyss, and convinced her to let him cross. He had wanted to be with her, no matter what happened, as they tried to save the city from Abernathy's dastardly plot. Because he *loved* her.

That was why she was still in London. That was why she hadn't gone back with Claudette. It was all because of Thaddeus and that moment. Yet they hadn't spoken of it since.

Rémy felt her opal pendant shift slightly against her skin – a small, mystical sliver of stone with a life of its own. Most of the time she wasn't aware of it, but every now and then it would make itself known. There would be something like a tingle, a tiny, insignificant buzzing in her head. And then, filtering like new mortar through the bricks of her thoughts, there would be others. Thoughts that weren't hers; the thoughts of people passing in the street, of J in his sleep... of Thaddeus trying to find something to say to her and mentally crossing out every sentence before it even got to his lips. His eyes, that odd mixture of one blue and one brown, clouding with a confusion that she wanted to understand but couldn't bring herself to talk about.

She stood, shaking off this sudden, unsettling feeling with a flick of her shoulders. She hadn't seen Thaddeus for days. The last time he had visited, it hadn't even been to see her. He'd been looking for J, as he always seemed to be now that the boy was his unofficial eyes and ears on the ground in the East End. She and Thaddeus had stood in front of the fire together, awkwardly, neither quite meeting the other's eye. They talked of nothing at all because all the things they should have been talking about had flooded the space between them and turned it into a fathomless, impassable ocean.

And that, she thought, *was what I abandoned my oldest friend for? Where are you, Claudette? Why don't you write to me?*

To occupy her mind, Rémy decided to go to the theatre and practise her new routine. She wasn't due on stage that evening, which was just as well. After the exertions of the previous night, Rémy knew she wouldn't be at her best. But she needed something to distract her, both from her worries about Claudette and from thoughts of Thaddeus, and there was nothing better for that than mastering a new trick. J was still hammering frantically behind the closed door of his room as she stepped from the noise of the workshop into the roar of Limehouse.

When Rémy had first begun living at the workshop, she'd tried to work out what time of day the dock was busiest, but

25

had soon given up. The place never seemed to settle; there was always work to be done. That morning, a clipper had arrived, travelling up the Thames on the morning tide from whatever far-off place it had begun its journey – India, perhaps, or maybe even further. Now the ship's sails stood furled as men of all sizes and colours rushed up and down her gangplanks, hauling crate after crate back down onto the solid, wet-sluiced stone of the dockside. Rémy paused beside one of the wooden boxes, wondering what was inside. Tea? Spices? Silk? Everything came through Limehouse, though little of it stayed. It was for richer folk in richer places than this.

The bustle danced to a different tune as she turned onto Whitechapel Road and began heading north. The dosshouses had turned out their penny-chair renters hours ago, and now the scramble to earn enough to find a warm place for tonight was in full swing. The cutpurses were on the lookout for the unwary; the women who could do no better were trying to find men with whom they could do worse.

Under the pale, miserable London sun, the stink of the streets was rising to meet the stink of the people who lived there. Rémy had grown used to it over the months. She knew this place now, and she knew that what the people did, they did because they had no choice. Take J, for example – their chance encounter had been driven by his need to steal her bag, but the first chance he'd been given, he'd dropped all that thievery and become a model citizen. He'd even travelled as far as some of those clippers, to India and back with their friend Desai.

The East End was a strange place, a wild place, a dangerous and sometimes even a kind place. It was the sort of place that someone like Rémy found very easy to make home.

The theatre was quiet, its lights dimmed for the daytime. The old doorman let her in with a black-toothed smile that was really more of a leer. She slipped up the stairs to the dressing rooms to change before heading for the stage, only to find that the stage was already occupied. Rémy could tell that the performer was a magician, even from where she stood in the wings. He was wearing the ubiquitous black top hat and tails combination that workers of stage magic seemed to favour. There was only one person in the audience. Mr Richards, the owner of the theatre, was sitting in the stalls, three rows back so as to get the best view. He had obviously offered the magician a chance to try out for a coveted spot on the playbill.

"Come on then, lad," Richards bellowed at the tall young man on stage. "Show me what you've got, and be quick about it. I haven't got all day, y'know."

"As you wish, Monsieur," said the magician, with a French accent as elegant as his outfit. "Since your audience will be unacquainted with The Magnificent Yannick and his astounding talents, it would be best to start with–"

At the sound of his name, Rémy's mouth fell open in astonishment.

"*Mon Dieu* – Yannick?" she exclaimed, the words bursting from her before she'd even thought them. "Yannick! Is it really you?"

The magician turned sharply towards her. His face was partially cast in shadow by the rim of his hat, but Rémy would have known her childhood friend anywhere.

"*Mon Dieu!*" Yannick exclaimed, whipping off his hat to let a flash of white-blond hair free. "If it isn't the very excellent Rémy Brunel! Where on earth did you spring from?"

Rémy laughed, dancing forward onto the stage to pull

The Magnificent Yannick into a hug. "I perform here, you idiot! Three times a week. I'm the star attraction!"

"Ahem." They both turned towards Richards, who was on his feet, looking at them both with raised eyebrows. "That is a matter for debate, Miss Brunel," he said, "and in that debate, I will always have the deciding vote. Perhaps you'd both like to stop wasting my time so that I can see whether Yannick is as 'magnificent' as he'd have us all believe?"

Rémy bit her lip, nodding as she retreated to the wings again. She watched as Yannick got into his part with gusto, laughing quietly and willing him on. He was better than she remembered, with more stage presence and a nice turn in tricks. He'd even added in some hypnosis. Richards evidently thought he was good, too. Not that he clapped once Yannick was done, but he did book the magician for a trial week, which was even better.

They embraced again once Yannick came off stage, Rémy's face fixed in the permanent grin she had worn since she'd first realised who he was. It had been so long since she'd seen anyone from home – anyone from that life.

Yannick pulled back from the hug to look at her, though he didn't let her go. His bright blue eyes were twinkling, just the way they always had. "I wondered what had happened to you," he said. "I heard that Gustave had... how shall we say it? Got his comeuppance, at last."

Rémy smiled grimly at the memory of her old circus master, the devil who had forced her parents into a curse that tore them apart and made her into his pet jewel thief. "*Oui*. Well, he had it coming, wouldn't you agree?"

Yannick laughed. "Oh, I would – I would, Little Bird."

Rémy felt a jolt at the sound of her old circus name.

No one called her by it now, not in her new life in London, and she realised that she missed it. And it wasn't just the name she missed. A wave of homesickness rolled over her as she thought of Claudette and Amélie, of her pony Dominique, of the whole company helping to put up the circus tent at each new place they visited, of nights around the circus fire, laughing and eating and just… being together. She swallowed, hard, to stop the memories engulfing her heart.

"Hey, what's the matter?" Yannick asked, his hands still on her arms.

Rémy stepped back and smiled a watery smile. "Oh, nothing. Nothing at all! It's just so good to see you, and such a surprise! What are you doing in London?"

Yannick glanced at the toes of his shiny black shoes and shrugged. "The circuit in France isn't what it used to be. I thought I'd try my luck here. Cross your fingers for me."

Rémy grinned again. "Ach, you'll be fine. The Magnificent Yannick always falls on his feet, isn't that so?"

Yannick grinned back, and Rémy realised with another shock that he had grown up since she had seen him last. He wasn't the floppy-haired, awkward boy she'd known when they were both small and trying to learn their trade. He was a man now, and he was handsome with it. She wondered for a moment what Yannick saw when he looked back at her, and wished suddenly that she'd thought to brush her hair instead of just scrunching it all up into a ball to get it out of the way.

"Where are you staying?" she asked, to pull herself away from the unexpected thought. "Not too far away, I hope? We must catch up, Yannick!"

"Ah, well," the magician said ruefully, turning to point at a

29

battered old suitcase that was propped against the wing. "In that respect, I'll take any advice you care to give me, Rémy. As long as it's cheap, that is."

"Oh, well, if you don't have anywhere, you must come and stay with us," Rémy blurted, almost before she'd even realised she'd been thinking the words.

Yannick raised a quizzical eyebrow at her. "Us?"

"Yes – J and I live in a place in Limehouse Basin. It's huge, big enough for you too, of course, if you've still got your bedroll and aren't too proud to sleep on the floor!"

Yannick looked doubtful, and also a little curious. "And this… J… won't mind my intrusion into your… lives?"

Rémy laughed, "No, of course he won't." Then she realised what Yannick had really been asking, and laughed again. "J's just a boy, Yannick, a street boy who needed a home, just like me. It's a long story, but now we're friends, and we share an old workshop. Come and stay there with us, at least until you find those famous feet of yours again. It'll be fun – like old times!"

Yannick grinned along with her, and nodded. *"D'accord."*

New Trouble

It was early evening when Rémy and Yannick walked back to the warehouse, winding through the throngs of people crowding the East End streets. Yannick had swapped his elaborate stage clothes for a pair of brown trousers and a rough cream shirt, topped off by a cap that made him look far younger and much more like the boy he'd been when they'd first known each other. As they chatted, Rémy thought back to those days, when life with the circus had seemed to be one long, hot summer of fun. That was before Gustave had realised her talent for stealing jewels, before her life had been as much about breaking into houses as it was about performing on the trapeze. She laughed at another of Yannick's circus tales and realised that, in his company, she was completely relaxed. This, thought Rémy, was how all friendship should be – easy and undemanding.

"Do you remember that time outside Rouen," Yannick said, laughing even as he remembered, "when Marta the elephant took fright and went on the rampage, right into that woman's vegetable patch? I thought Gustave was going to have a fit!"

Rémy laughed. "I do remember! She only calmed down because of you. Marta loved you."

31

Yannick shrugged. "I felt sorry for her. She shouldn't have spent so much time in that leg iron." He glowered for a minute. "Gustave never understood that she would have stayed of her own accord, as long as we showed her love. He always preferred that animals – and people – obeyed him through fear. He was a fool."

"He was," Rémy agreed, "but he is gone now, and we are making our own lives, at last. Look, here we are!"

They had arrived outside the workshop, which Rémy realised must look like a corner of nothing to Yannick. It was just a rotten old wooden door beside a stinking, salty lock. But of course that was what the Professor had always intended it to seem, to disguise what was hidden beyond.

Inside, the fire that burned fiercely in the big fireplace had warmed the space, and the room smelled of fresh cooking.

"Aha," Rémy said, cheerily. "Looks as if someone was ready for us, Yannick. J's been cooking stew again!"

"Wot do you mean, again?" asked J, sticking his head around the door to his room. The boy's face was almost completely hidden by a contraption that looked a bit like a metal globe. He wore it as a hat, making his unruly fair hair stick out all over the place. It seemed to be combined with a pair of the Professor's night-glasses and two sets of conjoined compasses that met in the centre of the wearer's head. It jangled slightly as the boy pulled it off. "You want something else, you only 'ave to say so."

"I wouldn't dream of it," she said.

"Oo's this then?" the boy asked, putting down the device and shuffling into the room as he looked Yannick up and down.

"J, I'd like to you meet an old friend from my circus days in France. Yannick, this is J, a very good new friend of mine."

"It's wonderful to meet you, J," said Yannick, bowing lavishly and holding out a hand for the boy to shake.

J looked confused by the elegant greeting, and flushed as he grasped Yannick's hand. "Er – likewise, I'm sure," he said. "You stayin' for dinner?"

"Actually, J, if you don't mind, Yannick's going to stay not just for dinner, but for a few nights. He's on trial at the Albert Saloon, you see. I said it would be all right. It is, isn't it?"

"Oh," said J, a tad awkwardly. "Yeah, o' course it is. Any friend, et cetera. You'd better be happy bunking on the floor, though."

"You are very kind," said Yannick, smiling. "I cannot tell you what a relief it is to find a friendly face – more than one – in a new city such as this. I am in your debt."

"Ah well, none o' that," J muttered, turning back to retrieve his spoon. "Dinner'll be ready in a mo. Make yourself at home."

There was a knock at the door. With barely a pause, it creaked open on its old hinges to reveal Thaddeus Rec, his battered hat under one arm and a bunch of bright yellow daffodils in the other. The first person he saw as he stepped into the room was Yannick. He stopped dead.

"Oh," he said, after a moment of silence. The policeman's eyes flicked from Yannick to Rémy and back again. "My apologies. I didn't realise you had visitors."

"He ain't a visitor. He's a *friend*," J said, raising his eyebrows significantly as he stirred the pot. "Just like you are, Mister Rec. Come on in, grub's nearly up."

Thaddeus continued to stare at Yannick. Yannick stared back. Rémy, confused by the sudden and unexpected hostility that had entered the room, took a step between them.

"Ah – Thaddeus Rec, this is my old friend, Yannick. We used

to be in the circus together. He's a magician – he's just arrived in London and has got a spot at the Albert Saloon. Isn't that amazing? We're going to be colleagues again!"

Thaddeus nodded curtly at Yannick, but didn't relax for a second. At a loss for something else to say, Rémy pointed at the flowers. She'd never seen Thaddeus with any such thing before.

"You are visiting family later?"

"What?" Thaddeus tore his gaze away from Yannick and looked at her for the first time. Then he looked at the flowers, still clutched in his hand. His cheeks flushed a little. "Oh. No. These – these were… are – for you, actually."

It was Rémy's turn to blush. Flowers! No one had ever given her flowers before.

"Ahh," said Yannick, a knowing smile in his voice. "So, you are the type of girl who likes flowers now, *oui?*"

Rémy flushed deeper, embarrassed as she saw the amused look on her old friend's face. Beside her, she felt Thaddeus tense even more and knew he had taken Yannick's jibe as if it were aimed at him. It wasn't – Yannick had always teased her in the past and it looked as if the present would be no different.

"You don't have to have them if you don't want them," Thaddeus said with a carelessness he obviously didn't feel, dropping the daffodils and his hat on a nearby table. "They're a shameless bribe, really. I'm–" he cleared his throat, "I'm on official police business. Well," he added, "in a manner of speaking, anyway."

"Police business?" Rémy asked. "Then you'll want to talk to J, I suppose. Thaddeus is an Inspector with Scotland Yard, Yannick," she explained.

Yannick's eyebrows shot up into his fair hair. "A policeman!"

he said. "Well, you really are moving in exalted circles now, Rémy Brunel. I will really have to – what is it you English say? – mind my Ps and Qs." He strolled towards the fireplace and sank into a nearby armchair. "Isn't that so, Monsieur Policeman?"

Thaddeus glanced at him, an expression of annoyance briefly passing across his face. "That depends on what you've done that I might be interested in, Mister – Yannick, is it?" he said, coolly. Then he turned back to Rémy again. "Actually, it's not J I wanted to talk to this time. I was hoping you might help me. I need a fresh pair of eyes on this case, and I can't think of anyone better. You know, given your… previous, um… occupation."

Thaddeus seemed to suddenly realise what he was saying, and looked away, embarrassed. Her criminal past as a jewel thief was something else they never, ever talked about.

"Well, don't mind me," said Yannick, apparently oblivious to Thaddeus' discomfort. "I'm just going to sit here quietly and wait for J's delicious-smelling stew."

Thaddeus frowned. "Perhaps we can talk privately?" he suggested to Rémy.

"Anything you have to say you can say in front of Yannick, Thaddeus," she said, with a touch of irritation. "I've known him for many years. He is completely trustworthy."

Rémy saw Thaddeus' eyebrows flick up slightly. He looked at Yannick again. "Have we met before?" the policeman asked suddenly. "You seem familiar, somehow."

Yannick shrugged. "Not that I know of. Perhaps we passed in the street once."

"Perhaps." Thaddeus frowned, and then turned back to Rémy. "There's been a burglary, a strange one, and the second of its kind. It happened last night – well, early this morning, really.

One of the big houses in the West End. Hanover Square, to be exact. Jewels taken from a locked safe in a locked room that's only accessible through the gentleman's locked study."

"Hanover Square?"

"Yes. It's a very well-to-do place. Lots of toffs live there. You wouldn't believe the way they live on that side of town."

Rémy nodded. "Little men in uniform to open doors for you... more jewellery than clothes..."

Thaddeus looked at her curiously. "How do you know what it's like? You've never been there... have you?"

The opal tickled, moving against her chest almost as if in warning, just as Rémy saw the policeman's gaze fall upon the huge ruby ring given to her by Lady Sarah. She loved the red stone so much that she hadn't taken it off since.

"Where did you get that?"

And there it was, clear as day, his doubting voice in her head... *Where did that come from? Could Rémy be the thief?*

And then, just as quickly...

No. No, she wouldn't do that. She's changed...

But the damage was done.

Rémy leapt towards him. She only came up to Thaddeus' shoulder, but even so he took a step back in the face of her towering anger.

"You think it was me!"

"What?" Thaddeus asked, holding up his hands. "Of course I don't! I just wondered where the ring came from, that's all!"

"And you assumed I must have stolen it! As if I am still a thief! As if I hadn't done enough to prove myself to you!"

"Rémy, wait! That's not what I meant!"

"But it's what you thought! Isn't it?"

"No! No – not really."

"And here I thought you actually wanted my help, but no, you just wanted to find someone to pin your case on. That would be so easy, wouldn't it?"

Rémy saw the anger flicker into Thaddeus' eyes, the brown and blue darkening as if thunder had rolled into the room. His jaw tightened and he shook his head.

"How can you say that? How can you even think that, after everything? Do you even understand how difficult this entire situation is for me? You're still a wanted criminal, Rémy! I am a Detective Inspector of the Metropolitan Police! Do you know what would happen if they found out–"

"Then what are you doing here at all, little policeman? Why associate yourself with a disgusting criminal like me? Eh?"

"I don't think you're disgusting. Of course I don't – you *know* I don't!"

"But I am a thief, yes? And you are sworn to put people like me in jail. Why else would you be here, eh?"

"I came because I thought you could help me," Thaddeus bellowed. "I thought, stupidly, that you might want to help me solve this case. I thought – God knows why – I thought we might work well together!"

"How can we work together when you think I am the criminal you are searching for?" Rémy yelled back.

"I don't! I never even said that!"

"You didn't *have* to!"

They both stopped, breathing hard, staring at each other through seething eyes. Something electric sparked between them, and just for a second, Rémy remembered the kiss they had shared, all those long months ago, and thanks to the opal, she couldn't work out if she was the one thinking about it, or he was.

"Ahem…" The discreet sound came from Yannick, still seated in the chair across the room. It cut through the tense silence in the room like the crack of a whip.

Thaddeus jumped, as if he'd forgotten that they were not alone. He stepped away, scowling as he took a deep breath.

"I am sorry," he said, in a cold voice, "that I intruded on your reunion with such unimportant matters. Good evening. J, I'll see you soon."

He turned on his heel and stalked to the door, snatching up his hat with such violence that the discarded bouquet tumbled to the floor. A moment later he was gone, but Rémy was too angry to let Thaddeus get away so easily. She followed him.

"That's it?" she hissed, incensed, catching him outside on the street. "You're going to walk into my home, accuse me of theft, and simply leave?"

Thaddeus spun around to face her. "I did not," he said, in a harsh whisper, "accuse you of theft." He paused for a moment, as if hesitating over something.

"What?" Rémy asked, jutting out her chin and crossing her arms. "What now?"

"Does he have to stay here? With you, at the workshop?"

Rémy frowned. "Yannick? Why shouldn't he?"

Thaddeus made an annoyed sound in his throat. "I don't trust him. I don't think you should either. And besides…"

"Besides – what?" Rémy asked, as he trailed off.

Thaddeus shook his head again. "I just don't like it."

"You don't like it?" Rémy asked, her voice rising in annoyance. "You want me to turn a friend out on the street because you don't *like* it?"

"He *was* a friend, Rémy. How long is it since you've seen him? When you were both children? Who knows what kind of man he is now? I've seen his face before. I can't place where, but it worries me."

Rémy stepped away from Thaddeus, angry. "Only an Englishman could demand I turn an old friend out on the street when they have nowhere else to go. How can you ask me such a thing? First you accuse me of theft—"

"I. Did. *Not*," Thaddeus hissed.

"And now you try to tell me who I should keep as my friends. Well, you have no right! You have no right, and I will not listen to you. Go back to work, little policeman. You are not wanted here."

She watched as Thaddeus set his jaw, gritting his teeth. "Fine," he said, his voice stony. Then he turned on his heel and was gone, disappearing into the night-time murk.

Five

Catching Up

Back inside the warmth of the workshop, Yannick was attempting to regale a somewhat downcast J with a tale of their shared past. The boy stood up as soon as she stepped back inside. "I fink I'll go to bed meself," he muttered. "Lots to do in the morning."

Rémy nodded. "Night, J."

"A pleasure to meet you, J," said Yannick, with his warmest smile. "And thank you for letting me stay."

J half shrugged a response. The next moment, the door to his room was closing behind him. Rémy expected the sound of hammering to start up again, but all was silent.

"Well," said Yannick, wryly, "that's two of your friends I seem to have upset already, and with only one evening gone. Perhaps tomorrow I should make more of an effort and try for three?"

Rémy sighed as she sat down opposite him in front of the fire. "Thaddeus and J are really the only friends I have, here in London. The three of us have become very close over the past few months. We've been through a lot together."

"Really?" asked Yannick. "You wouldn't know it from the way that policeman of yours spoke to you. Let me guess, in that little chat you two had out there, he warned you that I shouldn't be staying here with you. Am I right?"

Rémy scrubbed her short thumbnail against the frayed material of the chair's arm. "Something like that. He says I don't really know you any more. I suppose he's right, really."

"Tsk!" exclaimed Yannick. "What rubbish! I know you better than some English boy you met just a few months ago, Rémy Brunel. How many years were we on the road together? Can I really have changed so much?"

Rémy raised her eyebrows at him. "I hope so. You used to be so clumsy you'd fall over your own feet."

Yannick laughed, and then she did too, and Rémy's discomfort at Thaddeus' words faded. They had only spent an evening together, but already she felt more at home, more comfortable, with Yannick than she ever had with Thaddeus. Yannick put her at her ease whereas, around Thaddeus, Rémy always felt as if she had to be better than she ever could be.

"I don't know why you put up with him coming around here," Yannick said, almost as if he knew what she was thinking. "That sort are never good news."

"Thaddeus is a good man, really. He's – it's just not… I don't…" Rémy sighed, and tried again. "It's difficult, that's all. Anyway, I don't want to talk about Thaddeus. I need news, Yannick. Tell me what has been happening in France."

"Well, of course everyone's excited about the Jamboree," Yannick told her. "It's this week, you know."

Rémy stared into the fire, imagining the gathering. Once every four years, circus troupes from all over France – and sometimes beyond – gathered in one place, just outside Paris. It was a chance to catch up with old friends and make new acquaintances, to learn news and, for some, to change jobs. When she was younger, she had always looked forward to the week-long festival of noise, magic, fire and fun. Yet this year, she'd hardly thought about it. London was her home, and where she was meant to be now. Or so she'd thought.

"I suppose Claudette and the circus will be living it up there."

"I don't know." Rémy rubbed a hand over her face. "I'm sure it's nothing, Yannick, but I haven't had a letter from Claudette for ages. We were supposed to write to each other every week, but... she hasn't returned word for a while."

Yannick stared into the fire. "That seems strange. I always remember you two being so close."

The well of unease that had been flooding Rémy's stomach bubbled a little. "I know. To tell you the truth, I am worried. But I don't know what to do."

Yannick sighed. "Ah, Claudette. I will not lie to you, Rémy – when I was a boy I had a little crush on her. She's so... so different to the rest of us circus folk, isn't she?"

Rémy laughed faintly, thinking of her friend's beautiful face and chestnut hair, of her way with languages and her ability to write, which was almost unheard of in circus life. "She is. She was beginning to teach Amélie to read when they went back to France. You never met her daughter, did you?"

"No," said Yannick, "though I heard about her. Poor Claudette, and the baby – to be left like that."

Rémy thought back to those months before Amélie had been born. Once Antoine had gone, Claudette refused to speak his name. Her belly had swollen along with her grief, and then Amélie had been born, as beautiful as her mother, but as mute as a swan. And though Claudette never said it, Rémy knew her friend blamed herself. Claudette thought that somehow, her grief had poisoned the baby in her womb. Not once had Amélie spoken, in all her six years, not until the day Rémy's opal had woken and allowed her to hear the little girl's thoughts. But Rémy hadn't told Claudette about the opal's powers. She hadn't known how to, and while Rémy was still trying to find the right words to explain, Claudette and her daughter had gone back to France.

She and Yannick were silent for a moment, both staring into the flames as memories swallowed them both. The feeling of homesickness overcame Rémy again, as she thought of her friend so far away. London suddenly seemed a very strange place for her to be.

"I'm sorry, my dear friend," said Yannick, his face full of concern. "I did not mean to make you think of worrying things. If it helps, I do have word of a more jolly nature."

"Oh?"

"Indeed. It seems as if the fabled Lost Comtesse may soon be found at last."

"No, surely not?" asked Rémy. "I thought that was just a fairy tale that parents told their children. You know – 'Don't run off, you know what happens to naughty children who run off… you'll end up like the Lost Comtesse'…"

Yannick shook his head. "It's not just a story. Bits of it might have been made up, but she's out there somewhere, for real. The new Comte de Cantal de Saint-Cernin has issued a reward, and says he's determined to find her once and for all. He says he has studied his family's records and she is his cousin, so now that his father is dead and he's the new head of the family, he thinks it's time he put all his efforts into finding her."

Rémy shook her head, thinking about the old story. It was

one all circus children grew up knowing, because it was what marked them out from the rest of the world. In it, circus people were a bad lot, kidnapping unwary children who strayed into their path. The story went that there was once an old circus couple who were desperate to have a child but, year after year, the wife remained barren. This saddened her beyond measure, and the husband could not bear to see his beloved wife bowed double by the grief.

One day, a rich governor gave a huge party for his wife's birthday. The entire city turned out for the celebration, which attracted many performers and circuses from miles around, and continued late into the night. The governor had a daughter, a young girl who did not go to bed as she had been ordered, but begged her maid to take her into the town instead. The maid was persuaded, but then became distracted and forgot her charge. The little girl wandered off, straight into the path of the old circus performer, who snatched her up and claimed her for his wife. The girl had never been seen since.

"The story never really made sense to me," said Rémy. "Surely the girl could have screamed as they dragged her away. And it's not as if they could have kept her locked in their caravan forever – she would have been able to run away at some point. So why didn't she?"

Yannick shrugged. "Not every girl is as able as you are, Little Bird. I heard tell that they'd built a tall tower in a secret forest and locked the child in it. They bricked up the door so there was no exit except for a high window that was too far from the ground to escape."

Rémy laughed. "That's the fairy tale of Rapunzel, you idiot!"

"Ahh," said Yannick, waggling his eyebrows and making her

laugh even more. "But *is* it? Seriously, though, Rémy – imagine being the Lost Comtesse. Imagine having that entire inheritance sitting there, just waiting for you to remember who you are and come forward. How extraordinary would that be?"

Rémy smiled. "Very," she said.

They were silent for a while, staring at the fire and thinking their own thoughts. Rémy's homesickness returned, and she wondered again where Claudette and Amélie were, and what they were doing at that moment. Yannick sighed and, stretched his legs out towards the fire, his face pensive and a little sad, as if remembering all their childhood adventures and wishing it were possible to relive them all.

"Are you sure this is where you belong, Rémy?" he said, at last. "What are you doing here, in London? What – or who – is keeping you here?"

Rémy stared at the fire.

"I don't know," she whispered. "I don't know any more."

An Impossible Case

Thaddeus sat at his desk, his notes on the case spread out in front of him. None of what he had read made sense. Two burglaries, both of jewels, both as inexplicable as the other. Lord Theakston's and Lord Bolsover's valuables should have been as safe as... well, he wouldn't use the saying 'as safe as the Crown Jewels' ever again, not after what had happened a few months ago, but they were as safe as a very safe thing. As he had told Rémy, they seemed to have been taken from locked strongboxes in locked rooms, which had remained locked even after the thefts. Thaddeus had no idea even of where to start. The more he turned the facts over in his mind, the more impossible both events seemed to be. After his argument with Rémy, Thaddeus had known he wouldn't sleep. So he'd gone back to his desk, where he'd been sitting all night.

Lord Theakston had taken his wife and daughter out to the Adelphi Theatre. Two of the servants had been granted the night off, but the rest of the household had remained at the residence. All of the servants had exemplary records, and neither Lord Theakston nor Lady Theakston believed that any of their household would steal from them. Indeed, it seemed a remarkably happy home, both upstairs and downstairs. Thaddeus was beginning to agree that the thief must have been an outsider, which only served to make the policeman's job all the harder.

As for Lord Bolsover, that case was even more difficult. Those jewels had also been within a safe in a locked room, this time one with no windows and only a single door, which opened into Lord Bolsover's private study, and for which only he had the keys. And, as with Lord Theakston, Bolsover swore blind that the keys had never been out of his sight, not even long enough for an enterprising thief to have made an impression of them.

How do you steal a jewel through three locked doors? Twice?

The more he thought about it, the more Thaddeus was convinced that the only person who could help him solve the case was Rémy Brunel.

The policeman sighed and rubbed his eyes. His Rémy Brunel. At least, he'd thought she was at one point, but now… they could barely be in the same room together. Every time he tried to say something about what had happened in that cave – about what he'd said to her when he'd thought she was about to die – something passed through her eyes that made him think he'd be better off not saying anything at all. And after last night…

Thaddeus stood up and began to pace. There was something just not right about that Yannick fellow turning up out of the blue. Besides, the policeman was sure he'd seen the man's face somewhere before, and until he could place it, he wouldn't be happy. And of course Thaddeus hadn't really thought that Rémy could be the thief he was searching for. It was only that she'd suddenly been wearing that ring – a ruby that, if sold, could buy the workshop and everything in it several times over. And after how they had met, it was natural that he should be a little

47

suspicious, wasn't it? But he believed her, unreservedly, when she protested it wasn't her. He just wanted her help.

Because how do you steal a jewel through three locked doors, as if by magic?

Thaddeus blinked, staring at the mass of notes on his desk. A cog turned in his head. A switch flicked.

Magic.

* * *

Rémy woke with an ache in her head that echoed an even more painful one in her heart. Getting up, she looked in the mirror and saw dark circles beneath her eyes. It wasn't just the worry about Claudette, or the homesickness that had enveloped her since meeting Yannick again. It was the argument with Thaddeus. Their bitter words had rolled around and around in her head all night. If only she'd not heard what he was thinking in that split second. If only she'd just been able to listen to what he actually had to say: *I thought we might work well together.*

But how? she thought. *How would we ever be able to do that, when you think I'm still capable of being the thing you most despise?*

Her fingers went to the opal. It hung on a thin gold chain around her neck, just as it always had. Claudette had given it to her as a child, saying it was a gift from the mother she'd never known. *The gift has turned into a curse*, she thought. Not for the first time, Rémy wished she'd found the time to talk to Claudette about what her opal could do. Before they'd come to London, it had just been a talisman given in love. Now it was something entirely different. Rémy didn't know how to deal with it.

Reaching for the clasp, Rémy took the necklace from around her neck and coiled it into her palm. The opal glinted, a thousand threads of colour in a milky sea of white. Through its centre ran the great split that had been there ever since the night she had almost died. She had never taken it off before. Without it she felt naked, and yet with it came such a burden now that it was almost a relief to be free. Reaching out, Rémy opened the drawer of the old dresser and hid it carefully in an old matchbox.

When Rémy had finished dressing and left her room, she discovered that Yannick had already gone out. J didn't know where, and didn't seem particularly bothered by the fact.

"You don't mind him staying, do you, J?" Rémy asked as they shared some bread and cheese over a subdued breakfast.

J shrugged. "I s'pose not. It's a bit of a coincidence, though, innit? Him finding you in the whole of London. Some might say he knew what he was about, going to the very theatre you perform in, eh?"

Rémy frowned. "You sound as suspicious as Thaddeus."

J sighed. "I'm not suspicious, no more than usual. I just don't like seeing you and Thaddeus fight, that's all. And I's got a feeling that if Mr Yannick stays around, there'll be a lot more fighting."

Rémy shrugged. "Well, Thaddeus has only got himself to blame for that."

J put down his chunk of bread and leaned over the table towards her. "Now, why would you go and say a thing like that? What's Thaddeus to blame for? Ain't 'e helped us both out?"

"Yes, J, he has helped us out – a lot. But he's still a policeman. And police and people like us never mix. We're like oil and water. You can swirl us around and it'll seem like we're one. But we always separate eventually. That's just the way of the world."

"Ballcocks!" scoffed J. "That's total rubbish, that is. You and Thaddeus, you're two of a kind. Or you were, before that Mr

Yannick turned up." J set his jaw in the stubborn line Rémy had become used to, and shook his head. "I just don't know what's up with you and Thaddeus. Honestly, after all that stuff that happened in Abernathy's caves, you'd think—"

Rémy covered her face with her hands. "Not now, J. D'accord?"

"All right, all right. You've got to admit, though — that's some whopper you've got there. Ain't really surprising Thaddeus thought it might be nicked, is it?"

Rémy dropped her hands, and saw that the boy was pointing at Lady Sarah's ruby, still sitting heavily on her index finger.

"That's a right beauty, that is."

She shrugged. "That's what I thought, too. Now I think I'll throw it in the Thames."

"Don't do that! It's just what I need. Can I borrow it for a bit? I'll give it back, promise."

Rémy pulled the ring from her finger and threw it to J. He caught it one-handed, staring into the red jewel with wide eyes.

"Keep it," she told him. "I wish I'd never seen the damned thing."

* * *

Thaddeus spent most of the day following a hunch that took him deep into London's West End. Once there, he called at the Adelphi, where Lord Theakston and his wife and daughter had spent the evening before the jewels had disappeared. Once he had taken a look at the playbill and spoken to the establishment's owner, he moved on to another theatre called the Vaudeville, where, he had discovered, Lord Bolsover had visited the night of his robbery. There, he looked again at the playbill and spoke to the theatre owner. By the time he had completed these tasks, Thaddeus felt not only that his hunch was proving itself to be a solid line of enquiry, but also that it was leading him uncomfortably close to home.

He returned to his office, footsore and perturbed. Sitting down, he spread his notes out across his desk again and tried to find a clear path to follow through the fragments.

He was still deep in thought when a strong knock sounded at his office door. Thaddeus glanced at the clock to find with surprise that it was after six, and the police station was almost empty. He stood and opened the door to see his friend Maandhata Desai standing patiently outside. The policeman smiled as he bid him come in, noting the slight frown on his friend's face.

"Desai," he said, in greeting. "It's good to see you."

"And you, Thaddeus," said the older man, his floor-length cloak rustling as he took a seat. It was a rich blue, embroidered at the edges with foreign flowers that made Thaddeus' drab office seem even duller than usual. Desai pulled the hood down, and the young policeman saw a new touch of grey in his friend's long hair and beard.

"You look worried," Thaddeus observed. "Something I should know about?"

"I am afraid so, my friend, and worse than you will be expecting." Desai let out a sigh.

Thaddeus and Desai had first met during the Abernathy affair, when Desai's men had rescued the policeman from one of the mad lord's malfunctioning machines. Thaddeus had heard Desai's name whispered before that, though, and had assumed that he was just another gang lord making money from the misfortunes of the poorest in the East End. This had turned out to be far from the truth. Desai had proven to be a great ally in helping

Rémy and Thaddeus thwart Abernathy's plans to destroy London. Afterwards, he had taken J under his wing, even letting the boy accompany him to his homeland of India to release Rémy from her family curse. Since he'd been back in London, Desai had been a great help in keeping an eye on the criminal workings of the city.

"Well, tell me," said Thaddeus, beginning to tidy his desk. "Perhaps it is something that, together, we can put right."

Desai smiled. "My young friend, your optimism and positive spirit are a valuable gem in these injurious times." He leaned forward. "You know that my men have been, as you would say, keeping an eye on the rivers?"

Thaddeus frowned, alert at once. "Yes, of course. Why? Has something come of it?"

Abernathy's plan had been to attack London from below, using terrifying machines of war that could navigate the city's submerged rivers. The would-be despot had died trapped inside one such contraption. It and the others had sunk into the silt deep below the streets when Rémy successfully disabled their power source. They were still there now. Desai had made it his mission to see that the machines never again saw the light of day.

Desai nodded. "At first my scouts believed they were interrupting salvage-seekers who had simply stumbled on some remains by accident. But now I am convinced otherwise. Over the past month, we have tracked three or four larger-scale operations that have specifically targeted the Black Ditch, where Abernathy's largest machines lie."

"'Specifically targeted'?" Thaddeus repeated. "That would mean that someone else knew what Abernathy was doing."

Desai nodded grimly. "Indeed, my friend. As I said, worse than you were expecting, no doubt."

"But how?" Thaddeus asked. "How could anyone know?"

The other man pulled a folded piece of paper from his pocket and passed it to the policeman. Thaddeus opened it. The paper bore two columns in Desai's neat handwriting. One was of names, the other a list of countries.

"What's this?"

Desai leaned back in his chair, steepling his fingers. "Besides monitoring the rivers, I have also been examining Abernathy's past, starting with that first fateful meeting with the Professor. My inquiries have turned up several disturbing facts, the chief among them being that Abernathy was not alone in his insanity. He had friends. The names you hold in your hand are his consorts, his encouragers, and, I am sorry to say… his investors."

Thaddeus stared at the note again, his stomach beginning to churn. Among the names listed were counts and princes, noblemen all. Their countries ranged from Bavaria to France, from Turkey to China and even beyond. He shook his head, reeling in a revelation he was only just beginning to grasp.

"Are you saying that these men may also have the machines the Professor designed?" he asked hoarsely. "What could they possibly want them for? War?"

Desai unsteepled his fingers to raise his palms. "This I do not know. At least one of them has been trying to recover what he can from the scene of Abernathy's failure."

Thaddeus looked up. "Surely that's a good sign? Perhaps it means that they have also failed in their own attempts and are clutching at anything."

Desai smiled wryly. "We can but hope. Alas, I think it more likely that at least one of these men is eager to see a return on his investment."

Thaddeus shook his head, staring again at the paper. "But what can we do? These men – they are powerful, and so spread out. Where do we even start?"

Desai sighed, a soft sound that filled the room with melancholy. "Ah, Thaddeus, this is where I must burden you further. Whatever must be done, must be done by you alone, at least in the immediate future, for I must return to my homeland to deal with a problem I had thought long quelled."

Thaddeus stared at Desai for a moment, unbelieving. "But... you've only just come back," he began. "And what problem could possibly be greater than the return of Abernathy's machines?"

The older man smiled sadly, his face creasing into a harmony of fine lines around his eyes and mouth. "There are things about my past you are unaware of; ancient responsibilities that cannot be ignored. But it is nothing you should burden yourself with, my friend. The Sapphire Cutlass is a worry for me alone." He reached out a hand, grasping Thaddeus' own firmly. "I am sorry to leave you at such a time. But in my absence, I wanted you to be aware. In case I do not come back–"

"What do you mean, in case you don't come back?"

"If I do not come back, my men have been ordered to report to you. In fact," Desai added, "I am informed that one of these–" he pointed to the paper Thaddeus still held, "is to meet with the salvage hawkers tonight. As yet, we do not know who, but finding out is vital. I feel it would be prudent for you to attend yourself, since I cannot."

"Tonight?" Thaddeus asked, looking at his watch. The evening was already drawing on. "You must leave so soon?"

"I am afraid I must. If you had plans this evening, I apologise, my friend, but–"

"It's nothing like that," Thaddeus interrupted quickly. "But a case I am working on – a difficult case – I finally have a lead... What time is the meeting?" Thaddeus asked, glancing at his watch again. "If it is late, as I'm sure it must be..."

"It is late, indeed," confirmed Desai, "for who conducts nefarious deeds in daylight? We believe the meeting is set for midnight – though, of course, it would be prudent to be in place beforehand in order to observe."

The policeman shut his eyes briefly. He had hoped never to enter the dank underworld that lurked beneath the city again. But it seemed he had no choice.

"I should be free from ten o'clock," he said quietly.

"Excellent." Desai stood up. "Where shall I have my man meet you?"

Thaddeus stood, too, his stomach churning. "Outside the Albert Saloon Theatre, in Britannia Fields."

"Very well." Desai dipped his head, a slow gesture full of dignity. "I am truly sorry for this abrupt departure, Thaddeus. With any luck, I will return swiftly and with a better plan of how to proceed. But for now, I must take my leave."

Once Desai had gone, Thaddeus sank back into his chair. He'd thought Abernathy's madness to be far in the past, but now it seemed that what they had battled was only the tip of the iceberg. He stared at the list of names Desai had given him. One drew his attention more than the others. Comte de Cantal de Saint-Cernin. Had he heard it, or something like it, before?

After another moment's thought, Thaddeus stood and reached for his coat. Desai's problem was not the only issue he had to deal with. Tonight he would come closer to finding out whether his hunch about the 'impossible' burglaries was correct.

Dark Deeds

Yannick was already on stage when Rémy arrived at the theatre that evening. Even without seeing them, she could tell from the buzz of the crowd that they loved his act. But that wasn't surprising – she'd always known Yannick was going to be a great magician once he'd honed his craft, in the same way that he'd always told her she was going to be an amazing trapeze artist.

Rémy stood in the wings and watched. "Is there someone out there willing to volunteer?" Yannick was saying, standing at the front of the stage and addressing the audience. "I need someone of strong mind; someone not easily swayed."

There was a chorus of calls from the seats. Rémy peeked out from the curtain to see a flurry of hands. Yannick picked a fat old wheezing man in a black dinner jacket who struggled slowly to the stage with the help of a carved, dog-headed cane.

"Welcome to the stage, Mr..." Yannick greeted him, his voice carrying sharply through the auditorium.

"Sir," said the old man, coughing slightly. "I am Sir Johnson."

"Sir Johnson, it is an honour to have you as my guest this fair night," Yannick corrected smoothly. "Now sir, I ask you again – are you of strong mind? If you are not, I fear..."

"Oh, I have a strong mind, damn you," boomed Sir Johnson. "Do your worst, trickster; you'll see you can't fox your betters. Stuff and nonsense, hypnosis – it'll only work on the weak. Not me, my boy, not me!"

Rémy smiled. So that was what Yannick needed the old goat for – to hypnotise him! A smart move because, unlike other tricks, hypnosis performed by one truly skilled in the art was no illusion – it was real, and it worked best on those who swore blind they could never be controlled by it, just as Sir Johnson had done. It was what made the turn so hilarious for the rest of the audience, and it was why they loved it. There was nothing better than seeing the pompous taken down a peg – or a dozen.

Rémy scanned the audience as Yannick prepared his hapless helper. They were animated, interested, excited. Good, that meant that when Rémy herself took the stage to finish off the night, the audience would be nicely warmed up and ready for–

Rémy froze, her gaze falling on a familiar figure in the fifth row. Oh, he was without his battered top hat, but she'd know that face anywhere. Thaddeus! What was he doing here? Had he come to see her perform? It was a sweet gesture, but it wouldn't…

Then it hit her. No, he wasn't here to see her. He was watching Yannick too intently for that, his sharp policeman's eyes following everything her friend did, taking it all in, filing it all away.

Thaddeus suspected Yannick! He still couldn't find the real culprit behind his blasted burglaries, and since he couldn't pin it on her – because she was innocent – he was going for the next best thing: Yannick, whom he'd hated on sight.

Rémy was instantly furious. How dare he? *How dare he?* Was Thaddeus going to pursue all her friends? Did the great and pure

Thaddeus Rec of Her Majesty's police assume that all former circus acts were criminals?

Rémy didn't see the rest of Yannick's act – she was too blind and deaf with rage. It bubbled in her ears, an angry roar that didn't diminish even when the audience exploded with applause as the curtain came down on a humiliated Sir Johnson.

"Rémy? What on earth's the matter?" Yannick asked as he stepped from the stage. He gripped her shoulders. "What is it? Tell me! You look as if the fires of hell itself burn behind your eyes this evening!"

"They might as well, too," Rémy hissed. "Yannick – we don't belong here. Not in this theatre, not on this stage, not in this stinking, godforsaken city."

"Rémy – what's happened?" Yannick asked, rubbing her arms in an attempt to calm her down. "You can't go out on the trapeze like this, you're too tense. You'll do yourself a mischief."

"I'm not going on," she spat out. "Not here, not ever again. Let's go back to France. Right now. We can get the last train from Waterloo and be on the first boat back home in the morning."

"But–" Yannick began.

"I mean it, Yannick," said Rémy. "We're not welcome here. Don't ask me why, but I know something bad will happen if you remain in London. We've got to go. Now."

Yannick stared into her eyes for a moment, and then away at the wall, frowning. *"D'accord,"* he said, finally. "Just give me a moment – I have an errand I must attend to."

He stepped away from her, motioning to one of the backstage boys who was lurking in the shadows. They conversed in low voices for a moment. Then the boy nodded once before vanishing back into the shadows.

"Right," said Yannick, returning to her. "Let's go."

They left the theatre quickly and quietly, slipping through the night as eels would through the murky sediment of the Thames.

* * *

Thaddeus did not stay for Rémy's performance. Instead, he left as soon as Yannick had exited the stage, having first noted Sir Johnson's name on the notepad he had tucked into his top pocket. That line of enquiry would have to wait for tomorrow. For now, he had even darker deeds to observe.

Desai's man fell into step with the policeman as soon as he left the theatre's main doors. He was hugely tall and broad-shouldered, with his dark hair swathed in a deep blue turban. As the policeman had expected, his escort had little to say, merely introducing himself as Satu.

"Follow," Satu said, then took off at a brisk pace to lead Thaddeus back east.

What Thaddeus had not expected was to find himself on the path beside Regent's Canal, heading towards Mile End. As they passed St Anne's, a vague suspicion of just how they would enter the remains of Abernathy's underworld began to occur to him.

"Wait," he said, pausing as a bridge loomed out of the darkness. "I know where this is. We're not – we can't be…"

Desai's man turned to look at the policeman, smiling slightly. "Please," he said, his deep voice rumbling in the darkness. "We are not far now."

Thaddeus began walking again, though reluctantly. He knew they weren't far away, because he had travelled this route before. He'd been in the company of Desai's men then, too – as well as

Desai himself. Rémy had been there, wounded by a gunshot and a terrible fall, and J, too. They'd all been prisoners of Abernathy's thugs, who had dragged them down into the darkness.

As they reached the bridge, there was a rustle in the undergrowth to his left. Thaddeus started as two eyes blinked out at him, but Satu seemed unperturbed. He nodded silently to the watcher, who nodded back and melted back into the verge. *A sentry*, Thaddeus thought. *One of Desai's own.*

His escort pulled an ancient, heavy key from beneath his dark robes and fitted it to the rusted lock of a door set in the side of the bridge. The door looked so old and disused that Thaddeus imagined most passers-by failed to even glance at it. But for those in the know…

The key turned and the door swung inwards. Beyond was an inky darkness that made Thaddeus shiver. Desai's man did not hesitate, stepping over the threshold and disappearing from view almost immediately. Thaddeus swallowed hard and then followed him, pushing the door shut and casting them both into pitch darkness.

There was the sound of a match being struck. A second later a yellow flame bloomed as Satu lit two sturdy candles and handed one to Thaddeus.

The dim candlelight revealed a set of wooden steps that twisted down and out of sight. From somewhere there came a slow, incessant *drip-drip-drip*, and the air reeked thick with rot. They slowly began to make their way down the stairs, for the steps were slippery and as degenerate as the air around them. As they reached the bottom, his guide turned to him, his face sallow in the weak candlelight. "Be careful," he said. "The way here is difficult. Watch your feet."

Satu was right. Thaddeus could feel slime beneath his shoes, and here the stink of old water was far worse. The drip had become a modest trickle – a remnant, no doubt, of the flood that had burst the underground banks of London's Black Ditch.

The policeman was beginning to think that they would walk forever when Satu stopped abruptly. Desai's man appeared to listen intently for a moment, and then turned to him.

"Thaddeus Rec," Satu said, in a low voice. "You must trust me now. Place your hand here." He turned his back to the policeman and patted his shoulder. When Thaddeus had done as instructed, Satu blew out his candle. "You, too, please."

Thaddeus hesitated for a moment, and then snuffed out their one remaining light. The darkness was instant and cloying, and he had to take a breath to steady himself. He felt Satu step forward, and followed – after all, the only alternative was to be left entirely alone in that dank passageway.

His guide continued to walk, without the aid of light. Thaddeus soon lost all sense of how far they had come and what direction they had taken, but his initial bout of panic had subsided. He was just beginning to think that his eyes had adjusted to the incessant gloom when he realised that, in fact, there was a light somewhere far ahead of them. It was tinged greenish-blue, eerie and dim, but it was definitely a light.

Satu stopped at the mouth of another turn. The light had grown strong enough that Thaddeus could see ahead now, and dropped his hand from his guide's shoulder.

"You see?" Satu asked, nodding towards what lay ahead.

Thaddeus did indeed see. Beyond the tunnel in which they stood, the passageway opened out, dropping several feet to form a wide, shallow cave. It was lit with torches burning with a strange green light that cast the place in peculiar, flickering shadows. Through this cavern cut a fast-running channel of water, formed with wide banks of stone on either side. It was what was in the water, though, that gave the policeman pause.

"That's one of Abernathy's underwater boats," he whispered, making sure that his voice didn't carry.

Satu nodded grimly. "It was found two nights ago. Whenever they salvage something like this, they bring it here. It is... a marketplace, of sorts."

Thaddeus rubbed his face, weary and worried. He'd only ever seen one of these machines before, but that had been enough to etch it into his memory. Its bottom half was almost like the normal hull of a boat, though it had been hammered from gleaming golden metal rather than wood. Above what would have been the deck, however, the contraption was encased in glass, so that it looked a little like a supernaturally strong bubble. The entire machine could be submerged. Abernathy had built several of them as war machines, intending to attack London from below, via the city's underground rivers.

"It's not in good shape," Thaddeus observed. The machine's glass was cracked. Its once shining metal was dented and dull. The policeman wondered what had happened to the crew, but thought the answer was probably obvious. He shivered. Thaddeus had thought he was going to drown that night, and that had been bad enough, but to have been stuck inside one of those things...

A noise echoed up from the cave, interrupting his dour thoughts. Satu crouched beside the wall, pulling Thaddeus down with him. Voices drifted up from below, along with the sound of echoing footsteps as a group of people entered the cavern. There were five of them, the leader a small, wiry man with ragged trousers and a dirty shirt. At his right hand was an individual that Thaddeus guessed was a bodyguard. His size would be enough to make anyone considering violence think twice, let alone the large pistol he could see jammed into the man's belt.

These two were a pair of the kind Thaddeus had seen many times in the East End, but the remaining three were something different. For a start, he instantly recognised the first as the Comte de Cantal, who had mocked him so mercilessly at Sir Henry Strong's table. *Of course,* Thaddeus thought. His name had even been on the list Desai had given him earlier – his *full* name, Comte de Cantal de Saint-Cernin. The Comte stood straight with his chin raised, his figure exuding a swagger that had nothing to do with movement and everything to do with expectation. This man was used to being obeyed. The Comte was dressed in a richly tailored suit matched with a long, dark coat of fine wool. In one hand he held a thin and elegant walking stick.

The party stopped beside the wreck of Abernathy's wondrous ship.

"Well?" said the thin man who had led them in. Thaddeus assumed he was the seller. "Told you the truth, didn't I? Didn't I say I'd hit the jackpot this time?"

The Comte regarded the contraption for a moment. He made a show of walking this way and that, looking it up and down.

"It is damaged," he observed, in his cool French accent.

"That ain't my fault, is it?" said the seller. "Not my concern, neither."

After another moment, the Comte nodded slowly. "I will give you two thousand pounds for it."

Thaddeus couldn't help drawing in a sharp breath. Two thousand pounds? That was more than he'd earn in years. It was an insane amount of money.

But the seller simply laughed. "You must think I were born yesterday," he said. "I won't take a shilling less than four thousand."

The Comte de Cantal made a disgusted sound in his throat. "Obscene. I will give you two thousand five hundred, and you will be grateful for it."

The seller shook his head firmly. "This ain't a negotiation, mister," he said. "I got another buyer, ain't I? And he's already agreed to the four thousand, like I asked for. Problem is, he's a bit far away, like, so I'd have to wait a few months for 'is payment. So if you stump up the cash sharpish, you can have it. If not, say toodle-pip to the find of a lifetime. Your call, yer lordship."

"Don't call me that, you impertinent whelp," said the Frenchman, through gritted teeth. "I will get you the money."

"When?" the seller asked. "Cos I got fees, you know. I got expenses. I can't be hanging around for the likes of you forever."

In a flash, the Comte had twisted the grip of his walking stick and had drawn out a slim but pointed sword, and was holding it at the seller's throat. He'd moved so quickly that the thick-necked bodyguard had had no time to react.

"Listen to me, you lowbred scoundrel," the Comte hissed, his angry voice echoing around the cave. "By rights I should not need to pay you at all. By rights, I should slit your throat and simply take this and everything else you have, for I have already paid. Paid, and paid, and paid. But, because I am a fair man, a good man, I will—"

The sound of running footsteps interrupted the man's flow. A boy, dressed all in black, entered the cave, out of breath and puffing hard. He went up to one of the Comte's men, who bent down so that the child could whisper in his ear.

"Well?" asked the Comte, his blade still at the seller's sweating throat. "What is it?"

The boy vanished again, his footsteps echoing back the way he had come.

"A message, sir." The man stepped forward and whispered in the Comte's ear.

There was a moment of silence. The Comte's face changed, relaxing as it lost all hint of the fury. Abruptly, he dropped his sword arm, releasing the seller to cough and splutter, supported by his useless bodyguard.

"Well," said the Comte, his voice soft and full of danger. "Well, well, well. How... unexpected." He contemplated for another few moments, seemingly lost in his own thoughts. Then he laughed, coldly, the unexpected sound bouncing around the chamber.

"It is your lucky day, it seems," he said to the seller, who was still recovering. "How about this, eh? Five thousand. I will give you five thousand, payable in cash. But you must wait for a month. Understand? In one month, I will have the money. Perhaps sooner. But you will wait, yes? You. Will. Wait."

The seller nodded. "All right, mister. But remember what we agreed on. Five thousand. We've got witnesses here, see?"

The Comte laughed again, the sound grating against the stone walls like nails down a blackboard. He sheathed his swordstick with a flourish. A moment later, he swept from the cave, the rest of them following in his wake.

Flight from London

Rémy hadn't spent much time on boats, but she liked them. She liked the feel of something solid under her feet that could still move however it pleased – it wasn't unlike being on the trapeze, but with less chance of falling. She stood at the stern, watching the white chalk cliffs of England fade into the low cloud and mist of early morning.

Yannick was off finding them something for breakfast. The crossing would take a few hours and they wouldn't reach the port of Calais before lunchtime. They were both already hungry, having forgone supper the night before. Rémy should have been feeling pleased that her plan had worked so smoothly – she'd rushed back to the Professor's workshop, hurriedly stuffed a few things in her battered old travelling pack, written a quick, guilty note for J and left. They'd narrowly caught the last train out of Waterloo station and stepped off it in Dover at about one in the morning. Then all they'd had to do was wait until the first boat left the harbour at six o'clock.

At first it had been exciting – Rémy had spent all her life on the move – and fleeing so suddenly had felt exhilarating and familiar. But now, as she stood watching the shores of England draw away from her, Rémy couldn't stop the melancholy seeping into her bones. She was accustomed to leaving places behind, but she usually took the people she loved with her on the journey.

Rémy pushed her unhappy thoughts away with a shrug. She had to get over it. She had thought there was something for her in London – she had thought there was something for her with Thaddeus – but it had not been the case. Now it was time to return to her real family – the circus – and to make sure that Claudette and Amélie were safe and sound.

She took the sheaf of letters from her pocket – the ones that Claudette had sent before her long and worrying silence – and was rereading them as Yannick returned.

"There wasn't much on offer, I'm afraid," he said, holding up a cloth-wrapped loaf and two battered-looking apples.

"It's fine," Rémy told him with a faint smile, taking one of the apples as he tore the bread in half.

They sat on the deck with their backs against the rails, facing the distant shores of France with the wind whipping around them. "What have you got there?" Yannick asked around a mouthful of bread.

"Claudette's letters. I thought that maybe she'd said something I hadn't noticed the first time, or that there might have been a hint that something was wrong, but…" Rémy shrugged and shook her head. "I can't find anything."

"I'm sure she's fine," Yannick said. "Claudette always struck me as someone who could look after herself. Like you."

Rémy smiled at the compliment. "Thanks – although Claudette's about a million times smarter than I am."

"I don't believe that for a second," Yannick told her. "Although –

there was always something... I don't know, a little mysterious about Claudette, wasn't there?"

Rémy took a bite of her apple. "What do you mean?"

Yannick shrugged. "She always seemed too well-educated for the circus, for one thing. All those languages she could speak." He waved at the bunch of papers in Rémy's hand. "And how many of us can write like her? Apart from you – and that was only because she taught you."

Rémy shook her head. She couldn't pretend she'd never wondered about her friend. Claudette *was* unusual for a circus woman. It wasn't just her knowledge of languages and history; it was the way she carried herself, her elegance and poise. Rémy had asked her where she came from once, but Claudette had dodged the question with one of her quiet smiles.

"And the more I think about her," the magician continued, "the more I think..."

"What?" Rémy frowned at the intense look on Yannick's face.

"Well," he said, "you're going to think I'm mad, but... all those strange things about her – they'd make sense if she were the Lost Comtesse."

Rémy nearly choked on her bread. She laughed out loud. "What – Claudette? *My* Claudette?"

"Why is it such a funny idea, Rémy?" Yannick asked, leaning forward. "Think about it. What do we know about her, really, other than the fact that she's far too educated for a circus brat? She's always vague when you ask her about her parents... And you remember the story – the old woman who raised the princess was supposed to be a palm-reader. Well, Claudette's a fortune-teller as well as a pickpocket, isn't she? She could have learned that from the old woman."

Rémy shook her head. "Claudette might have learned pickpocketing at the circus, but the fortune-telling isn't a trick. She can really do it. I've seen it happen – she sees things. It's part of her, not something she learned." Rémy stared at her bread for a moment. "Besides, she can't be the Lost Comtesse," she muttered, as much to herself as to him. "She'd have told me."

"Maybe she doesn't know," Yannick pointed out. "If she did, she wouldn't be lost, would she? Who in their right mind would carry on scraping a living in the circus when they're heir to that fortune?"

"I suppose," murmured Rémy. "But still…"

"You haven't ever noticed a birthmark? The Lost Comtesse is supposed to have one, isn't she?"

"Oh, yes – that's right. A dark mark that looks like a sea serpent. Well, there you go then," Rémy said, her relief taking her by surprise. "Claudette has no such mark."

"You're sure?" Yannick asked. "It was supposed to be on the child's back, wasn't it? Would you have definitely seen it?"

"Well – yes," said Rémy, frowning, although now she thought about it, she wasn't sure if she'd ever seen her friend's back properly. Claudette had a habit of keeping a long garment on, even when swimming. It was to protect her arms from the cold, she said, and Rémy had never questioned it. "I mean – I must have done. At some time…"

"Ah, well – I suppose when we get to the Jamboree and you find the Circus of Secrets, you can ask her, eh?"

"I don't think the Circus of Secrets will go to the Jamboree this year," said Rémy, as she shooed away a gull that was a little too interested in their breakfast.

Yannick sat up with a frown. "Oh? Why not?"

"I've been looking at the postmarks of the towns these were sent from," said Rémy. "Claudette seemed to be working her way south, taking the circus away from Paris and the Jamboree, not towards it."

Yannick brushed the crumbs from his fingers before reaching for the letters. "May I?"

Rémy passed them over and he went through them one by one, studying the stamps and marks. "Which was the last one you received? This one?" He held one up.

"Yes," she said. "It was posted from Moulidars."

The magician nodded with a smile. "Well then," he declared. "That is where we shall start, Little Bird. Then we'll follow the trail until we find the Circus of Secrets. We'll catch up with them in no time!"

"But – I thought you'd want to go to the Jamboree," said Rémy. "Don't you want to find a place with a new circus?"

"Yes," said Yannick, "although to tell the truth, Rémy, I'm hoping that my new circus might turn out to be my old one." He grinned at her and raised his eyebrows. "Wouldn't it be great if I could join the Circus of Secrets? It'd be just like old times."

Rémy laughed. "Except that we're much older. And wiser," she added.

"Yes," agreed Yannick, watching the hopeful gulls still darting into the boat's wake. "Yes, that we are."

* * *

Rémy and Yannick reached Calais at midday, stepping from the ferry and into sunshine. Rémy was momentarily flummoxed to find herself surrounded by people speaking her native tongue. It had been so long since she'd spoken French properly that for a few moments it felt strange to hear the lilt of it everywhere, instead of the blunt vowels of English curled around the cockney tongues of the East End.

"It's good to be home, isn't it?" said Yannick, watching her with a smile. "Smell that bread! See that sun! Good God, Rémy, what on earth were we thinking when we left this for decrepit little England?"

Rémy laughed along with him, but still she felt a brief pang in her heart. She wondered what Thaddeus was doing at that moment. J must have found her note and told him of their departure by now. Rémy had thought about leaving one for Thaddeus, but what could she have said? At the time she'd been so angry about seeing him there in the theatre, blatantly lining up her friend as his next target, that she'd not even wanted to say goodbye. And now…

"Rémy!"

She jolted out of her reverie to discover that Yannick was no longer by her side. Instead, he was standing under the sign that pointed to the train station.

"What are you doing?" she asked, as she hurried over to him.

"Train, Rémy. We need to catch a train. If we take it as far as Angoulême, we'll be pretty close to Moulidars, the last place we know the Circus of Secrets stopped."

Rémy shook her head. "I can't afford a train ticket, Yannick! I used most of my money to get us this far. I was thinking we could find a cart or something going in that direction…"

Yannick shook his head firmly. "It'll take too much time. Leave it to me. With any luck, we won't have to wait long for the next train."

"But…" Rémy started, but Yannick vanished into the crowds

before she had a chance to say anything else. He reappeared a few minutes later with two tickets in his hand.

"We're out of luck, I'm afraid – there's an hour's wait until the next one."

Rémy shrugged. "It doesn't matter. Yannick, listen. Thank you so much, but how did you afford the–"

He cut her off with another smile. "Rémy, it's nothing. Really. Now come, let's go and wait on the platform. It'll be quieter there."

The station at Calais had only two platforms. They fought their way through the crowds to Platform Two. Yannick showed their tickets to the guard waiting by the entrance. The guard scrutinized their tickets before waving them through.

Beyond the barriers, the platform was almost empty, though on the other side stood an engine just arrived from Paris. It gleamed red in the midday sun, disgorging a final stream of hissing steam into the cloudless blue sky as passengers spilled out of its doors. Rémy watched them scurrying about, hauling bags, gripping hats, calling for children in danger of being lost in the fray. It reminded her of an audience at the end of a performance, and another wave of homesickness struck her. Whatever she had left behind in England, Rémy was looking forward to being back with Claudette and the circus. The further away she got from London, the more those six months felt like an unearthly dream.

"Rémy?" asked Yannick, from the bench he'd found. "You are far away again."

She smiled. "Sorry," she said. "Just a lot to–"

She stopped dead as she saw the poster. It was pinned to the post behind the bench, there for all to see.

"What is it?" Yannick said, the look on her face making him leap to his feet. Together they stared at the poster. A sharp sketch

72

of Rémy's face stared back at them. The words below the picture read 'WANTED FOR THE THEFT OF JEWELS'.

"Ahh," said Yannick.

Rémy dipped her head and pulled her hair around her face, glancing quickly around them. "Someone's going to see me! We have to get out of here."

Yannick laid a hand on her shoulder. "Don't panic, Little Bird. There's no one here at the moment except us and the chubby guard who let us in, and he didn't even look at our faces. When our train arrives, people will be too busy with their own affairs to even notice us, and once we're aboard, we'll find a quiet carriage and keep ourselves to ourselves. There is nothing to worry about."

His reassurances did nothing for Rémy. "We should never have chosen the train," she muttered. "It would have been safer by road."

"And slower," he reminded her. "Really, Rémy..."

She looked around, spying a sign for a ladies-only toilet. "I'll be back," she told Yannick, walking quickly towards it.

Inside, Rémy locked the door. *Stupid*, she thought. *How could you forget that you are a wanted girl here in France, as well as in England? Welcome home indeed, Little Bird!*

With one quick tug, Rémy let her hair fall down around her shoulders, and then opened her bag, searching for the nail scissors she had found in the Professor's workshop and always carried with her. They most definitely weren't for cutting hair, but this was an emergency and they were all she had.

Taking a breath, Rémy grasped the first strands and snipped.

* * *

She emerged as their train pulled into the station. It wreathed the platform in thick white steam that billowed around her as she headed towards Yannick. He was examining something in his hand, and only glanced at her when he first looked up. A second later he looked back, his eyebrows raised, with a slight smile on his face.

"You never were one for doing things by halves, were you, Rémy Brunel?" he said.

Rémy ran her fingers through her newly short hair. "Different enough?" she asked.

"Different, but still beautiful," he told her. "As always, of course."

Rémy flushed at the compliment and how easily it had been given. Wouldn't life be simpler if all men could say what they were thinking just as easily? Pushing away the turn of her thoughts, she looked up at the poster of herself. It had gone.

Yannick moved closer to her as the passengers began to disembark around them in a cloud almost as thick as the engine's smoke. He showed her what was in his hands – the poster.

"So no one else sees," he told her. "Everything will be fine, Rémy. Trust me."

She was about to reach for it, to tear it into pieces so small that no one would ever be able to tell it had been her face that was drawn there, but before she could, Yannick moved. He turned towards their train as he folded the paper, tucking it into his pocket before looking back at her.

"Shall we, Little Bird?" he asked, offering her his arm.

Nine

A Rude Awakening

Thaddeus had finally reached his bed as the clock was touching one in the morning, and so was asleep when J arrived at his lodgings a few short hours later. A distant banging disturbed his dreams. He opened his eyes to see the door to his room vibrating on its hinges as Mrs Carmichael pounded at it, yelling at him to wake up.

Thaddeus dragged himself blearily out of bed and pulled on his dressing gown before opening the door to his landlady.

"For goodness' sake, Mr Rec," she snarled, her coarse grey hair beginning to escape her hairnet. "I will not be having these goings-on in this respectable establishment!"

"I apologise, Mrs Carmichael," Thaddeus said automatically. "May I ask to which goings-on you are referring?"

"There is… there is a… a *street urchin*," the woman said, her lips curling around the words as if they were filth itself sticking between her crooked teeth. "He's downstairs. I tried to shoo him away, but he won't go. I even threatened to call the police, but the little monster still won't budge."

Thaddeus stepped into the shabby hallway outside his room. "Perhaps because I am, in fact, the police, Mrs Carmichael?" he suggested mildly. "I think I know the boy you mean. He must have good reason to call at," he looked at the clock, surprised to find the hour barely touching five, "such a disagreeable time."

His landlady followed him down the stairs. "I don't know what you think you're playing at, Mr Rec," she said.

Thaddeus stopped on the bottom step and turned to her. "I could find other lodgings, Mrs Carmichael. If that would suit you better?" He raised an eyebrow, though he already knew her response. Whatever her gripes, in Thaddeus Mrs Carmichael had by far the most respectable tenant she could hope for.

"Less of your lip, if you please. I'm the owner of this house, not a washerwoman or such." She pushed him out of the way and, grumbling, headed back to her own room.

"Oh, Thaddeus," said a breathless J, as the door opened. "Sumfin' right awful's happened! It's Rémy. She's gone!"

Something like a millstone thumped into Thaddeus' stomach and rested there. He said nothing for a moment, and then nodded once. "J, I'm going to get dressed. Give me two minutes. Then we'll go and get breakfast."

* * *

Thirty minutes later, they were seated in the murky bow window of The Grapes, each with a plate of ham and eggs and a pint of strong, hot tea in front them. Neither of them, however, seemed to have much of an appetite.

"They must've left last night," J said miserably. "I didn't hear 'em go. They must 'ave got back from the theatre early, like, when I was still working, and just upped and went."

Thaddeus stared at the brief note, written in Rémy's haphazard handwriting.

76

I'll miss you, J. I'm sorry not to say goodbye in person, but I don't think I can stay in England any longer. I will remember you always. Take care of yourself and be good.

Rémy

There was no mention of Thaddeus at all. He wondered for a moment if she might have left him his own note, at the police station perhaps, but dismissed that notion as soon as it arose. He already knew she hadn't. Why would she, when he was what she was running from?

"This was all they left?" Thaddeus asked.

"Nearly, but not quite." J pulled out a crumpled roll of paper from his bag. "They forgot to take this with 'em."

Thaddeus took the sorry scroll and unfurled it. It was a poster, proclaiming in large red and yellow letters that something called a Jamboree was about to happen. The images depicted all manner of circus performers, from high-wire walkers to elephant riders.

"It's some big circus event that's going on in Paris," J said eagerly.

"Right," said Thaddeus heavily, letting the scroll roll back into itself and dropping it onto the table.

"Don't you see?" J asked. "It's where we'll find 'em!"

Thaddeus picked up his mug of tea and stared into it. "We won't be going to find them, J."

"Why not? It'll be easy! They're two circus folks, heading back to the circus. Where else would they go?"

Thaddeus shook his head. "That may be so, but there's the little thing of getting there. I don't have any money. Do you? Certainly not enough for the train and then the boat that we'd need to take. And say we do get there – say we do find them. Then what? What do we do then?"

J stared at the policeman. "We get her back," he said slowly, as if he were talking to a simpleton. "You get her *back*."

Thaddeus sighed. "I don't see why she'd be willing to listen to me, J," he said. "She never has before."

"Yeah, she has," said J, staring at Thaddeus intently. "That time you told her you loved her. I was there, 'member? She listened to you then, didn't she?"

The policeman felt his cheeks go red at J's words. "That was... they were extreme circumstances, J. It's not—"

"It ain't what? It ain't true?" J made a disgusted sound in his throat. "Poppycock. You ain't pulling that one, Thaddeus. I know you love 'er. Just like I know she loves you, even if she ain't smart enough to sort that out in her own head, yet. I don't know what you two've been playing at over the past few months, honest I don't. I thought, once you'd found her again, you'd be happy – both o' yer. But you've been dancing around each other like two fish in the net."

"J–" Thaddeus began, uncomfortable.

"Don't you 'J' me," said the boy, warming to his theme. "You's both as pig-headed as the other. And then this Yannick bloke comes along and catches you napping, and now he's carried 'er off and you're just going to let 'im get away wiv it?"

Thaddeus laughed at the notion of anyone carrying Rémy off. "J, you know as well as I do that Rémy never does anything she doesn't want to. If she's gone back to France, it's because it's where she wants to be, and if she's gone with Yannick, it's because she wants to be with him. I'm not sure what you think I can do about that."

"Sumfin'!" J exclaimed, thumping his hand on the table and causing his uneaten fried eggs to wobble wildly on the plate.

"Sumfin', instead of nuffin'! How can you just let her go, especially with that Yannick bloke? He's as dodgy as the pope's cloak is long, and what's more, I think you know it. Don't yer?"

Thaddeus grimaced. "Yes, J, I think he might be. But all I've got are theories and a hunch."

"Why don't you trust him?" J asked. "What is it you fink 'e's done?"

Thaddeus glanced out of the window at the busy high road. "There hasn't been time to investigate properly."

"Come on," J insisted. "Out wiv it. No other beggar's going to listen to yer, are they?"

Thaddeus laughed, though there wasn't much mirth in it. "All right, then. These robberies – there've been two of them now. Impossible thievery, right through locked doors. Tell me, J – how do you steal something through several locked doors when the keyholder swears the keys never left their sight?"

J shrugged. "Can't see how you would do it, to tell you the truth. I surely wouldn't try, that's for sure."

"Exactly. Because it's impossible. And yet it happened. So what does that tell us?"

"Yer've got me there. What?"

Thaddeus leaned back, his breakfast forgotten. "You don't do it, J. You don't."

J stared at the policeman for a moment, and then blinked. "Have I missed something? Cos–"

"The only way those jewels got out of those strongboxes and through those locked doors is if the keyholders either never put them in there in the first place, or they took them out themselves. Nothing else makes sense. You can't do the impossible."

J stabbed a piece of burnt toast with the point of his knife and shoved it into his mouth, chewing thoughtfully. "You sayin' these rich fellers stole their own baubles? For the insurance or sumfin'? Cos I can't see that theory going down too well."

Thaddeus shook his head. "No. No, I think whatever they did, they did willingly, but without realising it. That's why there's no sign of a break-in – because there wasn't one."

J looked perplexed. "I've got no idea what you're on about."

Thaddeus sighed. "Well, anyway, it's irrelevant. It's just a theory, and I don't have any way to prove it."

"But you fink it was Mr Fancy-Pants magician, right? Yannick, you fink 'e was behind it?"

Thaddeus stared into his rapidly cooling tea. "I don't know what I think. I'm pretty sure that he's been in town longer than he let us assume. I spoke to two theatre owners who both say they've employed a hypnotizing magician with a French accent over the past month. Both of them had different names, but they fit Yannick's description and both burglary victims visited those theatres on the nights their crimes were committed. Now I won't know if there wasn't another burglary because Yannick's not my man, or because he left town before he could complete the third. None of that proves anything, anyway. Maybe I just want it to be him. Maybe me suspecting The Magnificent Yannick has nothing to do with police instinct and everything to do with me being..." He trailed off.

"Jealous?" J prompted shrewdly. When Thaddeus didn't reply, he went on, "Well, what about the Frenchie coppers? Can't you check in with them, find out a bit more about 'im? If they've got gripes as well, they might give us a bit of help tracking him and Rémy down. You won't even have to go yourself. Problem solved."

Thaddeus looked at J seriously. "You're right, they might help. But what about Rémy, J?"

"What *about* Rémy? This is perfect – the police'll go looking for Yannick and lead us straight to her."

"Exactly. Rémy's hardly what you'd call a clean character, is she? She's a wanted woman, most likely in every country in Europe. And you want to send the gendarmerie after her?"

J sat down again, his face glum. "That's a good point."

Thaddeus nodded. "There's something else, too," he said, after a moment's hesitation. "Desai came to visit me yesterday."

J's eyebrows shot up at the sound of his mentor's name. "Why? More trouble?"

Thaddeus sighed. "You could say that." He quietly outlined what their friend had told him about the list of names, adding a description of the Comte de Cantal and his late-night visit into the bowels of the city. J's face paled as Thaddeus went on, the boy's fingers gripping his knife and fork until they turned white.

"Blimey," J muttered, when Thaddeus was done. "That's not good. That's not good at all."

"The worst thing is," Thaddeus added, "after I saw Yannick last night on stage in his top hat and tails, I finally remembered where I'd first seen him – why he looked so familiar. He was the man who brought the Comte a message during Sir Henry's dinner. He was talking to the Comte as I left."

"Hang about," hissed J. "You're telling me that rotter Yannick is mixed up with Abernathy's lot?"

"I don't know that exactly, but..."

"Wait, wait, wait," said J. "Go back a mo. You mentioned this Comte feller, that he needs money, right? And you reckon

Yannick's in league wiv 'im, on top o' which, you fink Yannick's the one who's been nicking all these jewels. See where I'm going 'ere? What if this bloke the Comte has gone and got himself a way of picking up all the money he wants – he just gets his tame hypnotist to nick him a new bauble to flog every time he needs the cash, right?"

"Right," said Thaddeus. "That does make sense, because otherwise it'd be Yannick who was living it up like a prince, instead of bunking down with you and Rémy at the docks."

"Yeah," said J, raising his eyebrows. "Unless there was a *reason* 'e was looking for the greatest jewel thief in Europe... Rémy got away from that Gustave bloke, but I bet there are loads out there just like him who'd kill to have a pet jewel thief as good as she is. How much money do you fink it'd take for Yannick to be willing to hand her over to one o' them, eh? Like this feller, the Comte?"

Thaddeus stared at him, the cogs whirring around in his mind. "The Comte told the seller of Abernathy's machine that he'd have five thousand pounds for him within a month..."

J speared a piece of ham and stuffed it into his mouth. "Sure sounds like he needs someone who can nick 'im sumfin' big in a hurry, don't it? We know anyone who fits the bill, d'ya fink?"

Thoughts whirled in Thaddeus' head. He'd always seen Rémy as a free spirit – strong-willed, able to do whatever she wanted. But he hadn't known her before, when she'd been part of that circus of villains, all kept on a nasty kingpin's leash.

"That'd be awful, wouldn't it?" J probed. "If that's what Yannick's about? And you know what'll be even more awful? The fact that if you don't go after her, you'll never know. Will yer?"

The boy was right. Thaddeus knew he was right. And, moreover, Thaddeus wanted to go after her – he did. Of course he did! How could he live the rest of his life without her in it? How could he let the Comte de Cantal use her to become the kind of threat he would be with one of Abernathy's awful machines? But it was no good.

Thaddeus shook his head, staring at the congealed mess of his wasted breakfast. "There's no way to get there, J. I just don't have the money."

J grinned. "Tell you what, I might be able to help you there." The boy leapt up. "Meet me at the workshop tonight. The later the better. And be ready to have the biggest adventure of your life!"

"J," Thaddeus began, but the boy was already halfway to the door, weaving between the tables. "J – wait! What–"

"See you later!" J shouted, just before the door banged shut behind him.

Ten

An Unexpected Departure

It was well after eleven o'clock that evening when Thaddeus headed for the Professor's workshop. As he walked, he wondered how long they would continue to call it that. It seemed to have stuck, despite the man being dead these six months now, and despite Thaddeus being the only one of the three that had ever really known him. Or at least, Thaddeus reflected, he had *thought* he'd known the Professor.

The workshop was in darkness when he finally reached it, the door firmly locked. Thaddeus slipped his key in, and the door swung inwards with a familiar rusty squeal.

"J?" Thaddeus called into the room beyond. The fire had burned to embers and the dinner table was empty. He tried not to look towards the door to Rémy's room, but failed. It was half open, as if she'd just stepped out for a moment. "J," he called again, turning away. "Where are you?"

Thaddeus was about to knock on J's bedroom door when it opened. J's face appeared around it, speckled with grime and grease and wearing a pair of oversized glasses with metal surrounds, rather like the Professor's revolutionary night-vision goggles, but far more substantial.

"There you is," said J, with a sigh of relief. "When I said late, I didn't mean tomorrer."

"Sorry," said Thaddeus. "There was a lot I had to do at the station." In truth, Thaddeus hadn't known how to leave. J had seemed convinced – though Thaddeus couldn't imagine how – that they would be setting off for France tonight. For Thaddeus to take a sudden leave of absence in the middle of such a difficult case was impossible, so in the end he'd just left two notes on his desk for Collins to find in the morning. One was a list of tasks for the sergeant to get on with while he was gone, and the other simply saying, 'Following urgent leads. May be away a few days. Will be in touch when I can.'

At least two of those three sentences were lies, though Thaddeus tried not to think about which they were. If he had a chance of saving Rémy and thereby thwarting the Comte's plans, what other choice did he have but to abandon his post? With any luck, he'd also be able to reveal Yannick as the perpetrator of the robberies, and thus return with the case solved and the criminal in custody.

"Ah well," said J, with a shrug. "You're here now. Best come in then, hadn't yer?"

Thaddeus frowned. Neither he nor Rémy had ever been inside J's bedroom. They understood that the street boy, never having had a home before, wanted his own private place. "Into your bedroom?" he asked. "Whatever for?"

The boy grinned. "For a copper, you ain't always very observant, are yer? You ever see me sleep in 'ere?"

"Er, no. But–"

J disappeared for a second, and there was the sound of a winch being turned, the faint squeak of rope winding over rope.

85

And then, much to Thaddeus' astonishment, the wall of J's room began to fold back on itself. What he had always assumed to be solid walls of wood zigzagged together, moving along cunning metal tracks embedded in the floor and ceiling, until the whole wall had neatly removed itself to one side.

"So then, Mr Rec," said J in a theatrical voice. "What do you fink of the Professor's greatest invention?"

It took Thaddeus a moment to move, and even longer to draw his next breath. Inside the now-open room was another workshop. It was as cluttered as the main room of the warehouse, but a space had been cleared right in the centre of the floor, and it was what stood here that had made the policeman's mouth fall open and his eyes bulge in naked shock.

The huge structure looked a little like the hull of a boat, though it was like no boat Thaddeus had ever seen. Made of wood as well as scraps of metal riveted together, the vessel looked like a large, sealed tube with two smaller tubes connected at either side. Three small round windows had been cut into the wall along the length of the main cylinder, with wooden shutters that fastened to close them. There was a hatch, too, currently sealed shut. At one end of the vessel – which Thaddeus took to be the front – was a semicircular window. Below this, pointing out like the sharp nose of a deep-sea creature, was a twisted spindle of metal that tapered to a lethal-looking point. At the other end were fixed several small but powerful-looking propellers.

"J," said Thaddeus, slowly walking forward in wonder. "What on earth is it?"

"It's a ship," the boy said, with unmistakable pride. "But it ain't any old sailboat, oh no. This here is an airship."

Thaddeus turned to look at J in astonishment. "An airship? What do you mean?"

"It flies, Thaddeus!" J said, proudly. "Now d'yer see what I meant earlier? We don't need no train or boat to get us to France! We can just take off right from here and fly ourselves there."

Thaddeus blinked. "Fly to France? How? I've heard of balloons crossing over to the continent, but this is no balloon…"

Chuckling, J beckoned him over to a cluttered workbench that ran along the left wall. In the centre of the bench, an oil lamp burned gently, illuminating the pages of a large, open book.

"See this?" J said, pointing to it. "This here book has got all the Professor's inventions in it – whether he got around to making them or not. I found it the first week me and Rémy moved in and I've been trying to work it all out ever since."

Thaddeus paged through the book, taking in the intricate sketches and scrawled notes. There were detailed plans for everything, from the night-glasses to the terrifying mechanical armour that Abernathy had put his hired thugs into. Further in, Thaddeus came across another version of the mechanical armour. He stared at the helmet, which seemed to have no space for a human head. Beside him, J shuddered.

"Now, these I'm glad he never made," said the boy. "These would 'ave been nasty blighters, and no mistake. Best as I can work out, they're metal soldiers with clockwork bits inside, instead of brains. Imagine that! A soldier who don't even 'ave to think. Can't get scared, can't stop, doesn't feel 'urt. Just goes and goes, and is stronger than an ox." He shuddered again.

The policeman shook his head, turning the page to yet another scrawl of scribbled words and pictures. "How on earth did you manage to decipher all this, J?"

The boy huffed a little. "Just cos I was raised on the street don't mean I'm silly in the 'ead. You should know that right enough. The Sally Ann, they used to teach me my letters a bit – after they'd read the Good Book, o' course. And then Mr Desai, he taught me some more. The rest I've just been working out for meself."

Thaddeus patted the boy on the shoulder. "I didn't mean the reading part, J," he said. "I meant, how did you understand all this? It doesn't make a whit of sense to me!"

"Ah, well," said J. "It don't always make sense to me, neither. You might say there's been a fair bit of trial and error, like. That's why I never showed you and Rémy this before. I wanted to get it right. I wanted you to see that I ain't a waste of space, or nuffin'."

"You'd never be a waste of space, J," Thaddeus said, but the boy had already moved on.

"Anyways, I was struggling with what you said – how this thing flies," he said, waving at the airship. "Far as I could make out from the pictures, it needed some big jewel to power it. But I ain't exactly walkin' round with a stock o' diamonds, am I? But then, couple o' nights ago, Rémy came home with that big old ruby on her finger, and it all came together."

"What did?" Thaddeus asked, trying not to remember what had happened when he'd seen that ring for the first time. The thought of that encounter was still bitter.

"Just stay here and watch. You's got to see this from the outside," said J, with another grin. He went to the hatch in the side of the vessel and pulled a wooden lever. The hatch eased down to reveal a small flight of wooden steps that led up into the ship. The boy went up the stairs and disappeared into the airship.

Thaddeus waited outside the strange vessel. Nothing happened. "J?" he called. "I can't see anything."

"Hold on, why don't yer!" came back a muffled cry from inside the great contraption. "Give an airship 'alf a chance!"

Then, slowly, something began to happen. There was a hissing sound, faint at first but then louder. A moment later, something began to rise from the top of the ship. At first Thaddeus couldn't work out what it was – it seemed to be a sail that had been packed away somewhere out of sight – but then he realised. It was a balloon. A great oval balloon was slowly rising above the roof of the airship. It was bigger than the ship itself, and it eventually began to press against the workshop's ceiling.

"Pretty amazin', huh?" said J, appearing beside Thaddeus and looking up at the balloon with his hands on his hips.

"It really is," agreed Thaddeus. "But–"

"Hang on a mo. I'll just stop that there balloon filling for a bit so it don't get caught on them rafters." The boy was about to disappear into the airship's interior when he turned to wink at the policeman. "About time you saw inside, don't you fink?"

Thaddeus didn't need a second invitation. He climbed the narrow steps, ducking to avoid bashing his head on the low lintel at the top. Inside, the curved walls enclosed a space that was far smaller than had been suggested from the outside. Thaddeus found that he couldn't stand up straight except for in the very centre of the room, or else his head would press against the wood. The floor was a patchwork of mismatched wooden planks, all lovingly polished to a high shine.

At one end of the airship were four narrow bunks, two on each side, one above the other. One of the lower bunks had obviously already been claimed by J, as it also had a pillow and a crumpled blanket atop it. At the other end of the airship was the window that Thaddeus had seen from outside. Set in front of it, reaching up from the floor to about halfway up this window, was a semicircular cabinet overlaid by and riveted together with brass, tilted at an angle like a writing desk. Into its golden surface were set various knobs, levers and handles, all currently being manned by J. The boy sat in front of the controls on a small wooden chair that had been connected to a spindle so that it could pivot in a circle. He was busily whirling a handle. The hissing that had filled the cabin slowed and then eventually stopped.

"There," said J with a beam of pride, as he swung around to face the policeman. "Well?" he asked. "What do you fink? Shall we make for France?"

Thaddeus surveyed the airship again. There were basic wooden cabinets for storage, small oil lamps for light, and a barrel full of water. On one wall, a stepladder led up to another hatch that would open onto the roof.

Thaddeus shook his head. "All of this is amazing, J. But even with that great balloon, I can't see this thing ever lifting off. It must be incredibly heavy."

"Ah," said the boy, holding up a finger. "But you see, that balloon ain't just filled with air. That's where the ruby comes in."

Thaddeus shook his head. "You've lost me, J."

J headed back towards the control panel, and then knelt on the floor in front of it. "You know what the old Professor was like. He had that thing about precious stones, didn't he?" said the boy, as he heaved up another hatch, this one set in the floor. "He believed they had powers. Like the ones Abernathy was trying to use for himself, right? Well, take a look," he advised.

Thaddeus knelt and stuck his head into the hole. There was just enough light for him to see a complicated tangle of tubes and wires. They led to and from a central apparatus – a large glass canister full of a filigree of copper, enclosed at one end and open at the other with another glass pipe connected to it at the mid-point. Above its open end hovered a clamp, and held by the clamp was Rémy's ruby ring.

"Watch this," said J, standing up and reaching for the ship's controls. He pulled one lever and then wound the circular handle he'd undone just moments before.

Thaddeus watched as the ring lowered slowly, pushing into the glass canister until it was only millimetres from the copper filaments. The filaments began to vibrate, faster and faster, until they were moving so swiftly that Thaddeus could hardly see them. The ruby began to glow, and then, as if by magic, a pale green smoke began to coalesce against the glass. It filled the canister and billowed up the connecting pipe before disappearing in the tangle of tubes. The hissing returned, growing louder as the ruby glowed even brighter.

"And there you 'ave it," said J, shutting down the reaction again. The ruby retracted on its tiny winch, its bright cherry glow fading slowly. "It ain't air in that balloon at all. It's stuff that came straight out of the Professor's brain, and that's good enough for me."

Thaddeus stood up as J closed the hatch back over the ruby's encasement. He shook his head. "This whole contraption is astonishing, J. But even if you did trust it to fly, how would you ever get it out of the workshop?"

J grinned, heading for the hatch and leaping down the steps to the floor in one bound. "Ain't you learned yet? The Professor thought of everything, so he did."

Thaddeus followed as J disappeared around the airship. There came the sound of metal being forced against metal, and rope crossing over rope. There was a moment of silence, and then, from far above them, came a long, slow creak.

"I could do wiv a bit of a hand here, Thaddeus," yelled J.

Thaddeus ducked under the ship's hull and saw J turning a huge wooden handle that was housed against the far wall. He gripped the opposite side and together they heaved.

"That's it," yelled J. "She's working – she's working!"

Suddenly Thaddeus felt a draught. Then it was more than a draught – it was a wave of cold night air crashing over his shoulders. He looked up to see one of the roof panels flopping back on itself, just like the wall had done.

"Brilliant, ain't it?" yelled J, over the slow squeak and squeal of the moving roof. The final panel fell back with a *whump*, and J's bedroom-cum-private-workshop was entirely open to the night skies, ready to let the airship take off.

"Well, I'll be…" muttered Thaddeus, turning around below the festival of stars he could now see through the London smog.

"See? The old Professor, he thought of everything. There's even a switch I can throw to shut it behind us once we're out and about. Right then. Ready to go, are yer?"

Thaddeus looked at the boy. "Now? Right now, just like that?"

J shrugged. "Why not? We'd best get going now, before some smart Joe outside comes to see what all the noise is about."

"But–"

As J disappeared around the hull, Thaddeus made his way up the airship's short gangplank and followed him inside.

"J, wait," Thaddeus began, as the boy turned the handle to inflate the balloon with the ruby's mysterious gas. The sound of hissing returned. It seemed even louder than before, and somehow more insistent. "J, now just hold on a minute…"

J turned to him with both eyebrows raised. "What's the matter? Didn't bring enough spare undies? I did tell you to be prepared, didn't I?"

"Yes, J, you did, but…"

"Oops," said J, as the ship shuddered slightly. "Before you settle in, Thaddeus, I'm going to need your help. You saw the ropes tying us down, right?"

The airship gave another judder, this time rising a few inches off the ground. Thaddeus reached for the wall to brace himself. "What, outside?"

"Yeah. They need cutting. Do the honours, could yer?" J pointed to a small axe secured against the wall. "No need to be dainty or nuffin', just chop 'em off and we'll be ready to go, like."

"Hold on," said Thaddeus. "If I'm outside when we cast off, how do I get back in? Can you stop the ship from rising?"

"Ah," said J. "I don't think so, no."

"You don't think so?"

"It'll be fine," yelled J over the hissing of the gas. "Just be quick, and you'll make it to the gangplank, no problem. Better do it now, though," prompted the boy as the ship lurched and bounced, "cos she's fair raring to go!"

Thaddeus shook his head and grabbed the axe before heading for the gangplank, where the wooden stairs were already a few inches off the ground. He jumped out and ran for the aft tethers first, striking the rising rope. The axe was sharp and sliced through with just one strike. The airship immediately pulled upwards, its nose still tethered to the ground but the stern swinging up towards the open roof.

"That's the stuff," yelled J from inside the ship. "Quick now – gotta cut the other one before she does 'erself a mischief!"

The airship was lurching from one side to the other, knocking into the crowded walls of the workshop. There was a crashing, clattering noise as he ran for the other rope – one of the ship's fins had caught the edge of an over-piled shelf, sending its contents smashing to the floor. He chopped at the second rope, but missed as the ship slewed away from him.

"Hold it steady, J," he shouted.

"I'm trying!" came J's voice back again. "Hurry up!"

Thaddeus' second blow missed again, but the third was enough. The rope broke with a twang and the ship immediately lifted off so fast that Thaddeus had no time to make it to the gangplank. He grabbed for the rope instead, clinging on as the airship made a bid for freedom through the open ceiling.

"Thaddeus!" J shouted from within. "Where are you?"

"Put her down, J!" Thaddeus yelled as the airship continued to rise. Every second took him higher. He looked down to see he was already several feet from the ground.

"I can't do that!" said J. "The ruby will be all used up if I do! It'd take hours for it to charge again!"

Thaddeus looked around wildly, trying to work out what to do. The gangplank was still hanging open, moving slightly as the ship bumped its way skyward, almost out of the workshop now. Thaddeus twisted on the rope to look over his shoulder and saw the edge of the open roof looming nearer. He swung towards it, his weight enough to jerk the airship.

"Watch it!" J cried as the nose dipped, but Thaddeus ignored him. He swung the rope again towards the roof. His feet connected with it, just long enough for him to brace against the edge and spring away. Thaddeus flew through the night air, using his momentum to reach for the gangplank. He crashed into it, letting go of the rope to cling to the wood. The boards creaked and groaned beneath his weight.

"J!" he shouted. "I really need some help!" The airship lifted ever higher as Thaddeus held on for dear life.

"Bleedin' 'eck," J proclaimed, as he appeared in the doorway. He turned away for a moment, grabbing a rope and throwing one end to the policeman. "There's a hook," he shouted over the roar of the air around them. "It's on the end of the hatch. It'll be somewhere under your belly right now. Loop this through it and throw the end back. Come on, Thaddeus, you can do it!"

It took the young policeman a moment to gather the strength. The air around them was astonishingly cold and they were still rising. From the corner of his eye Thaddeus could see Limehouse spiralling away beneath them at an alarming rate of knots. Then he rolled sideways, letting one arm take all his weight as he grabbed J's rope and did as he was told.

"Good man!" shouted J as the rope came back to him. He threaded it through another hook and pulled on it. Thaddeus, hanging helplessly on the gangplank like a fish being landed, saw the boy dangling all his weight on the rope, drawing the walkway up, bit by bit.

Eventually Thaddeus tipped down it, rolling untidily into the airship's hold to lie, gasping, on the patchwork wooden floor.

"Blimey," puffed J, "that were a close one!"

Eleven

Suspicions

The train was quieter than Rémy had expected; she and Yannick were able to find an empty carriage to make their own. This seemed the height of luxury to the trapeze artist. She was more than happy to relax against the soft, comfortable cushions as they steamed through the countryside. Yannick, however, seemed distracted. Several times he checked his watch and then glanced out of their carriage into the corridor.

"What's the matter, Yannick?" she asked. "Expecting someone?"

She had meant it as a joke, but when he looked at her, Yannick's gaze was sharp. Then his face softened into a smile and he laughed. "You know me, Rémy. I'm a circus boy at heart – happier plodding along on the road than travelling like this. The speed makes me nervous."

"We could have gone by road, or even by water," Rémy pointed out. "It would have been far cheaper. I still don't think you should have spent all this money. Not on my account, anyway."

"Well," said Yannick, leaning back, "I'm happy to help an old friend. Especially when she first helped me by giving me somewhere to stay in London."

"Oh," said Rémy. "But that was nothing..." *And you told me then that you had to live cheaply,* Rémy thought. *And now it turns out you didn't have to at all. Why? Where did all your money come from?*

"I am grateful nonetheless, Little Bird," Yannick said, oblivious to her thoughts. "Now, it might be best to sleep while we can. At the end of this line, we will have to do the rest of the journey by less comfortable means."

Rémy pushed her troubled thoughts away. It was she who had wanted to return to France, after all. She settled back against the cushions and let the train rock her slowly to sleep.

She woke some time later to find the carriage in darkness. Yannick was gone. Disoriented, Rémy stood up, stretching. Her brain felt fogged, her thoughts rolling thickly in her head.

Rémy pushed open the door and looked out into the corridor. It was empty. The rest of the passengers, she supposed, were long since asleep. She slipped out and headed for the restaurant car.

As she approached the door to the first carriage, she saw Yannick through the window. He looked as if he were deep in conversation with a man dressed in an elegant black frock coat, a white dress shirt and smart, polished black shoes. The man nodded at something Yannick said, and the dim overhead light of the carriage gilded his cheek for a second. Across it snaked a thin, pale scar. To Rémy, this man looked too richly dressed to know a lowly stage performer such as Yannick.

As Rémy watched, Yannick took something from his pocket – a dark-coloured cloth with something wrapped inside it – and passed it to the stranger, who immediately tucked the package inside his coat. The entire encounter made the hairs at the back of Rémy's neck prickle. She slid open the compartment door.

Yannick saw her and immediately walked away from the stranger, who moved in the opposite direction as if they had not been talking at all.

"Aha," said Yannick, with a smile. "How was your sleep?"

"Who was that?" Rémy asked.

"Who?" Yannick glanced back down the corridor. The man in black had vanished into the next carriage. "Oh, no one. We just had the misfortune of reaching the same point in the carriage at the same time. These trains are so very narrow, aren't they? Another reason I shall be relieved when this one stops."

Rémy nodded, slowly. Yannick walked past her with a smile and she followed him back to their own compartment. She was unsettled, and suddenly felt oddly wary of him. "Yannick, have you got that wanted poster? The one of me? I'd like to see it."

"Oh, that," he said. "I tore it up, Little Bird, and threw it out of the window while you were asleep. The fair countryside of France is home to it now! I thought it for the best. Don't you?"

Rémy did not sleep again. Instead, she watched the dark landscape pass the window while Yannick snored gently in his seat. A sense of foreboding had settled over her again. She thought she'd pushed it away, but it had seeped back into her mind since the peculiar exchange between Yannick and the other man. She played it over and over in her mind. What was the package Yannick had passed to the stranger, who was the man and, more importantly, why had Yannick lied to her so blatantly?

The more she looked at him, the less Rémy believed she knew him as well as she thought she had back in London. The Yannick she'd known would never have lied to her. And what about the money for this trip? In London, he'd been as poor as she was, but suddenly he had enough money for train tickets? Had he just been lying to her about that, as well? Or had something happened that meant he now had the resources to travel how he liked? *Thaddeus was right,* she told herself. *He is not the boy you knew.*

Glancing at Yannick's sleeping face, Rémy reached for the secret pocket she'd added to her corset a few weeks ago. She'd sewn it herself, thanks to Claudette's insistent tutoring. It was tucked above the hem so that it sat securely above her navel, only big enough to store something very small within. In this case, it was her opal necklace, coiled inside a fold of paper. Rémy took it out and looked at her talisman. It seemed duller than usual. She wondered if not wearing it was somehow damaging the jewel.

Well, Little Bird, perhaps now is the right time to wear it again. And to use its powers, too…

Before the thought had even had time to echo in her mind, Rémy fastened the opal around her neck, and let the gem fall against the skin at her throat. It was almost as if the stone was connected to her heart. The opal possessed a pulse that Rémy had felt so often she had forgotten it even existed. Now it was there again, passing between the stone and her body like electricity.

She sat still for a few moments, letting the opal settle. Then Rémy looked at Yannick, with no real idea of how this should work. She had never deliberately attempted to direct the opal's powers before – hearing other people's thoughts had always been accidental, an intrusion. But now the opal could be the key to knowing whether she could truly trust Yannick or not…

Something swelled in her mind, like the flame of a candle bursting into life for the first time. There was something there, something below the surface. She tried to follow where the opal was leading her, down a path into Yannick's mind, yet something wasn't right. Usually she heard a person's thoughts straight away.

Yannick's were muffled, as if behind a veil that the opal was trying to break through, but...

Yannick opened his eyes. He was staring straight at her, wide awake, as if he'd not been asleep at all. The flame Rémy felt in her mind was snuffed out, the opal quaking suddenly against her skin before falling still. There was silence.

"Aha," said Yannick, smiling and nodding at her throat. "So there's your opal! It's what I remember most about you from when we were children – how you never, ever took it off. I wondered where it was. I was worried to ask, in case it had been lost."

Rémy breathed hard, feeling sick to her stomach but trying to hide it. The opal had not been able to let her into Yannick's thoughts, but not only that – had her effort woken him? Had he known that she was trying to see into his mind?

"Rémy? Are you all right?" Yannick asked, and she realised he was watching her with what appeared to be simple concern.

"Sorry. Yes, I'm fine," she managed. The train began to slow. "Oh – I think we must be coming to a station. Is this our stop?"

As he stood to look out, she unfastened the opal and hid it away again, tucking it into the pouch beneath her corset hem.

In Pursuit

"How are you supposed to steer this thing?" Thaddeus asked, once he had recovered enough.

J had returned to his seat at the front of the ship, closing off the gas and dulling the hiss. The airship ceased its rise, drifting over the night sky of London like a concentrated cloud.

"It's got propellers," J said, standing on tiptoe to reach a circular control at the very top of the control desk. "Didn't you see 'em? Rudders, too, one left and one right. Sorry, I mean, one starboard and one port. Right nifty, this is – watch."

He turned the handle. The cabin filled with a whirring sound and the ship nosed forward over the murky waters of Limehouse.

Thaddeus got to his feet, feeling the gentle rocking of the aircraft, and leaned over J's chair, looking out of the window at his first view of London from the air. It was an extraordinary sight, despite the darkness. The sparse gas lamps of the East End were burning brightly, illuminating splashes of the surrounding streets with the curdled yellow of too-old milk.

"Look, there's The Grapes," J pointed. "Here, looks like they're havin' a lock-in. And they didn't even invite us, cheeky beggars!"

"J, mind the paper mill," Thaddeus said. "It's coming up on your right."

"Don't worry yourself," said J, with a confidence Thaddeus didn't share. "All's I need to do is twist this handle here..."

J thumbed a lever on his left. The airship began to turn to the right – straight towards the tower of the biggest factory in Limehouse.

"J!" Thaddeus barked. "Left! We need to go left, not right!"

"I'm trying," J insisted, yanking on another of the levers. "This one seems to be a bit stiff, that's all! Give me a minute..."

"We don't have a minute," Thaddeus yelled, gripping the back of the chair as the mill loomed like a dark behemoth through the glass. "We're going to hit it!"

"Hang about a tick," J muttered, concentrating hard. He yanked the lever down again and the airship moved left.

Thaddeus held his breath as the red bricks of the factory tower came close enough to count.

"Yes!" yelled J in triumph, as they cleared the building with mere inches to spare. "That's got her, all right!"

"J," said Thaddeus, rubbing an anxious hand over his face. "Please tell me you know what you're doing in this thing."

"I do, Thaddeus. I absolutely, truly do," said J. "And what I don't know, I can read in the Professor's book."

"But have you ever flown this thing before?"

"Not as such, no. But I have practised, I promise. I've sat here in this very seat and done exactly what I'm doing now. It was just – on the ground, like."

Thaddeus stared at the boy. "Right," he said, weakly.

"Sorry," said J, sounding a tad defensive. "But I wasn't to know there'd be an urgent call to use her so soon after I'd finished putting her together, was I? Otherwise I might 'ave 'ad a chance to do a proper test and all."

Thaddeus blinked. "After you'd finished… putting her together?"

J glanced up at the policeman with a frown. "Yeah. I only finished greasing in the last propeller earlier today, y'see. And up until yesterday I was still trying to get the ruby mechanism to work."

Thaddeus suddenly felt the need to sit down, which was unfortunate, since there was a distinct lack of chairs. He settled for staggering to one of the bunks instead. "J, are you telling me… that *you* built this?"

"Well, not prexactly, no. I just finished her. The Professor, he must have got her started, because when I found her, the metal bits had been done. To tell you the truth, I think the Professor had in mind that the ship would be all metal, but obviously I didn't have any o' the right stuff."

"Obviously," Thaddeus echoed, weakly.

"So I decided to use wood for the rest," J explained. "Snaffled it from around Limehouse, I did. There's bits of about a hundred boats from a hundred countries in this tub." He rubbed the control desk affectionately.

"Right," said Thaddeus, rubbing his eyes again. "So we're sailing over London in what amounts to a pile of firewood."

"Well, technically," said J, "we ain't over London any more."

Thaddeus stood up and looked, and saw that the boy was right. They had left behind the dark conglomeration of the city and were heading out towards the leafy, unlit countryside, the Thames on their starboard side, reflecting the hard glint of the stars above.

"So," said J. "Next stop France then, eh?"

"How do you know which way to go?" Thaddeus asked. "Have you got a compass bearing?"

"Sort of," said J, looking up at him with a grin, "but even better." He leaned forward on the control desk and pressed a square of wood. It sprang up beneath his touch, rising an inch or so clear of the control panel.

"Sprocket and hinge," J said, casually, as he flicked up the surface of the square to reveal that it was a tiny wooden door, set on the vertical. Within the raised column was a complicated gadget of the like Thaddeus had never seen before.

"What on earth is that?" the policeman asked. Whatever it was, it looked as if it had been repurposed from a ship's barometer. It was still in the glass housing, but the original dial had been removed and repainted. As Thaddeus leaned closer he could see the Professor's small and neat handwriting, marking out regular intervals around the new face. The words ran from left to right, from the centre of the dial where the barometer's original hands remained, to the outside edge.

Each of the words painted in that tiny hand was the name of a city. At least, that's what Thaddeus assumed they all were, though only because some of the more exotic names he'd never even heard of were arranged alongside ones that he had. London, for example, was flanked on one side by Innsbruck and on the other by somewhere called Kathmandu.

"Amazin', innit?" said J. "I mean, have you ever heard of Manaus? I surely ain't, but it's there, so it must exist and this ship must be able to reach it. Anyway, watch this…"

J reached over and turned the tiny filigree metal dial in the centre. Thaddeus watched as the barometer's hands moved.

J adjusted them until one was pointing at 'London' and the other at 'Paris'. Then he pressed the dial in. It clicked, locking into place.

Immediately, there was a whirring sound from above them. Thaddeus looked up to see two spindly metal arms descend out of the ceiling above the control desk. They were hinged in several places, and on the end of each arm was what looked like a single lens from a pair of small, round pince-nez. The arms adjusted themselves, whirring happily, until they settled against the glass of the airship's window. J pulled one lever and pushed another, and Thaddeus felt the craft move slightly, turning away from the Thames completely to head out over the open countryside. As they did so, the metal arms readjusted. J kept manoeuvring the ship until both lenses were aligned, right in the middle of the window.

"There," J said, with a satisfied sigh. "We're on the right track now. All we have to do is keep those two arms dead centre, with one lens over the other just like that, and we'll sail right into Paris. Or over it, I should say, eh?" He laughed.

Thaddeus shook his head. "Astounding. It's truly, truly amazing, J. How do you know how all this works?"

J jerked his thumb over his shoulder to where the Professor's book lay open on his bunk. "It's all in there. Glad I didn't have to build these bits, though, and there's the truth. The fiddly scientific fings the Professor had already built. I just had to put 'em all together, like."

"Well, I'd say you've done a pretty good job."

The boy beamed, and then yawned. "Thank you kindly. I'd like to think the old Professor, he might have been proud to see her a-sail on the winds."

"I'm sure he would have been. In fact, I know he would have been." Thaddeus looked out of the window, into the night. "Why don't you show me how to fly her, J? Then you can get some rest. It's going to be a long night."

* * *

J was asleep in his bunk, snoring, when the airship struck out over the Channel. The sun was beginning to rise, a pale blush of pink on the far horizon. Thaddeus looked out on a rose-coloured sea that chinked and guttered like a flame. He was so mesmerized by the waves below that he forgot about keeping their heading steady. The lenses drifted apart, slowly, as the airship's nose turned lazily in a direction of its own making. Thaddeus cursed when he realised, and grasped the rudder controls, fighting against a headwind to bring the ship right again. When the ship was in drift, she felt weightless, but in trying to control her, Thaddeus realised the craft was anything but. He wondered how long the ruby's gas would last, and thought about looking it up in the Professor's book. Then he decided against it – it was probably better not to know.

"'Ello," came a sleepy voice from over his shoulder. "We there yet?"

Thaddeus looked up to see that J was awake, rubbing his eyes,

"Not quite," he replied. "But I'm already wanting breakfast. Did you bring anything to eat? Because I didn't."

J nodded, hopping off the bed, his hair even more askew than usual. "Always come prepared, that's my motto," he said, through a yawn, before reaching up to a cloth bag that hung on a hook above his bunk and pulling out a bread roll. "These are yesterday's, but they'll be better than nuthin'–"

His words were drowned out by a noise like screaming. Thaddeus and J were on their feet in an instant, forgetting the stale bread and their hunger. There was a sharp thud and the ship shuddered, and then another thud, and another, as if it were being hit by rocks. The airship juddered and jerked, dropping lower and lower in the sky with each thud. J tried to pull the ship straight, but her nose sank into a dive.

"What is it?" Thaddeus yelled. "What's happening?"

J didn't need to answer. Outside the window, there came the sudden flurry of small, white bodies. A flock of seagulls came crashing down, screeching as they fell, then righted themselves and swooped away.

"Oh, lawks – they must have run straight into the balloon!" J cried, fighting the rudders as the ship continued to fall. The metal steering arms were fluttering wildly, waving about as if in a thunderstorm, the direction lenses clattering against each other. J thumped the directional gauge back into its panel. The arms folded safely back into the ceiling, out of harm's way, which was more than could be said of Thaddeus and J.

"Pull her up," Thaddeus shouted, as they continued to plunge. The sea below had darkened as the sun rose, and now shone blue-black. The waves that had seemed so tiny just moments ago were rearing up like fully grown horses.

"What the bleedin' 'eck do you fink I'm trying to do?" J yelled back, wrestling with the controls, wrenching them back as the ship bucked away from him. "There's vents that open when you want to deflate the balloon – they let the gas out. A bird must have run right into one. We've lost gas – we're too heavy!"

"What do we do? Can't you reinflate it?"

"Not mid-flight. Oh, no," J's voice could barely be heard above the fierce cacophony that filled the airship, but Thaddeus knew exactly what he was talking about.

Out of the window, directly in front of them now that the ship was taking a nosedive, was another ship. This was the normal variety, one that floated and bore sails rather than a balloon, and was coming up before them fast. The sailors were all standing on the deck, waving their arms as if to shoo away a giant bird.

"If we crash into them, we'll burn," J screeched, still trying to yank the ship back under control.

"What do you mean, burn?" Thaddeus asked, shouting over the growing maelstrom of noise and fear.

"The gas in the balloon," J panted. "It's pretty – what you call it – it burns really easy, like."

"Volatile?"

"That's the one!"

Thaddeus wiped a hand over his face.

"I might have forgotten to mention that bit during our tour," J managed, through gritted teeth.

"Yes," said Thaddeus. "Yes, J, I think you might have."

Thirteen

Home Truths

The station that Rémy and Yannick stepped into when they left the train was far less grand than the one in Calais. It was nothing but a raised wooden platform, with a small shack for the ticket office. Rémy looked around as they walked from the station to the town, searching for the man in black, but she saw no sign of him. Part of her wondered whether she'd dreamed the entire thing, but then she thought about the incident with the opal and knew that her misgivings were real.

What was I thinking? she asked herself silently, as Yannick led her towards a small bakery. *Why was I willing to trust Yannick more than I was Thaddeus? Stupid, stupid, stupid.*

"Come on," Yannick said cheerily, interrupting her thoughts. "I think we need a decent breakfast to set us up for the day ahead."

"I have hardly any coins left, Yannick," Rémy said. "Just ask for yesterday's bread at the boulangerie – I have enough for that."

"Tsk," said Yannick, "that's not enough to travel on, Little Bird. Leave it to me."

"Yannick–" Rémy began, but he cut her off.

"No arguments, eh?" the magician chided. "Let a friend help a friend. Sit at that table while I go inside."

Rémy did as she was told, sitting at a wooden table outside the bakery in the town's main street. It was a pleasant scene, but her thoughts were increasingly troubled, and darkened further when Yannick returned with enough fresh, delicious pastries to feed an army, along with a large pot of good coffee. But before she could comment on the extravagance, Yannick started talking, enthusiasm bubbling through his words like a brook through a forest.

"Good news, Little Bird," he said brightly. "I thought I'd ask the baker if he'd heard of the Circus of Secrets."

"Oh?"

"He had," said Yannick, biting into a croissant. "He went to see it two weeks ago when he was visiting his daughter in Périgueux. That's about sixty miles away from Moulidars. That was where Claudette's last letter was sent from, wasn't it?"

Rémy leaned forward, a twinge of excitement struggling through her anxiety. "Yes, that's right. Périgueux is south of Moulidars, isn't it?"

Yannick grinned. "It is. The good thing is, now that we know the circus was in Périgueux, we don't have to go all the way right into Moulidars. We can skirt around it and head straight for Périgueux. Assuming that Claudette is moving the circus on once every week, we should be able to find it from there. I think we have a trail to follow, Little Bird."

"Not a very good one. And that's a long way away."

"True," said Yannick, starting on another pastry. "Which is why I think the next thing we need to find is a map and some horses."

"Horses!" Rémy exclaimed, almost choking on her coffee. "Don't be ridiculous, Yannick! How on earth are we going to find the money to buy horses? We'll hitch a lift on a cart or two. That will be fine."

Yannick shook his head. "And what if there are no carts to be had today? Or tomorrow, or the day after? Or what if they are not going in the right direction, Rémy?"

"Then... then we'll walk," said Rémy, with a shrug. "I've done it before, I can do it again."

"It'll take too long. By the time we get to wherever the Circus of Secrets was, it'll have moved on. And on, and on... we'll never catch up on foot. No, we need horses – leave it to me."

Rémy crossed her arms. "I refuse to believe you have enough money for horses," she said. "I can't even understand how you managed to pay for this." She waved her hand at her half-eaten breakfast. "I couldn't have!"

Yannick narrowed his eyes. "That would never have stopped you in the past, Little Bird."

Rémy set her jaw. "I'd steal instead, you mean? Well, I don't do that any more. It's not who I am."

"Oh? Why not? Because of your black-hearted policeman?"

"Thaddeus doesn't have a black heart. He's one of the best men I have ever known. Probably *the* best man."

"Then why are you here, Little Bird?" Yannick asked, his voice suddenly holding an angry challenge. "Why are you here, back in France with me, instead of in London with him?"

Rémy looked down at her hands, her fingers tangled together on her lap. She frowned. "Because I am the one with a black heart," she said quietly. "And I don't know if it can ever be anything else – in his eyes, at least." Rémy looked up, surprised that she had spoken such thoughts aloud. She cleared her throat. "Anyway, it doesn't matter now, does it? Here I am, back in France, trying to get back to my old life. But I don't want to be a thief any more, Yannick. Gustave turned me into one, but it's not who I am."

Yannick sighed, his anger fading. "Well, neither am I."

Rémy made a disgusted sound in her throat. "You must think I'm an idiot, Yannick. No circus performer earns enough to spend the way you have done since we left London. Where, I might add, you most definitely didn't have this kind of money."

"I did not steal it," Yannick insisted.

She crossed her arms. "Then where did it come from?"

"We both have our talents, Rémy. Yours is on the wire. Mine is... different."

"What is that supposed to mean?"

Yannick shrugged. "I am good at... persuading people. At making them think they want to help me."

Rémy shook her head. "I knew it! You're using your skill as a hypnotist to steal!" She pushed her plate away. "That's how you could afford this food, is it?"

"No!" Yannick protested. "Go and ask the baker, if you like. I paid him every centime he asked!"

"Oh yes?" Rémy said, outraged. "And where did that come from, hey? You still haven't answered me that."

Yannick fell silent again.

"It was you, wasn't it?" Rémy probed.

"What was?"

"The thefts in London. The impossible break-ins that Thaddeus was trying to solve. You were behind them."

Yannick rolled his eyes. "Ach, Thaddeus again."

"Yes, Thaddeus again. He worked it out, didn't he? Or he was beginning to."

Yannick shrugged. "So what if he had? It's not thieving if someone gives you something willingly. Especially if they don't even really need it."

Rémy couldn't believe what she was hearing. "So that's how you did it, is it? Those people came to your show, and you hypnotized them into giving over their jewels? That's what's paying for this journey of ours?"

Yannick stared back at her with angry eyes. "I don't know what you're getting so high and mighty about, Rémy Brunel. I remember you once boasting to me about how you were the best gem thief in Europe – no, in the world, you said. You could break into anywhere, and steal any jewel you wanted. And you loved it. What's so different about you and me, eh? And don't pretend you didn't know, anyway. Hypocrite that you are."

"I *didn't* know!"

"Of course you did! Maybe you didn't *want* to know, but you knew. You were quick enough to get me out of Thaddeus' reach when he got too inquisitive, weren't you? You wanted to come back to France, and I was a convenient way to afford the trip. And I suppose it's better, isn't it? To let someone else do the stealing? That way you can tell yourself you had nothing to do with it."

"I didn't know!" Rémy shouted, though Yannick's words pricked at her like the point of a knife. "He's going to think it was me. He already suspected it, and when J tells him that I ran away with you–"

"Oh, in the name of all that's holy," said Yannick scornfully. "Stop talking about your ridiculous boy policeman. He's long gone. As if you two could have stayed friends, anyway. You're a born circus rat, Rémy Brunel. It's the only thing you're good at. What did you think you were going to do? Marry him? Become a respectable little London housewife – hold polite dinner parties under a glass chandelier? Get your husband to take you to the theatre and watch people like us perform like dancing monkeys?"

"Shut up," Rémy said, through gritted teeth.

Yannick sat back in his chair with a disgusted shake of his head. "You can look down on me all you want, Rémy," he said. "But at least I don't pretend to be something I'm not. And you know where you belong, really. Isn't that why you came back?"

Rémy stood up, pushing her chair back so angrily that it almost tipped over. "I came back to find Claudette," she hissed. "And I can do that without you. I don't ever want to see you again, do you understand? This is where we part ways, Yannick."

"No – Rémy – wait!" Yannick said, as she grabbed her pack and stalked away from the table. "I'll help you find Claudette. Don't leave!"

"Don't follow me," Rémy warned, not even looking back.

"I'm sorry," Yannick called after her, his voice suddenly desperate. "Rémy – wait!"

She didn't listen, even when his footsteps began to follow her. Instead she turned a corner into another quiet street, and then another and another, until the sound of Yannick's footfalls faded away. Rémy paused for a moment, thinking. Yannick hadn't been wrong when he'd said that following Claudette's trail would be long and difficult without horses, and she had but a few centimes left. Which meant the only way she was going anywhere was by begging – or stealing.

I will not become a thief again, she told herself firmly. *I will* not.

Determined, Rémy headed for the marketplace. With a bit of luck and some charm, she'd be able to hitch a lift on one of the carts as they headed out of the village. There was no way she'd find one to take her all the way, but anything would be a start.

The market, when she found it, wasn't much busier than the rest of the village. Five or six farmers had driven their carts into

114

the small central square to sell their piles of fruit and vegetables to the townsfolk. Rémy's heart sank as she realised how few people there were to ask. What was the likelihood that any of them would be going in the direction she needed?

She'd just approached the first farmer when a shout went up from the north end of the square. Turning, Rémy saw two men in police uniforms, standing next to a fat man in a flour-dusted apron. He was pointing right at her.

"There!" the man cried. "She was eating at my bakery, just minutes ago. I tell you it's her. It's the jewel thief from the posters!"

Rémy turned and ran, her nimble feet carrying her swiftly over the uneven cobbles as she headed for another route out of the square. But as she reached it, a group of townsfolk closed it off, unwilling to let her escape.

She slid to a stop and then ran again, south this time, scrambling for another narrow street as her ears filled with the shouts of the townspeople and the shrill sound of the gendarmes' tin whistles. Someone rolled a barrel at her, trying to slow her down, but Rémy leapt over it and up onto one of the carts, scattering apples in her wake as she plunged off the other side, almost losing her footing on the cobbles in the process.

She dodged one policeman and sidestepped another, but there were too many people trying to stop her. They had closed off every way out. Rémy launched herself at one of the houses that lined the square, trying to claw her way up the stone walls and to the roof. But before she could make it, she felt someone clutch her leg and wrench her backwards. She tumbled to the ground, where she lay, winded, on the dirty street. The market people surrounded her, threatening to block out the sky as the policemen looked down at her.

"Ah, *tant pis*, my girl," said one of the gendarmes. "You have lost your touch, now, eh?"

The two policemen pulled her to her feet, one of them snapping tight cuffs around her wrists as the other waved the gathered crowd away.

"Nothing to see here, *mesdames et messieurs*. Time to move on."

The townsfolk dissipated, gossiping among themselves. Rémy tugged against the cuffs, but it was no good – she was well and truly caught. She tried not to panic, her eyes roaming the square as she searched for a way out, but there was none. Except...

Rémy caught a glimpse of something – someone that seemed out of place, at least to her. It was a man in black coat-tails. He had no hat, but still, he was dressed too smartly to belong in that market square. What was he doing here, among the vegetables and fruits?

"Nowhere for you to fly to this time, Little Bird," said the policeman at her shoulder merrily, as he pushed her forward. "You will not get the better of us. Quickly," he added to his companion, "let's get this one to the station and into a cell. Go ahead and tell them we're coming."

The other man did as he was told, disappearing off across the cobbles and under the stone arch that led out of the square.

Rémy looked again for the overdressed man she'd seen a moment before. He'd been hovering beside the horses hitched to one of the traders' wagons, as if he were fiddling with the animal's harness, but now there was no sign of him.

"Go on, get on with you," muttered the policeman who had cuffed her, pushing her so roughly that she almost stumbled.

Rémy was about to say something when the man in black appeared in front of her. Yannick! It was Yannick, in his stage clothes.

"Here," said the gendarme. "What do you think—"

Yannick held up a hand, his fingers moving strangely in the slight wind that gusted through the square. The policeman fell silent at once. Rémy felt him relax his hold on her, dropping his hand from her arm.

Yannick didn't even spare Rémy a glance. All his attention was on the policeman. "Take off her cuffs," he said, in a low, soft voice.

"I'm not—" the man began, but Yannick's fingers flicked a quick symbol in the air. The gendarme stopped speaking.

"I'll say it again," Yannick stated, calmly. "Undo. Her. Cuffs."

The policeman seemed to sag a little, his eyes losing focus. He shook his head, a small erratic movement, as if he were trying to clear his head. Then, without another word, he pulled a bunch of keys from his belt. He picked one out and fitted it to the cuffs around Rémy's wrists. A moment later she felt them loosen. She tugged herself free.

"Quickly," hissed Yannick, "he's not properly under, and I can't hypnotize everyone in the square. We've got to get out of here!"

They dashed to the cart that Yannick had been standing beside a moment earlier. Rémy saw that he'd loosened the horses from their tethers. A shout went up behind them as one of the market folk realised she was free. Rémy cast a glance back over her shoulder and saw the policeman blinking and looking around, as if he'd just woken from a deep, deep sleep.

"Go!" Yannick yelled, pulling one of the horses out from between the wagon's yoke and then going for the other, too. "Go, go, go!"

Rémy only needed one leap to mount her ride, vaulting over its rear and landing on its bare back. Wheeling the animal around, she made for the archway, the creature's hooves clattering on the rough flagstones hard enough to send up sparks. Rémy heard Yannick behind her, but didn't turn to look. She was too busy avoiding the market sellers who were brave enough to try to stop a charging horse. One managed to grip her ankle, but she saw him off with a kick that sent him sprawling to the cobbles.

A moment later they were through the arch and into the town beyond. Rémy had no idea where to go. As if he'd heard her thoughts, Yannick shouted for her to follow him. He clattered a sharp left, and then a sharp right, the tails of his stage coat flowing out behind him. Rémy followed as they wound through the small town, hearing distant shouts and the occasional police whistle as the search for them started in earnest. Eventually they reached the town gate and rode through it at a flat gallop, charging along the dirt roads and into the forest, leaving the town and its police behind them.

Terror in the Air

"J!" Thaddeus yelled, as the airship began to creak and quiver. "Tell me you've got an idea!"

"B-b-ballast!" J yelled back, his voice vibrating along with the ship as he held on to the shaking controls. "W-w-we've got to u-u-unload some – we've g-g-got to l-l-l-o-s-e weight – get h-h-higher!"

"Tell me how," Thaddeus ordered, over the now constant noise of wood and metal under strain. It felt as if the entire craft might come apart at the seams at any moment.

"Open the h-h-hatch," J bellowed. "Ch-ch-chuck anythin' out y-y-you's can g-g-get yer hands o-o-on! I'm going to l-l-link up the r-r-ruby again, see if s-s-she's got anyfing e-e-else left in 'er. H-h-hurry! They d-d-down there are c-c-comin' up q-q-quick!"

Thaddeus glanced briefly through the shuddering window. The ship below now filled it entirely. He thought briefly that they were lucky it wasn't a frigate, because Thaddeus was pretty sure that if it had been, he and J would have a primed gun trained on them right now. He wrenched the hatch lever open, but the airship was travelling so fast that, even unfastened, the wind kept it shut. He braced his shoulder against it, fighting against the element outside that whistled and screamed at their violent descent. For a moment his efforts were useless, and then the hatch disappeared from beneath him, torn open so fast that it almost took Thaddeus with it. The air outside sucked at him, trying to drag him out. If he hadn't grabbed at the lintel and held on for dear life, it would have succeeded.

Eyes blinded by a stream of tears, Thaddeus staggered backwards against the inner wall beside the open hatch. Through it he could see the gangway hanging in the air, flapping wildly in the current. The ship lurched in the direction of its open side.

"The barrel!" J yelled, not even turning around as he continued to wind the ruby's control. "That's heaviest!"

Thaddeus forced himself away from the door and towards their store of water. Reaching it, he paused to check the seal of the cork in the top before tipping it onto its side and pushing towards the hatch. It was heavy and ungainly, despite the now sloping kilter of the floor. Thaddeus tried in vain to aim it straight towards the gangway, but it crashed into one of the cabinets to the right of the hatch instead. The cupboard splintered like firewood, sending lethal shards of wood flying through the air. One struck him in the cheek. He felt blood as the blankets that had been folded inside rushed towards freedom, taking flight like huge birds and vanishing through the hatch.

"Get it out!" J yelled again. "Yer've got to get it out, or–"

Thaddeus dragged the barrel around, forcing it against the lip of the opening. For a moment it teetered there, as if hesitating before the leap. Then it was gone.

The airship immediately tipped up a little, buoyant without the weight, but it was still dragging to the side thanks to the open hatch. Thaddeus caught the end of the rope that would close it, but it was as heavy as dragging a dead body from the bottom of the Thames. He braced all his weight against it and pulled, the effort sparking lights behind his eyelids. Suddenly he felt another weight added to his – J had left his post to help. Together they heaved. At first it seemed as if nothing was happening, but then the gangplank lifted into view.

"One more pull, J!" Thaddeus yelled. "On my count – one, two – THREE!"

Their last effort was enough to put the walkway on the right side of the gale outside. It slammed shut with such force that they both crashed to the floor. The airship recovered and lifted a little more.

It wasn't enough. As they scrambled to their feet, they saw the mast of the ship below them coming up fast, threatening to hit the dead centre of the main window's glass. J swore, lunging for the control panel and yanking the airship's rudder hard to port. They swung, nose up at last, but not quite enough – the mast of the other ship struck them a glancing blow to starboard. They could hear it scraping along the airship's hull with a noise as vile as chalk dragged hard down a blackboard. J pulled at the rudder again, but still the mast gashed them from stern to aft. Thaddeus half expected to see it punch a hole right through, but somehow the airship tore herself free. She flew out over open water.

Neither of them could talk for quite a while after that. They simply stared out of the window as the airship gained altitude again, watching as the coast of France drew ever nearer.

Reconciliation

For the first few miles of their ride, both Rémy and Yannick were worried they may be followed, but they saw no riders behind them. Neither did they pass anything on the dusty road. They hadn't spoken much since their escape – at first, they were both too out of breath. Now, Rémy had no idea what to say.

"Why did you do it?" she asked eventually. "Why help me escape?"

Yannick looked over at her. He'd removed his top hat, but was still dressed in his stage coat-tails. The outfit looked rather odd, given that he was riding a thick-legged carthorse. "Do you really think I'd just leave you there?" he asked. "You should know me better than that, at least. We circus people have to stick together, no matter what, isn't that right?"

Rémy smiled wanly. "Well, thank you." Then, after a moment, she added, "Not that I couldn't have got out of there on my own."

Yannick raised his eyebrows. "Of course. You were just... waiting for the opportune moment."

"Exactly."

The magician grinned, and then raised his face to the sun.

"Smell that, Little Bird," he said, breathing in deeply. "Ah! That beats the stink of the East End any day, doesn't it?"

"That I can't deny," she agreed. "This does indeed smell a good deal better than Limehouse."

The magician screwed up his nose. "All those people squashed one upon the other," he said, "the stench of the opium dens, rising up to meet the reek of burning oil and dirty flesh. I am amazed you stayed for as long as you did, Rémy."

She shrugged. "A city is like a circus. It's about more than its parts, Yannick. It's about the whole."

Yannick turned to look at her, his eyes shadowed despite the sunlight. "Ahh," he said, "you are thinking of the best man you know again, are you?"

Rémy stayed silent. Yes, she was thinking about Thaddeus. How could she not? She missed him. She wondered what he was doing at that moment. Rémy could imagine him leaning over his desk, the usual frown of concentration creasing his forehead as he puzzled over some piece of evidence. Unexpectedly, she felt tears prick at her eyes, and blinked them away. If her last escapade had shown her anything, it was that she could never fit into polite society. Someone would always recognize her as a thief who should be behind bars. *What did you think you were going to do? Marry him? Become a respectable little London housewife?* Yannick's earlier jibe may have stung, but it was no less true for that.

Squaring her shoulders, Rémy urged her pony on. "Do you actually know where we're going?" she asked her companion. "Or are we guessing the way to Périgueux?"

Yannick grinned again. With a flourish, he produced a crumpled map from his pocket. "I've got a compass too," he added. "We'll be fine as long as we stick to the road."

Rémy nodded, and they rode on, towards the spreading, leafy green horizon of trees ahead. The sun was at its zenith when they turned along a valley ridge, the road loose with pebbles. On one side of the road, a precipice dropped abruptly to the dry riverbed far below. On the other, a band of scrubby young trees lifted over a rocky ridge and into a thicker, deeper forest beyond. Rémy dismounted and picked her way up the incline between the saplings to get a better look. The forest stretched into the foothills of further mountains, an impenetrable carpet of green, made all the deeper by the darkness beneath the branches. In the heat of the midday sun, Rémy thought it looked like the perfect place for a break, but Yannick shook his head.

"We should move on as fast as possible," he said. "Who knows what's lurking in there?"

Rémy smiled slightly. "Afraid of monsters, Yannick?"

"Not of the imaginary variety, no," the magician said dryly. "But I'd bet fair money there's plenty of the human sort skulking in that wood."

They trotted off again, the ponies puffing in the heat. Around them, the landscape grew rockier as the road rose higher and higher towards the pass.

"What would you have done?" Rémy asked, some time later.

"What do you mean?" Yannick asked, puzzled.

"If I'd got away from the gendarmes on my own, fled the town before you could get to me," Rémy expanded. "What would you have done? Gone back to Paris, to the Jamboree?"

Yannick was silent for a moment. Then he shook his head. "I would have carried on looking for the Circus of Secrets."

It was Rémy's turn to be puzzled. "Why?" she asked, as they turned a sudden corner in the road. Pebbles skittered, falling down the ravine, echoing as they chinked and kinked their way to a new resting place. "You'd have a better chance of a sure

124

position in Paris. What's so special about– What's that?" Rémy asked, pulling up her horse suddenly.

Yannick barely paused, urging his steed to plod onwards. "I can't hear anything."

"I can," she said. "It's music. Yannick! Stop and listen."

He did as he was told. After a few moments, he shrugged. "Perhaps some travellers in their camp," he said.

"No, I know that music," Rémy said, feeling as if she were dreaming. "That tune. I've heard it before." She pulled her horse around, heading in the direction of the sound.

"Rémy!" Yannick called after her. "What are you doing?"

"I must find it," she told him absently. "It's for me. I know it is."

"Don't be ridiculous," said the magician, riding up beside her. He caught hold of her arm and forced her to stop, before snapping his fingers in front of her face. Rémy blinked. "I know you're tired, but we've got to find our way out of this forest. Then we can rest for a while."

"Yannick, I'm telling you, I know that music."

"So what if you do? It'll be some tune you've heard in a bar somewhere – or around a campfire late one night."

Rémy frowned. "Yes," she said. "Yes, I think that's exactly where I've heard it. Around a campfire." She nudged the horse onwards again, more determined this time.

"Rémy," Yannick tried.

She stopped and turned to him. "Yannick, I want to know who's playing that tune. I swear to you, I know it. It's music I didn't remember existed until a moment ago, but I recognise it and I have to find out why. Come with me, don't come with me: that's up to you. But I'm finding the player, regardless."

Sixteen

New Friends

The ruby airship sailed over Paris like a jewel of the skies, glinting in the colours of sunset and causing quite a stir on the ground. As Thaddeus and J steered the ship over cafés and bars, restaurants and theatres, people of all sorts looked up and saw her, and began to give chase. They trailed the vessel, shouting and waving, knocking on their neighbours' doors to urge them to see this great wonder that owned the air as surely as a ship owned the seas.

"'Ere," said J, a little uneasily. "There's quite a crowd down there, y'know. What are they going to do when we land?"

"I don't know," Thaddeus said, feeling the same anxiety.

J blew out a breath. "Let's just hope they're all friendly, eh? Any sign of the circus field yet?"

Thaddeus squinted into the indigo sky, and then pointed at a glare of rioting light on the very edge of the city. "That must be it, mustn't it? Turn a mite to port, Captain J."

"Aye, aye," said J, pulling the right lever.

They sailed on, descending slowly like a bird on the wing coming into land. The ship headed towards the smudge of light, which, as the sky grew ever darker with the onset of night, slowly coalesced into thousands of large, white candles. Each was set atop a metal pole that had been driven into the ground to mark out a giant circle. The circle was big enough to encompass the hundreds of caravans that sat inside it, gathered in little clusters and knots. There were circus tents, too, a myriad of colours melding into the dusky evening light. Around and between these, people milled. There were clowns and stilt-walkers, fire-eaters and jugglers, acrobats and tumblers, all mingling together as if inside the circle was its own fantastical city.

"Better set down inside, if I can," J muttered, a look of concentration on his face. "Got a hunch it'll be safer than leaving this beauty outside."

"Think you can manage it?" Thaddeus asked. "There's not much room."

J nodded, but didn't answer, and Thaddeus didn't speak again. The boy continued to let gas out of the balloon in a slow, steady hiss. Thaddeus wondered how long it would take to refill it if they needed to lift off the ground again swiftly, but decided not to ask. It was too late to worry now – the airship had lost so much height that he could see the astonished looks on the faces of the circus folk below. Many had stopped what they were doing and were simply staring up at them, mouths agape.

The circus tents seemed bigger now, more like the Big Top where Thaddeus had first seen and tried to save Rémy all those months ago. He wondered if she was down there now, looking up at them with the same amazement as everyone else.

He scanned the astonished crowds, searching for her face, but could not see it. Perhaps she was mid-performance, flying through the air with the grace that made her seem as if she had been born with wings.

"Ahh," cried J. "That chap's got the right idea, look!"

Thaddeus saw that one of the circus men had spotted where J was aiming the airship – a patch of empty ground as wide as two caravans beside a scarlet-coloured tent. He was directing the surrounding caravans to move back, making more room.

"Easy," Thaddeus warned, as the ship slipped slightly to port, her stern swinging dangerously close to the scarlet marquee.

"I got it, I got it," J muttered, pulling her round even as they sank even lower. They were level with the tops of the caravans now, and a horde of gawpers had gathered, held back by the man who had seen that the ship needed more space. He was walking back and forth at the edges of the crowd, waving them back just far enough to keep them in line. Dressed in an elaborate scarlet coat studded with gold buttons that shone in the candlelight and with tails so long they almost trailed in the dust, Thaddeus knew at once he was a circus master, used to marshalling crowds.

The ship set down with a thump hard enough to judder their teeth. J let out a sigh of relief, resting his sweaty forehead against the control desk. Thaddeus thumped him lightly on the back.

"Well done, lad," he said.

"Bleedin' 'eck," J muttered, straightening up and wiping a hand across his face. "I won't be wanting to do that again in a hurry, and that's the truth."

The sound of the crowd was clear now, a great bubble of noise – shouts and cries of, "Come out! Let us see you!" The circus master suddenly appeared in front of the airship, smiling broadly through the glass and then bowing with a flourish to invite them out.

"Yer ain't got that ray gun the Professor used to spring yer that time, 'ave yer?" J asked, as they began to lower the gangplank.

"Afraid not."

"Pity," muttered the boy, through a large, fixed grin.

The airship's walkway opened to a sudden hush. Thaddeus and J took a step out onto the gangplank.

"Behold!" boomed a voice to their left. "The Magnificent Circus Maximus presents to you, all the way from Great Britain... the Caravan of the Air!"

Thaddeus and J looked to see the circus master signalling frantically to a little man pushing through the crowd. The newcomer held up a tiny trumpet to his lips, and played a loud, bright fanfare. The crowd exploded with applause.

"Circus what?" J asked out of the corner of his mouth as they both stepped warily to the ground. "Caravan of the where?"

"I think we've been appropriated," Thaddeus muttered back. "How does he know we're British? Why is he speaking English?"

"*Mes amis!* My friends!" exclaimed the circus maestro, barrelling towards them with outstretched arms. "What an entrance! What an act! What an amazing contraption!"

"Thank you, Mr..." Thaddeus began, feeling his hand crushed in a grip that could have been made of iron.

"I am the Great Constanto," declared their new friend. "It is my great pleasure to welcome our wonderful English cousins, yes?"

"Yes," said J, "but 'ow did you know we was from Britain?"

"Ahh – the flag, yes? The... how you say... Union Jack?"

J and Thaddeus both turned to look at the ship. "What flag?"

The Great Constanto pointed to the underside of the hull. Thaddeus and J both bent down to look. Sure enough, there was a Union Jack, in its bright colours of red, white and blue, emblazoned on the underside of the ship, tainted by the jagged scrape of the mast that had struck it earlier.

"You never noticed that before?" Thaddeus asked J.

"Never," J admitted. "That bit were already built, weren't it? And it's not like I ever lifted her before, is it?"

"*Mes amis,*" the circus master interrupted. "Your public awaits!" He threw his arms wide, indicating the crowd, which whooped and hollered in response.

"Actually," said Thaddeus, "we're just here looking for our friends."

"Then you are circus folk!" Constanto exclaimed. "I knew it! I knew such a marvellous beast of the air could be nothing else!"

"Not exactly circus folk," said J, eyeing the crowd. "But I bet you know our mate. Rémy Brunel?"

"She's a trapeze artist," Thaddeus added. "She sometimes performs as Little Bird?"

"Aha!" said Constanto, "I think you mean *Le Petit Moineau*. If you are friends of the great Rémy Brunel, you are friends of ours."

"Can you take us to her?" asked Thaddeus. "Her circus is called the Circus of Secrets now."

"Ah yes, *Le Cirque du Secrète,*" sighed Constanto. "But alas, they are not here – we are missing them from our number for this Jamboree. It is such a pity. We were all so looking forward to seeing this troupe under a new name, without that stinking cur, Gustave."

"They – they ain't here?" J asked.

"*Non,* my young friend."

"Well then, perhaps Rémy is here without a circus?" Thaddeus suggested. "She was travelling with a friend – a magician called Yannick?"

Constanto frowned and shook his head. "I am sorry, *mes amis,* but I have not heard of her being seen. Besides, if it were known that the great Little Bird was no longer travelling with a circus, there isn't a master among us that wouldn't try to buy her talents for themselves. It would be the talk of the circle – but I have heard nothing. Still, perhaps there is someone who can help you."

"Oh?"

"Yes – I have recently taken on a German violinist, a man by the name of Dorffman. Until recently he was travelling with the new circus of Claudette Anjou. Come, I will take you to him."

J and Thaddeus hesitated, looking back at the airship, unwilling to leave it unattended under the hungry scrutiny of so many unknown people.

"Do not fear, eh?" said Constanto, and put his fingers to his lips. He emitted a piercing whistle, which was answered by two large men who looked like prize-fighters. "They will take care of the Caravan of the Air, you see?"

Constanto made to move off. "Hang on a sec," said J.

He looked out at the crowd, and then back at the circus master. "Reckon they'd pay a bit for a squiz inside, like?"

"J?" Thaddeus asked. "What are you doing?"

"If we're going to be here for a bit, we're going to need some readies, ain't we?" he said reasonably. And then, to Constanto: "Two… what do you call 'em? Centimes? Two centimes for a peek. We'll split the take wiv you if your blokes make sure they don't touch nuffin'."

Constanto grinned. "I like the way you think, young master," he said, before barking a swift order in French to the two men the size of tree trunks who were now standing on either side of the door. "Any time you want a job, you come to the Great Constanto, no?"

131

Seventeen

Real Magic

The music was distant, drifting on a rising and falling breeze, but growing stronger. After a few moments, Yannick's horse appeared beside Rémy's. They fell in step and rode on in silence, listening to the sound of the melody that Rémy knew deep in her bones. Above them, they could see twilight filtering between the branches, a cloudless, starry night settling over the forest.

The music was coming from a caravan. It was wooden, hand-carved in the old Romany style, with a rounded roof and half-panelled door. The cross-planks had been painted cherry red, the mid-panels a yellow as bright as the sun. It was standing in a clearing that seemed as if it had been created by the forest itself, as if the trees had bowed and taken a step back to make room for it. Fireflies sheltered in their nooks and crannies, imitating the stars still waking up above. In the centre of the clearing was a small blaze, the low, curling flames cooking a scrawny wild chicken on a spit.

An old woman sat on the steps of the caravan, her ancient fingers tangled around a small wooden pipe that wove the tune as she blew through it. She looked gnarled enough to be part of the forest herself.

Rémy had never seen the woman before in her life, but she knew that music. She and Yannick stood, watching the old woman and feeling the melody grow into the world like a frond of fern uncurling for the first time. It was at once unexpected and familiar, and when it stopped, Rémy had no idea whether she had been listening for minutes or hours.

The old woman opened her eyes and looked at them as if they had always been there.

"Ah," she said. "The chicken will be cooked by now. Time for dinner." She looked at Yannick. "You, boy – make yourself useful. Take it off the spit. There are bowls yonder." She waved one finger at the fire. "Some tomatoes, too."

Yannick shrugged and did as he was told. Rémy took a step closer to the old woman. Her face was as creased and cracked as the bark of a tree, but her eyes were bright and blue. She pulled a purple shawl around her shoulders and shuffled towards Rémy.

"Ah, and isn't it good to see you again," the old crone cackled, her voice as scratchy as new wool. She raised one ancient hand to Rémy's face, patting her cheek. "Pretty, too, though I knew you were going to be from the moment you opened that mouth and bawled."

Rémy shook her head. "I'm sorry, old mother, but I don't know you."

"I know you don't, girl, but that's no matter. I know you enough for both of us. Come on, let's sit and eat before the chicken goes to waste."

She shuffled towards the fire, Rémy staring after her, confused. Yannick handed the old woman a bowl and she settled on her haunches, turning to look at Rémy. In the firelight she looked even older.

Rémy sat beside her, taking another bowl from Yannick.

"Can you tell me how you know me?" Rémy said. "If we have met, I must have been very young, I think?"

The old woman cackled between mouthfuls. "Oh yes, you were very young. Next to nothing, in fact. I remember you, though. Oh, how you and your brother made your mother howl."

Rémy sighed, her suspicions confirmed. "Ah, old mother. I am sorry, but you have me confused with someone else. I have no brother. My parents had no children other than me."

The old woman eyes twinkled blue. "Is that so?"

A twitch of annoyance tensed Rémy's shoulders. The old crone's tone was teasing, as if she knew what Rémy herself didn't.

"Yes, it is most definitely so."

Abruptly, the old woman put down her bowl, shaking her head. "Ah, what a thing, to go through the world without knowing your own kin."

"I told you," said Rémy, "I don't have any kin. You're confusing me with someone else."

"And I am telling you, Rémy Brunel," said the old woman, in a voice suddenly as clear as day and as straight as a plumb line, "that I remember you, and I remember your brother."

Rémy jumped at the sound of her name on the old woman's lips and drew in a breath. "H-how do you know my name?"

The old woman smiled again. "I have birthed babies for the circuses of France since I was thirteen years old. And I tell you, my girl, that I never forget one of mine." The twinkle was back in her eyes. "No one expected you, but out you flew, hanging onto your brother's ankle as if you were already performing in the tent." The old woman chuckled. "And what a scrawny little bird you were, and didn't I tell your poor mother so?"

"That's... that's what they call me," stuttered Rémy. "That's... that's always been my nickname."

The old woman looked at her steadily, the slight smile on her ancient lips telling Rémy that she already knew full well that Rémy Brunel was more usually known as Little Bird.

Rémy stood up, a little shakily. "I don't have a brother," she said again. "I – I don't. I would know if I did. Wouldn't I?"

The old woman shrugged. "The things we don't know in this world are enough to fill the spaces between stars," she said.

Rémy spun to face her. "But – if I do... where is he? Why don't I know him?"

"I did not stay long enough to be able to answer all your questions, Little Bird," said the old woman. "I am a midwife. I go where the births are and leave the babies behind me." She looked into the fire, the sparks illuminating a face that had grown sad. "I will tell you this – when I heard of your parents' misfortune, I wept over it. They were good people."

Rémy sank down again, her food forgotten. Her head was spinning. Had she really had – did she *have* – a brother, a twin? It was unthinkable. She was alone in the world, except for Claudette. Gustave had seen to that when he'd forced her parents to steal a jewel that had cursed them both, driving them apart and away from their daughter forever. Besides, how could the woman possibly remember every child she ever helped into the world?

Almost as if Yannick had heard Rémy's thoughts, he spoke.

"Tell me, old mother," he said, "if you remember all the babies you have ever birthed, do you remember bringing one into the world called Claudette Anjou?"

Rémy frowned, wondering why Yannick wanted to know. She glanced at the old woman, but she was staring into the fire, her lips set in a determined line. For a moment Rémy thought she hadn't even heard Yannick's question. And then:

"If there's one thing I can't abide, boy," came her cracked old voice, turning harsher, "it's a question being asked where the answer is already known."

Rémy looked at Yannick. He looked back, uncomfortable, and shrugged.

"You are not wearing your opal," said the old woman suddenly, as she crooked one gnarled twig of a finger at Rémy's neck.

Rémy's hand flew to where she pointed. "How do you know about–? No… I did once. Always. I never took it off, but…"

Something about the look on the old woman's face told Rémy she didn't need to say any more, that in fact she knew exactly the gift – and the burden – that the opal had bestowed. Rémy felt faint, the blood rushing from her face. If the old woman knew about the opal, then what else did she know?

"Let an old woman see it, eh?" she asked, tipping her head to one side. "It is such a pretty thing. It has been a long, long time."

Rémy nodded, running her fingers along her corset's hem. She felt for the pocket, and the pouch within it…

She leapt up. "It's gone!" Rémy cried.

"What has?" Yannick asked, standing up on the other side of the fire in alarm. "Rémy? What's gone?"

"My opal! It was here, in a pocket beneath my corset, but it's gone! It's gone!" She stared at Yannick, her heart turning cold. "You – did you take it?"

"What?" Yannick asked, aghast.

"You heard me, Yannick. Did you steal my opal?"

"How could you even ask me that?" he demanded angrily.

"How?" Rémy asked, with just as much fury. "Oh well, let's see

136

now. Between the two of us, who last stole a jewel? Remind me again, would you, Yannick?"

The magician shook his head in disgust. "I can't believe you," he hissed. "After what I did for you, saving you from the gendarmes. After what I *risked* for you."

They both fell silent, staring at each other across the flames. The old woman stayed where she was, watching calmly.

"Anyway, don't you always have it around your neck?" Yannick asked coldly. "Didn't I see it the other day? How would I be able to steal that?"

"I took it off," Rémy said, her voice cracking over the words.

"You took it off?"

Rémy was distraught. How could she have lost the only possession in the world that meant anything at all to her? "I sewed a pocket for it, to keep it safe."

Yannick made a sound in his throat. "Safer than around your neck? You took off your most valuable possession and put it in a pocket, and now you're accusing me? Any cutpurse could have got at it, Rémy. Has the pocket been sliced?"

"No," said Rémy, pulling up her shirt and turning up the edge of the corset to show the pocket. "I would have felt it. I would have–" She stopped. The corner of the pocket was open, the bottom seam of stitching neatly cut, as if with a knife or pair of scissors. Rémy stared at it in horror. She had been robbed by a pickpocket. She, who had spent her life with the lowest of the low, had been cheated by a common cutpurse.

Rémy covered her face with her hands and sank to the ground, the tears pricking at her eyes. She should have worn it always. She should have fastened it around her neck so that no one could get at it, ever.

Rémy felt something on her shoulder – it was the old woman's hand, squeezing her gently.

"Be of good heart, Little Bird," the old woman whispered in her ear. "The opal has only one true owner, and it will always return home, however long it takes."

Rémy sobbed a little. "Then I will never see it again," she said, her heart broken. "Because that wasn't me. My parents stole it, didn't they? From a raja in India. They did not own it, they stole it."

"Rémy Brunel, dry your tears and look me in the eye," the old woman demanded, her hand on Rémy's shoulder becoming an iron grip until she did as she was told. Rémy stared into the old woman's eyes, which seemed as deep and as blue as the ocean, and just as old. "Did no one ever tell you that you were an Indian baby? It's as clear as the pretty on your face."

Rémy swallowed her tears, her spine tingling. "Yes," she said. "Yes. Someone did, once. Not long ago. But–"

The old woman smiled again, letting go of Rémy's shoulder and straightening up. She said nothing for a moment, just stood beside the dwindling fire, looking up at the stars that pricked the sky, brighter than candlelight.

"It is time for an old woman to sleep," she said eventually, before beginning to shuffle towards her caravan. "Sometimes we *all* need to go home."

"But," Rémy began, getting to her feet. "Wait, I need to ask you so many questions. Please!"

The old woman turned to her with a smile. "I am not an oracle, Rémy," she said. "I do not know the world's secrets. I have simply lived a very, very long time and I have seen many, many things. Old women need their sleep, and now I need mine. Goodnight. Rest now."

The woman turned her back and walked slowly to her home and up its little wooden steps, shutting the door behind her without another word.

Rémy and Yannick settled beside the dying embers of the campfire, but it took a long time before Rémy could sleep. Her mind was full of questions and reproachful anger. She had no one to blame but herself for losing the opal. She should have been wearing it, as she always had, but her cowardice had got the better of her, just at the moment when it seemed she had met someone who knew about the stone and what it could do.

Eventually the rigours of the day caught up with her, and Rémy fell into a fitful slumber. In her dreams, the woods were on fire. She was trying to flee the blaze, stumbling after someone who kept turning to wait for her, despite the flames licking at his feet. Rémy thought it was Yannick, but the only time she managed to glimpse his face, she realised it was Thaddeus.

Eighteen

Troubling News

Thaddeus and J left the storm they had created, following the Great Constanto as he led them towards another circle of light. This one was the halo of a bonfire, burning in the centre of a small cluster of caravans. From one floated a haunting sound. A figure formed through the flickering darkness. It was a large man, sitting in front of the wooden wheel of his caravan with a violin beneath his chin. The music spun into the night sky, accompanying the crackle and spit of the flames.

"Dorffman," said Constanto, his voice softer now. "I have brought two people to see you."

The man stopped playing and opened his eyes, which were a deep and melancholy blue. He looked at Thaddeus first, and then J, before settling back on Thaddeus.

"You," he said, his thick German accent making heavy shapes of the words. "You, I remember. You came to the circus in London, the night that we lost Little Bird. You are policeman, ya?"

"A policeman!" Constanto exclaimed in horror.

Thaddeus held up his hands, eager not to lose the friend they had made. "No – I mean, yes. I am a policeman, in London. But here, I am just trying to find a friend. Have you seen Rémy Brunel?"

Dorffman looked at him with open suspicion. "You are searching for Little Bird?"

"Yeah," said J, "but for a good reason, nuffin' bad like I reckon you're thinking, Mister. We fink she might be in trouble, see. An' more than that, Mr Rec here, he loves her, like, and..."

"J!" said Thaddeus.

"Beg pardon," said J earnestly, "but we got to tell 'im the truth! Especially wiv 'im knowing you're a policeman and all."

There was a brief silence as Dorffman watched the discomfort on Thaddeus' face.

"Why did you think she would be here?" the German asked.

"Where else would she be?" said Thaddeus. "Once Yannick had shown her the poster for the Jamboree..."

At the magician's name, Dorffman's expression hardened. "Yannick? What do you know of him?"

"He met up with Rémy in London. They came back to France together. You know him?"

Dorffman stared into the fire, nodding. "That one. He is bad news." The German looked back at Thaddeus with narrowed eyes. "But I think you know that already, ya?"

Thaddeus swallowed, his mouth suddenly dry. "I have my suspicions, yes. What can you tell me about him?"

Dorffman shrugged. "Up until two weeks ago, I was still with the Circus of Secrets. Until a month ago, Yannick was there also."

Thaddeus blinked. "What do you mean, Yannick was there?"

"I mean exactly what I say, Englishman. When we got back to France, some of the acts decided to move on. They were not sure Claudette had it in her to create a new circus from the ashes of the old. We needed new talent. Yannick turned up as we moved towards Paris, and so Claudette took him on as a magician."

"What happened?" J asked.

"Nothing, at first," Dorffman shrugged. "We went on. We were doing well. Yannick's act was popular. Then one night, I heard an argument. It was between him and Claudette, though I do not know what about. Yannick stayed for a few weeks after that, but Claudette would hardly speak to him. Then he left, and Claudette lost her mind."

"Lost her mind?" Thaddeus repeated. "What do you mean?"

Dorffman sighed. "We were supposed to be building a new circus, ya? A better one than under Gustave – bigger, stronger. To be a big circus you must play the big towns, where there is money, ya? Claudette did the opposite. She avoided the cities, and then even the towns. She moved us further and further away from where they can afford luxuries like a night at the circus. Then she announced that we would not be going to the Jamboree, which was insanity itself. Instead, she said, we would go south. She intended to head for the mountains and beyond that – to Spain."

"And you think that had something to do with the argument with Yannick?" Thaddeus asked.

Dorffman nodded. "I think so, but I don't know what. Anyway, with regret, I told her I could not stay in the Circus of Secrets, and I left. If money had been no object, I would have stayed, but I could not. So I came back to Paris in time for the Jamboree, to find new work," he said. "Claudette is a good woman, a smart woman. But the summer will not last forever, and the mountains are no place to be when the snows come. Still, if you want my opinion, if you are to find Rémy Brunel, you must find Claudette. Those two are like sisters."

Thaddeus nodded, thinking hard. "Tell me, Dorffman," he

142

asked, after a moment. "Have you ever seen Yannick hypnotise someone to do something against their will?"

The big man laughed, but without mirth. "Of course," he said. "It is the best part of his act. It is also how he takes whatever he wants. Something else I think you know already, ya?"

"Yes," said Thaddeus. "Yes, I do. And this is the man Rémy is alone with."

Dorffman stood, and then, to Thaddeus' surprise, laid a huge hand on the policeman's shoulder. "Do not worry yourself too much, my friend," he rumbled. "I have never known Little Bird to do anything she did not want to do. A will like that cannot be broken by a mewling whelp like Yannick; God help him when she becomes wise to whatever plan he has. But I do worry for Claudette. She has a darkness following her, with Yannick at its head."

* * *

It was late when Thaddeus and J got back to the airship. The crowds of circus folk had returned to their homes. Constanto's two hulking men nodded at them and then melted away into the night. J paused, looking after them wistfully.

"Wish we 'ad the cash to hire those two," he said. "I didn't like what that chap Dorffman had to say in the slightest. Oh, well. Looks like it's just me and thee." J stumped up the gangplank and into the airship, Thaddeus following.

Inside, they found the ship almost as they'd left it, save for a cloth bag placed on the control desk. It was full of centimes – their take from the evening.

"Not bad," said J, yawning. "That'll keep us in bread and drippin' for a while, at any rate." He paused with a frown. "'Ere – do they 'ave drippin' in France?"

More Questions

Rémy woke to birdsong and the dapple of warm sunlight on her face. She sat up and looked around. The horses she and Yannick had stolen were grazing quietly. A blackbird cocked its head and regarded her from atop a fallen tree, but apart from that she was alone. The old woman, her caravan and Yannick were gone.

Rémy jumped to her feet. The blanket she'd covered herself in the night before fell around her feet, and with it something heavier. It clunked to the ground and lay still.

It was a cube, golden-coloured and covered in intricate patterns. Whorls and connected circles swirled across its surface like waves on a turbulent sea. Rémy sat cross-legged on the blanket, turning the cube over in her hands. It was small enough to fit into her palm, and wasn't heavy, though it felt solid. She looked closer, and saw a series of tiny hinges cleverly hidden among the patterns.

Something else caught her eye, too, discarded among the blanket's folds. It was a scrap of paper, folded roughly. Rémy opened it. A note was scrawled on it in untidy writing.

Show this only to the one you trust the most. Solve the puzzle. Find the truth.

Rémy stared at the words for a moment. Who had written them? Who had left her the box? Surely it must have been the old woman? She stood and looked at the patch of grass where the caravan had stood the night before, but already it seemed to be springing back into place. Even the cooking fire seemed to have sunk into the soft earth. Had the woman really been there at all, or had it all been a dream?

She got to her feet, picking up her pack and hiding the cube deep within it before looking around again. Yannick couldn't be far away – after all, his horse was still there. Rémy searched the small clearing and found a faint track. She was fairly sure that it wasn't the one they had used the night before, though it still didn't look wide enough for the caravan to have passed that way. She shouldered her pack and followed it into the forest, glancing behind her. It wouldn't do to get lost out here alone.

Rémy listened out for the sound of running water, thinking that Yannick had perhaps decided to bathe. The forest, though, was quiet apart from the rustle of wind in the leaves and the occasional creak from the trees. Rémy was just beginning to think that it might be best to go back to the clearing when she heard voices. She stopped, trying to place the direction they were coming from, and then realised that, actually, there was only one voice. It was low and speaking in short bursts, though the wind made it impossible to hear what was being said. Rémy followed the sound, stepping on the forest mulch as quietly as possible. She wove her way through the trees until, abruptly, they ended.

Yannick was crouching in the dust, his back to her. He'd changed out of his stage gear and back into his day clothes.

"Yannick?" Rémy asked.

He stood up quickly, turning to look at her. "Aha!" the magician said, with a quick smile. "I was going to come and wake you. Look – we've found the road again!" He was trying to conceal

145

something on the ground behind him, but it was too late – Rémy had already seen it.

"What's that?" she asked, walking around him to see the object more clearly. For a moment she thought he had been left a puzzle box, too. But it wasn't a box – or at least, not of the sort that Rémy had found in her blanket.

"Oh, it's nothing…" Yannick said, with a nonchalant shrug, as they both looked down at the small device.

Rémy bent down and picked it up. It was made of silver-grey metal – an oblong with a rotating cylinder set inside it and wand-like antennae sticking out of it. She looked at Yannick with a frown. "I've seen this – or something like it – before," she said. "It's one of the Professor's communication devices."

"Oh, is that what it is?" Yannick laughed, though to Rémy it sounded forced.

"Did you take this from the workshop?"

Yannick made a face. "Rémy…"

"You stole it?"

"I'm sorry," he said. "But there were so many fascinating things – I couldn't resist. I didn't think you'd ever notice."

"Who were you talking to, just now?" Rémy asked, still frowning.

Yannick looked confused. "Talking to? What do you mean?"

"I heard you, Yannick. You were using this to send a message."

The magician held up his hands. "Rémy, I didn't even know what it was for until you told me just now."

Rémy set her jaw and stared at him. "Don't lie to me, Yannick."

"I'm not! I swear! Come on – as if this little thing could be anything other than a useless pile of junk, anyway! Now, that really would be magic." He laughed again, and then said, "Look, it's going to make me sound stupid, but what you heard was just me talking to myself. It's a habit – when I concentrate, I end up muttering things, telling myself what to do. That's all."

Rémy stared at him for another moment before opening her pack and putting the Professor's device inside. "I can't believe you stole from me," she said. "I thought you'd said you'd never do that?"

Yannick sighed impatiently. "I didn't steal from you, I stole from the Professor. He's not going to miss it, is he?"

Rémy slung her pack over her shoulder and looked at him seriously. "Look, Yannick. I don't think it's a good idea for us to carry on together. I'm grateful for what you did, helping me escape the gendarmes. But I don't think you're a good fit for the Circus of Secrets. Claudette wants it to be within the law – she told me so. And you... I don't think you can help yourself, Yannick. You see an opportunity to steal, and you don't think anything of taking advantage of that opportunity. I don't think you even see it as wrong. So I think it'd be best if we part ways, *d'accord?*"

Yannick looked away for a minute, staring down the road and at the dusty horizon beyond. Then he looked at her and shrugged. The magician lifted one hand to rub it through his hair and opened his mouth as if he was about to say something, but then thought better of it.

Rémy felt a buzzing in her ears. She shook her head to clear it. Everything suddenly seemed a little distant. She felt tired – her sleep obviously hadn't been as sound as she'd first thought.

"Come on," she said, with a sigh. "Let's get the horses and go. We'll never catch up with Claudette and the circus at this rate."

Southwards

Thaddeus slept little, disturbed by more than just the snatches of music and raucous laughter that drifted on the shifting breeze. He rose early in the morning, giving up on trying to get any sound sleep. Might as well take advantage of the time they were spending on solid ground, Thaddeus reasoned, and stretch his legs before he was cooped up once again in the small airship.

The overgrown camp was all a-bustle with the business of morning, full of laughter and chatter as the circus folk prepared for another day of performance. Thaddeus tried to imagine what it would be like to have such a life – to be always moving on, always thinking ahead. He concluded that it was probably something you could not imagine unless you had lived it yourself. That was why circus folk always stuck together – only another circus performer could truly understand the nature of this life. Thaddeus stopped for a moment, thinking about Rémy. She'd abandoned all that when she chose to stay in London. At the time he'd not given it much thought. Somehow he'd assumed that it would be better than a life on the road. Now, he realised that perhaps that was not the case. Maybe he had taken her decision to stay in London for granted.

Sighing, he raised his head. Thaddeus' eye was caught by a

poster nailed to a fence post. It was so colourful that no one could miss it, the paper having been stained yellow and printed with bright blue lettering.

REWARD
BY ORDER OF COMTE DE CANTAL DE SAINT-CERNIN
FOR THE SAFE RETURN OF THE 'LOST COMTESSE'
ARRIETE DE CANTAL.
BRING THE COMTESSE HOME!

Thaddeus moved closer, frowning as a sudden chill washed over him at the sight of the Comte de Cantal's name. He pulled the poster down and read it over again. Instead of heading back to the airship, Thaddeus went to find the German violinist.

Dorffman was tying down the guide rope of a new tent that had miraculously appeared, like a mushroom, since the night before. He nodded at the policeman as he approached.

Thaddeus held up the poster. "What can you tell me about this?"

The German shrugged. "What do you want to know? The missing girl, it is an old wives' tale, made to scare misbehaving children. The Comte..." Dorffman made a hawking sound in his throat, as if he was about to spit. "Whoever she is, real or not, she'd do best to stay away from him."

Thaddeus nodded. "I agree."

Dorffman raised an eyebrow. "You know the Comte?"

"Our paths have crossed. And–" he hesitated. "I think Yannick is working for him. Thieving. We think that's why Yannick's with Rémy – they're going to use her to steal something really big, sometime in the next few weeks."

Dorffman frowned. "What is it they will take?"

Thaddeus sighed. "We don't know. That's why we want to find her – before they can force her back into her old life."

The German watched Thaddeus silently for a moment, and then nodded. "So the Comte de Cantal needs money, ya? That explains the search." He waved a finger at the poster.

"Oh? Why?"

"The story goes that the old Comte and his Comtesse settled everything on their missing daughter," Dorffman explained. "All their money is sitting in a vault somewhere. It has been for decades. It will not be released to any descendant until she turns up and claims it, or unless someone can prove without doubt that she's dead."

Another chill passed through Thaddeus as he looked at the poster again. "So the Comte…"

Dorffman nodded. "I would say that this search is more about proving she's dead than finding her alive, eh? Then he can inherit."

"What happens if he finds her alive?" Thaddeus asked.

"Then she will inherit, and he will get nothing." The German shrugged. "What fools these rich folk are, eh? What a tangle they make of their lives. For me, I am always happier poor. And now, I must get on with my work, or I will be too poor even for me."

"Sorry – yes," said Thaddeus. "Thank you, Dorffman."

The German nodded. "Good luck and farewell, Rec."

Back at the airship, J was up and about, readying her for take-off. Thaddeus could already hear the faint hiss as the ruby, recharged overnight, did its job.

"Wondered where you'd got to," the boy said as Thaddeus came aboard. "Didn't stop to get breakfast, by any chance? No?

Never mind, I'll pop out meself and grab some of them curly bread things the Frenchies are so partial to."

"Croissants, J," said Thaddeus absently, still thinking about the poster. "They're pastry, not bread."

"Whatever they is, I like 'em," said J. "A nice bit of bacon and eggs would be better, but... 'ere," he said, concerned. "What's up?"

Thaddeus sat down on a bunk, and gave the poster to J.

"What's this all about?" J asked. "I mean, I know this involves the Comte, and what not, but what has this got to do with us?"

"J," Thaddeus said, after he'd briefly explained what Dorffman had told him. "What if we're wrong about why Cantal wants Rémy?"

The boy blinked. "You ain't saying you fink Rémy's this Lost Comtesse, are yer? She's too young, ain't she?"

Thaddeus shook his head. "It can't be Rémy. We know the story of her parents. But what about Rémy's friend, Claudette? Think about it, J – Dorffman said she and Yannick quarrelled, and then after that, she started avoiding the cities and going south, almost as if she was running from something. And we know that the other thing the German said was true – that they're like sisters."

"Rémy ain't had a letter from 'er for weeks," J said. "They was s'posed to write each other all the time, but Rémy's been worried lately cos she ain't 'ad one."

"And then Yannick turns up," said Thaddeus. "Out of the blue, just like that, and persuades Rémy to go back to France. None of them are here. What if Yannick's using Rémy to find Claudette?"

They were both silent for a moment, thinking it all through.

"Why would she not want to be found?" J asked. "If she was this missing girl, like, and she could prove it, why wouldn't she want to do that? She'd be in for a mountain of money, wouldn't she?"

"Yes. I don't know the answer to that," said Thaddeus.

J sighed. "It don't change nuffin' for us right now, do it?" he said. "I mean, we still got to find Rémy. Maybe now it's for a different reason, but either way…"

Thaddeus nodded. "Exactly."

"Well, then," J said grimly. "Better get on wiv it then, 'adn't we?"

Another crowd gathered to watch the airship take off, drawn by the hissing of the ruby's gas as the balloon billowed and swelled skyward. There was a great cheer as they lifted away. J waved through the window at the enchanted spectators, who slowly shrank to the size of ants as the airship rose higher and higher.

"Come on," J muttered, wrestling slightly with the controls.

"What's the matter?"

J shook his head with a slight frown. "Prolly nuffin'. Just seems to be something off. You didn't see nuffin' caught beneath the hull, did yer?"

Thaddeus shook his head. "Nothing. We're probably just getting used to how she moves."

J nodded. "Right enough. She seems to be all right, anyway. It should even out once we're up. So, then, where'd Dorffman say we needed to head?"

Thaddeus spread out the map Constanto had given them and found the name of the town on the map. "Périgueux. That's where the circus was when Dorffman left it. The circus will have moved on by now, but it's a start."

"And that's south of here, right?" said J. "The Professor's dial ain't no good for anything but big cities, so we'll have to navigate our way there ourselves."

"Not to worry, J," said Thaddeus, "I'm sure we'll be fine. I've read a map before."

The ship tipped as J turned her into the prevailing wind, moving in a graceful curve over the city to bring her around. There was a clunk and the sound of something rolling briefly, bouncing across wood. Thaddeus and J both jerked around to look, but there was nothing in the cabin.

"What the bleedin' 'eck was that?" J asked.

"I don't know." Thaddeus went to the other end of the ship, searching for any sign of something coming loose, but there was nothing. "I can't see anything."

"It were under the floor, in the ruby chamber," J said. "Better take a look. If we've got a problem, we'll need to put down."

Thaddeus went to the hatch and pulled it up. There was nothing wrong with the ruby assembly – it sat peacefully in its coupling, glowing slightly. Everything else seemed to be in its rightful place, too. He leaned in further, peering into the gloom of the small space beyond. Was there something there, at the back? He couldn't make it out.

"Well?" J called, over his shoulder. "See anything?"

"I don't know," Thaddeus said, straightening up. "It's too dark."

"Hang on," J said, a determined look on his face. "Give me two ticks, then take another look."

The boy began to bank the ship again, hauling her around in a tight circle that forced Thaddeus to grip the edge of the hatch to stop himself sliding the length of the cabin. From below, there was another clunk. He ducked his head into the hole again. Through the darkness, Thaddeus saw something move, thrown to the other side of the airship's hold.

"There's definitely something there!" confirmed Thaddeus. "But it's just too dark to see what, and I can't fit down there."

"Odd," J said. "I can't think of nuffin' that could break down there and roll 'bout. It should be empty 'cept for the ruby and its fittings. 'Ere – you take the controls, I'll have a look."

Thaddeus swapped places with him and watched as the boy stuck his head into the hole. He wriggled down so far that he disappeared up to his waist. After a moment, J gave a muffled yell and scrambled backwards.

"'Ere," said J, pulling his head out of the hole and staring with outright indignance at Thaddeus. "You won't believe this – we've only got ourselves a bleedin' stowaway!"

"What?" Thaddeus exclaimed, but the boy had already gone back under the floorboards, this time vanishing completely.

"Oi!" J shouted. "You! Come 'ere! Think you can make this ship your own, do yer? Well, you've got another fing coming!"

There came the sound of a scuffle. The ship juddered slightly.

"J," Thaddeus shouted, trying to hold the airship steady. "Take it easy, would you? Whoever's down there, we're all in the same boat – literally!"

There came a muffled scream from below as J ignored him.

"Aha! Got you now, ain't I?" came J's triumphant yell. "Right – out yer come, sunshine!"

Thaddeus looked over his shoulder as, with great effort and not a little yelling, J hauled a tangled bundle of rags out of the hatch. He dumped it on the floor.

"There," J said, still scuffling with the bundle. "Let's see what we've caught, shall we?"

The bundle threw out an arm, tossing away the ragged old blanket it had wrapped itself in.

There was a moment of silence.

"It's... it's a... *girl!*" J exclaimed in horror.

154

And so it was. Their stowaway was a thin child, not much older or younger than J. Her hair was a mass of tight, jet-black curls under a headscarf. Angry green eyes stared from a bronzed face. She jumped sharply to her feet, scolding J in broken English.

"Stupid *bengel*!" she shouted, with a strong German accent. "You ruin my blanket! You owe me."

"Like hell I do!" J retorted, to which the girl responded by stepping forward and slapping him smartly across the face. J's shocked mouth formed a perfect 'O' as she stepped back.

"For language, *Blasphemiker*," she announced stoutly.

"She – she–!" J spluttered when he found his voice, holding one hand to his reddening cheek. "She hit me! God darn it, I'll–"

He took a step towards her.

"J," Thaddeus warned.

"Fine," said the boy. "Set the ship down, Thaddeus – let's get rid of her, right now." J stared angrily at the girl, who was standing with her chin jutting out in defiance and her arms crossed.

"We can't, J. How long did the ruby take to recharge last time – it was all night, wasn't it? We can't waste another day waiting."

"Oh, well, nuffin' for it then," said J. "I'll just open the gangplank and chuck 'er out as we go."

The girl took a step back, wary and scared despite her defiance.

"J, we both know you're not going to do that. Let's just all calm down, shall we?" Thaddeus checked that they were heading in the right direction and stood up. "Come and sit down," he said to the girl. "Tell us who you are and why you did this."

J made a grumbling sound in his throat, but Thaddeus held up his hand for quiet. The girl watched them both suspiciously.

"Please," said the policeman, indicating his bunk. "J, sit. We'll talk this out like civilized people. Understand?"

After another moment of complaint, J did as Thaddeus asked. They sat side by side on J's bunk. Their stowaway looked around the cabin for a moment, as if deciding whether there was some way to escape. Having decided there wasn't, she walked slowly to the bunk opposite and sat down.

She was small, Thaddeus saw — smaller than J. When she sat on the bunk, her bare brown feet didn't reach the ground. She held the torn blanket around her shoulders. Beneath it she wore a tattered dress. It looked a little too small, even for her. The sleeves, which would once have been wrist-length, were now hovering around her elbows.

"Good," said Thaddeus. "Well, that's progress of sorts, I suppose. Hello. My name is Thaddeus Rec, and this is J. What's your name?"

The girl set her jaw, as if she was about to refuse to speak, and then apparently changed her mind. She sighed, and shrugged, still with her arms crossed. "Dita," she said. "I am Dita."

"Dita!" J mocked, with a howl of laughter. "I never heard nuffin' so daft in my life!"

"And what kind of name is 'J'?" Dita spat back. "Nothing, ya? Because you came from nowhere and have nowhere to go. Yes?"

"Stop it, both of you!" Thaddeus ordered, before they could start another argument. "It looks as if we're stuck with each other for the time being, so at least try to be pleasant. Dita, why did you stow away on this airship?"

Dita didn't answer for a moment, looking around her. Then she shrugged again. "I wanted to see. Then I wanted to fly." She paused. "It is *herrlich*. Magnificent."

"Yeah, it is," chipped in J. "And it's *mine*."

"Yours," Dita scoffed. "Pfft. How can it belong to a dirty boy?"

"I ain't dirty, I 'ad a bath last week," J retorted. "And the ship's mine cos I built 'er, that's why, and that's more than you could do, useless hellcat that you are!"

"J," Thaddeus said, "please!"

A look of surprise had settled on the girl's face. "You built this? The truth?"

"Yeah, truly," growled J, and then added, "Well... bits of it."

Dita shrugged. "OK for a smelly boy like you."

"Dita," Thaddeus said, before the fighting could begin again. "Where we're going, it's not—"

"I know. I heard you talk to Herr Dorffman."

"You know him?"

She nodded. "He is good man. Kind to me, got me work at Circus Maximus." Dita wrinkled her nose at the thought. "Cleaning up after the elephants. Not a good job, but—"

J hooted with derision, pointing at the girl and slapping his leg. "A dung sweeper! And she calls *me* smelly!"

Dita glowered. "Better than starving, dirty boy. Not that you know what that means."

J stopped laughing and scowled. "I've been starving more often than you've had years of your life," he growled. "And proper starving too, like there's sumfin' eating your bones and—"

"Enough!" Thaddeus shouted, smacking his hand against the wooden bulkhead above him. "Stop squabbling this minute or I'll gag you both, do you understand?" J and Dita looked at him with faint reproach, but nodded. "Right. J, you will refrain from speaking until Dita has finished her explanation. Dita, what was it about our conversation with Dorffman that made up your mind?"

Dita bit her lip. "You are going south. I want to go south. My father was German but my mother, Spanish. Andalusia. I want to go to her village. My grandmother is there, and maybe other… *Sippe*." The girl looked down at her bare feet. "I want… *nach Hause gehen*. In English – to go home."

There was a brief silence. Thaddeus nodded. "I don't suppose the circus pays enough for you to travel there with money you have saved, eh?"

The girl shook her head, her ringlets flying. "And alone – it would be *riskant*. But this wonderful machine…" She shook her head. "Anyway, I can be useful to you. I can pay my way."

J let out a snort at this. "We ain't got an elephant, in case you 'adn't noticed."

Thaddeus sent him a warning glance. "Dita, what do you mean?"

"So far, you have luck," she said. "People in circuses speak languages. But down there?" Dita shook her head. "No one speak English. I speak it – you see?"

Thaddeus nodded. "I do. And French, too?"

"*Oui, tres bon*. And *Deutsch*. And *Spanisch*. So – I can earn my keep. You have room. If you don't want me up here, I will sleep down there." She pointed at the hatch in the floor.

"Not likely," muttered J. "First chance you 'ave, you'll be off with that ruby and we'll be stranded in Frenchie land without a pot to p–"

"Then perhaps *you* should," suggested Dita, her eyes flashing, "so we do not have to smell you."

Thaddeus sighed as the pair began to yell at each other, and wondered whether there was something aboard he could make into earplugs.

Twenty One

Swift Progress

The ruby airship flew south all day, over a landscape that bucked and sprawled between patchwork fields and the curlicues of towns and villages. Leaning beside Thaddeus' elbow at the controls, Dita had pushed herself up on tiptoe to see through the window to the land below. She pointed out towns she recognised – Angers, Saumur and others – displaying a sense of direction that Thaddeus found remarkable. J merely huffed and sulked, constantly telling the girl not to touch this and that.

"There's Poitiers," Dita piped up. "We are in Vienne now. I think we reach the mountains by sundown."

"You can't possibly know that," J scoffed.

Dita looked at him. *"In Ordnung.* We find out soon enough," she said serenely.

The landscape grew rockier as they flew on, chunks of grey granite littering the ground as if a giant had been playing jacks and grown bored. J and Thaddeus took turns at the controls, guiding the airship ever south. As the day drew onwards, a mountain range rose over the horizon to loom ahead of them. Dark rain clouds twisted around the peaks. They gathered with the dusk, turning the sky from blue into an indigo-blackened bruise, full of foreboding. With them came a strong wind that buffeted the airship. Below spread a forest that seemed to go on forever. It pooled around the feet of the mountains, blocking out the ground in an endless sea of deep green. Here and there between the thick branches they glimpsed a road meandering slowly between the ancient trunks, but more often it was invisible beneath the weight of leaves.

"Look," said Dita, at one point, leaning past J to stare down at the road. "What is that?"

J and Thaddeus leaned over, too. Through the trees came brief flashes – sunlight glinting on something beneath the leaves.

"It must be people on the road," said Thaddeus.

"Looks as if there are many," Dita remarked as the forest parted for a second to reveal a column of uniformed men riding quickly along it on horseback. *"Sie sind Soldaten.* They are soldiers."

"Well, if they carry on in this direction, they're going to get wet," said J, nodding at the horizon. "I don't like the look of that." A slash of lightning burst like a white-hot whip crack over the trees and shortly afterwards a roll of thunder rumbled after it.

"I don't suppose flying through a thunderstorm will be very healthy for this rig?" Thaddeus asked.

"Not very healthy for any of us, truth be told," the boy said grimly, as he glanced at one of the dials and pulled the left rudder around. "The wind's bad enough, but if we get swiped by a lick o' lightning, we're done for."

Dita craned to see out of the window. "There is nowhere to land. Just trees. I cannot see the road, or where it leads."

J pointed ahead, to a pass between two of the largest mountains they'd seen so far. "We'll 'ave to try and make for that," he said. "The road must go above the tree-line and over –

stands to reason. Let's just 'ope it's wide enough for us to land and that we can reach it before the storm does."

They stayed silent as J skirted the high edge of the storm, staying just out of reach. Thaddeus watched the skies, fascinated. It was like watching some kind of battle. The clouds roiled around each other, spitting out fury and bellowing at the ground. The airship shook, J's knuckles white on the controls as he fought against the winds pounding them. The ship dropped lower as the boy guided it towards the pass. The trees still hid the road, and for a while Thaddeus thought that J must have been mistaken – there was no pass, or at least no road that carts could cross over. But then, there it was, snaking out from beneath the forest canopy and up over the rocky incline.

"Yes!" J whooped in relief. "We're nearly there! Now, I think I can hold her just as long as that storm doesn't change direction… but hold on to your hats, ladies and gents, we're in for a…"

A huge *crack* sounded from above. A flash of white light filled the portholes. The airship jerked and hummed. Something hot raced along the metal bands that held the ship together. There was a groaning sound, as if the craft itself was screaming in pain. They began to pitch into a spin, sinking towards the ground as a hissing filled the air.

"We're hit!" J yelled, his arms juddering with the effort of pulling back on the controls.

The ground was rising towards them fast. Thaddeus looked up, seeing the hatch that led on to the roof. He wrenched at it, pulling it open to let the lashing rain cut across his face like icy knives. Through the open square above him, he could see the balloon, a ragged hole torn in its side.

"We're losing gas!" he shouted. "But we're not on fire!"

Thaddeus clambered onto one of the top bunks and then pushed himself out through the hatch. Outside, the storm had shifted, sucking the airship into its grip like a creature pulling food towards its maw. The dark clouds pressed down on them from above, spitting rain and fire. The wind raged, wild and angry, making it almost impossible to breathe. He stuck his head back inside, already out of breath.

"There's a tear in the balloon," he gasped, wiping icy water from his face. "If we could reach it, we might be able to patch it. But I can't. I'll never be able to steady myself long enough."

"Do sumfin', Thaddeus," J said, his arms shaking as he tried to hold the rapidly sinking airship steady. "Or we're done for!"

"*Lassen Sie mich,*" said Dita. "I can do it."

"No," Thaddeus shook his head, "you'll fly off into the storm. There's nothing to hold on to, Dita."

"Then you hold on to me," the little girl ordered. "My legs, yes? Come on, quick, quick!"

"If she can do it, better let 'er," J said grimly. "Ground's not coming up any slower while we chat!"

In a second, Dita was beside Thaddeus on the bunk, and in another, she had clambered through the hatch into the roaring maelstrom beyond.

"Legs," she shouted back to Thaddeus, her voice almost torn away by the storm. "Hold my legs!"

Thaddeus leaned out of the airship as far as he could. His arms and shoulders were exposed to the fury of the sky. He grabbed the girl's ankles as she scrambled across the wet wood. Above her, he could see the balloon's hole, small but rapidly releasing gas. Dita reached for the ragged edges, pulling them towards her and winding them around in her hands to close the gap.

"Refill," she screamed. "The balloon – tell the *Knabe*–"

Thaddeus understood her at once. "J," he shouted over the howling wind, "can you deploy the ruby? Refill the balloon?"

"I ain't sure she's got anyfing left to give, Mr Rec," J yelled back. "It might not work!"

"Try it, J – now!"

The boy did as he was told, winding the ruby machine's handle as fast as he could. Thaddeus watched as Dita was buffeted by the storm. She was already soaked through, her old dress sticking to her. Her hair had fallen out of her headscarf and was plastered across her face, but she clutched the balloon valiantly, the girl's small hands seeming even tinier against the huge contraption. More lightning strikes lit up the raging sky around them, the thunder an incessant drum roll right above their heads.

Thaddeus heard the hiss of the gas. The balloon swelled away from Dita, and she had to battle to keep her grip as it threatened to jerk away from her with every new puff of gas. Thaddeus held on to her, feeling his legs beginning to cramp. His hands were numb with cold. He couldn't see for rain, and several times he felt the hot crackle of electricity as the clouds continued to hurl spears of lightning. He felt Dita move, and blinked the rain from his eyes long enough to see that she had something in her mouth. He realised in a flash that it was her headscarf. Dita struggled to wind it around the torn fabric that she still clutched in her hands, tying it off in a complicated knot. The balloon was full now, bobbing and fighting to get away from her. She let go.

Thaddeus held his breath, but the knot stayed fast. All it had to do was last until J could bring them in to land.

Dita was scrambling backwards when the airship gave a tremendous jerk. The little girl screamed as she was flung flat against the slippery wood, only Thaddeus' grip stopping her from sliding off the roof.

"Dita!" Thaddeus yelled over the storm. He tried to pull her towards him, but she was a dead weight. His hands were so frozen he could hardly feel them.

"What's happening?" J shouted.

"Just get us down, J!" Thaddeus bellowed. "I can't hold her…"

A moment later, the ship touched down with a jaw-crunching jolt. Thaddeus' icy hands gave up and he lost his grip on Dita. She disappeared from sight, slithering down the side of the airship.

J appeared in the hatch. "Thaddeus! Are you–"

Thaddeus jumped to his feet, feeling the rain sluice down his neck. "Dita fell," he yelled. "Get out there!"

As J uttered a curse and vanished, Thaddeus struggled after him. He followed J down the gangplank and into the pouring rain, both of them running for the huddled figure. Thaddeus dropped to his knees beside the girl, feeling for a pulse.

"She's alive," he told J. "But I don't know how badly she's hurt."

"We gotta get 'er inside!" J shouted over the noise of the storm.

Thaddeus nodded, pushing his hair back again, feeling the icy water cascade down his neck and into his sodden shirt. He lifted the little girl up. She weighed almost nothing.

"Put 'er on my bunk," J said, when they got inside.

Dita groaned and opened her eyes as Thaddeus laid her down. "There you are," he said in relief, as her green eyes blinked at him, pained but at least clear. "Where does it hurt?"

Dita was silent for a moment, a look of concentration on her pale face, as if she were working out the answer to Thaddeus' question.

"My... my arm," she said. "I think it's just my arm..."

Thaddeus rolled up her torn sleeve as gently as possible. Beneath was a nasty wound, open and bleeding. It gaped its ugliness at Thaddeus, who took a deep breath and forced a smile.

"I'm sure we can sort that out in no time."

Dita smiled faintly, and then fixed her gaze on the ceiling. Thaddeus could see she was biting her lip. Against the pain or to stop herself from crying, he couldn't tell, but either way the policeman was astounded by the little girl's silent bravery. He'd seen grown men wail over far less.

J had vanished to one of the wooden cupboards at the other end of the cabin as soon as Thaddeus had revealed Dita's injury, dragging out a tin box and scrabbling around inside. He returned a moment later with a needle, thread and roll of bandage.

"It ain't much," he said, in a hushed, apologetic voice, "but it's the best I can do. Be careful wiv the needle, too – we're going to need it to fix the balloon later."

Thaddeus nodded grimly, taking the offered items. "Have you got any alcohol, J?"

J looked shifty. "A quart of cheap whisky, but don't ask me where it came from."

"I don't care where it came from; bring it here."

"Really? Is now the right time for a tipple, Thaddeus? I mean, I know we're all in shock and all, but..." the boy nodded at Dita, pale and still and trembling.

"It's not for me," Thaddeus snapped. "It's to clean this needle. Hurry!"

J scurried away again, coming back with a small bottle of amber-coloured liquid. Thaddeus grabbed it from him and uncorked the bottle, splashing the contents over the needle and thread, as well as his hands. He heard J stifle a squeak as a good deal of the whisky ended up on the floor.

"Right, Dita," said Thaddeus, as the crack and roll of thunder went on overhead. "This is going to hurt, but it's got to be done. I'll be as quick as I can, all right?"

Dita nodded, and then raised her arm across her mouth. It took Thaddeus a moment to realise that the girl had taken the thin fabric of her sleeve in her teeth and was biting down against the pain.

He splashed whisky across the girl's wound, hoping to clean the worst of it. She shuddered, squeezing her eyes shut. The first stitch was the worst – pushing the needle through the skin and out the other side. Thaddeus felt sick but, as he'd told Dita, it had to be done – the wound was too bad to heal on its own.

"Bleedin' 'eck," J muttered, slumping to the floor, white as a sheet.

Thaddeus sewed quickly and as neatly as he could, pulling the torn skin together. Then he splashed his hands with more whisky to clean them, and wrapped the girl's arm in a bandage. Dita had passed out towards the end. She lay still and quiet in J's bunk.

Once the wound was wrapped, J stood looking down at her. "She's a braver soul than maybe I's gave her due for," he conceded.

Thaddeus was inclined to agree.

Exhausted and drained, they just managed to stay awake long enough for J to stow the balloon's remaining gas in the storage canisters. Then they collapsed into two of the bunks, sleeping despite the storm raging on above their heads.

Regrets

The storm had raged all night, the cold rain pelting Rémy and Yannick hard until they eventually decided to find shelter under the trees. They turned off the road and secured the horses under the leafiest branches they could find before huddling, wet, bedraggled and hungry, inside the remnants of a dead oak tree.

Yannick managed to doze, but Rémy could not. A nameless worry niggled at her, a notion that something here wasn't quite right. But every time she almost caught it, the thought was engulfed by a buzzing that seemed to come and go inside her head. Rémy wondered whether it was caused by the storm, which seemed to be powered by the fury of heaven itself. She toyed with the idea of getting out the golden cube again, but resisted the urge. Rémy was still unsettled by the loss of her opal and the discovery that Yannick had stolen something – however insignificant – from the Professor's workshop. *Show this only to the one you trust the most*, the old woman's note had said – and that definitely wasn't Yannick. Not any more.

She wished Thaddeus were there to talk to about everything else she had learned in the past twenty-four hours. That she had met someone who had known her mother, and her father, too.

That perhaps she had a brother. That she had lost her beloved opal. Now that it was gone forever, Rémy kept touching her throat where it used to lie, wondering what had made her take it off. Why had she never explained to Thaddeus and J what it could do, or even Claudette and Amélie, before they had left? If Thaddeus had known, if they could have been more open with each other, none of this would have happened.

Rémy shut her tired eyes, willing herself not to cry. All of this was her own doing, and she had no right to feel sorry for herself. She knew the real reason she had kept the opal's powers secret: because telling Thaddeus the truth would have meant confronting what he had said in Abernathy's underground chamber. Now, Rémy couldn't even work out why that would have been a bad thing. Had she been afraid that he'd say he didn't love her after all? No, that wasn't it. The truth was precisely the opposite. She'd been afraid that he *did* love her – she knew it, in fact. Rémy knew that he loved her, and knowing that scared her more than anything else in her life.

Yannick's words rang in her head again. *What did you think you were going to do? Marry him? Become a respectable little London housewife?*

The answer was, in fact, no. No, that wasn't what Rémy thought she was going to do. But she was afraid it was what Thaddeus was expecting. And the circus girl knew, hopelessly and with absolute certainty, that she couldn't do that; she couldn't *be* that. It wasn't her, and it never would be. So she'd avoided any chance of him ever bringing it up, because that was better than losing him completely.

She'd done that anyway in the end, of course, thanks to her stubborn pride. Rémy had told herself that her anger back in London was justified, because Thaddeus had chosen the easy route and shifted the blame for the burglaries onto her old friend Yannick. And how dare Thaddeus imagine he knew her childhood friend better than she did? How dare he assume that because Yannick was of the circus, he must automatically be a crook?

What a rank fool you are, Rémy Brunel, she thought now, hugging herself and staring out into the rain. *Since when had Thaddeus assumed anything? Did you stop to ask him his proof? No. Would you have listened even if he had told you? Probably not. Your pride has always been your downfall, and so it proves to be again. And now here you are with a thief, just because you were too much of a coward to face up to the truth. Worse, you'll never see Thaddeus again, and he'll think you were a part of it after all.*

Still, there was nothing she could do about any of that now. And things could be worse, after all. At least she knew a warm welcome would be waiting for her once they finally caught up with *Le Cirque du Secrète.*

With that in mind, the sun was barely up when Rémy nudged Yannick awake. The storm had finally burned itself out, and the landscape was peaceful once again.

"Come on," she said. "Let's get back on the road. We've still got so far to go before we catch up. They must be at least two more towns ahead now."

Yannick rubbed his eyes and then looked at her carefully.

"What?" Rémy asked, suspicious.

"Do you feel all right?" the magician asked.

"What, other than being soaked through and very hungry?" Rémy asked. "I'm fine, why?"

Yannick grinned, jumping to his feet. "Nothing. Just wondered. Come on, then – let's go."

Rémy looked after him with a frown, almost remembering something. It faded amid another bout of buzzing.

Twenty Three

Repairs

Thaddeus woke to the delicious smell of coffee and to sun streaming through the portholes. He blinked sleep away as he looked up at the curved ceiling, when suddenly the events of the previous night came flooding back. Sitting up, Thaddeus looked at the opposite bunk. Dita was still there, and seemed to be asleep. Her skin was paler than usual, but her cheeks were rosy. He got up and laid a hand on her forehead, relieved to feel no signs of a fever. The little girl stirred and mumbled, but did not wake.

From outside came brisk whistling and the clatter of tin pots. Thaddeus ducked his head out of the gangplank to see J fussing over a cooking fire, smoke rising steadily into the blue sky.

"Morning," Thaddeus said, stepping out. "Storm's passed on, then?"

J looked up at him with a cheery grin as he began to pour thickly brewed coffee into three tin mugs. "Mornin'. Aye, looks like the weather's turned. Ain't it pretty out 'ere?"

Thaddeus had to agree. They had landed at the apex of a rough road that passed between two mountains. The thick forest that forced them to fly on dwindled into scrub, and beyond the pass, the road wound slowly down to the base of a fertile green valley.

Thaddeus turned as the boy offered him a steaming mug. "You're strangely happy after what happened last night."

"Ah, well," said J, "the little miss looks like she's going to be fine so, all fings considered, it could 'ave been worse. That's why I made coffee – thought she could do with a nice way to wake up."

The policeman raised his eyebrows. "I actually meant the airship. The damage, from the storm? It wasn't just the balloon, you know – the wood up there's badly gouged, too."

"Oh," said J awkwardly. A faint blush tinted his cheeks and he turned away to pick up the last two mugs. "Well, it ain't like it's not fixable or nuffin'. So, like I says, all fings considered..." He trailed off, looking at the two mugs he held. "Er... I'll be back in a tick."

Thaddeus smiled to himself as J disappeared into the airship, though his heart ached a little. J's abashed look reminded him of himself, and that made him think once more of Rémy. He sipped his coffee and gazed down into the valley beyond the pass, wondering where she was at that moment.

He still didn't really know what he and J were doing there, or what he was expected to do when – if – he found her. The further they got into their journey, the more Thaddeus felt he was on a fool's errand. If it hadn't been for his worries about the Comte and for Dorffman's concerns about Claudette, Thaddeus would probably have told J they needed to give up now. He thought it very likely that Rémy would simply laugh in his face when she saw him here, in any case. What did he have to offer her, back in London, compared to the freedom of this landscape he saw around him – compared to the country she called home?

"Little miss is awake!" J's voice shattered Thaddeus' melancholy thoughts. "She seems hunky-dory, apart from the arm, o' course."

Thaddeus headed back to the fire. "I'll change her dressing in a little while, once we've all finished our coffee." Shielding his eyes, Thaddeus looked up at the pierced balloon, flopping over the side of the airship like an old sock. "Tell me how we can fix the airship."

J dropped to sit on a boulder. "I've got spare scraps of oilskin and more needles like the one you used on poor Dita last night. We can patch the hole, but it won't be easy and it'll take a while. Trust me – stitching old animal hide ain't a job for the lazy!"

Thaddeus looked back towards the mountain pass. "I'm not too happy about being stranded here."

"Ah well," said J, "I'm afraid there's nuffin' I can do about that."

Thaddeus nodded, swallowing the last of his coffee in one gulp. "We'd best get to it then. Let's take a look at Dita first, though."

The little girl appeared before he could reach the gangplank. She'd tied her shawl in half around her neck to make a sling for her injured arm.

"Dita," said Thaddeus, "let's change the dressings."

The girl smiled and walked down the gangplank with a nod of her dark curls. "No need. J has changed bandage already."

Thaddeus raised his eyebrows and looked at the boy, who was staring at his feet with reddening cheeks. "Has he, indeed? Well, I'm glad he's being so attentive. How are you feeling otherwise?"

"I've felt worse," Dita shrugged. "Thank you for the…" she paused and indicated the stitching with her one good hand.

Thaddeus smiled. "You're welcome."

"Come on, you two!" J called impatiently. "Stop nattering. We've got things to do, ain't we?"

Dita blew a strand of hair out of her eyes with a puff of her cheeks. "Ah yes," she said, with a cheeky grin. "And you boys must do all the work, no?"

Twenty Four

The Homecoming

By lunchtime, Rémy and Yannick had made their way up and out of the lush valley that the magician had insisted was a shortcut. Beyond the narrow pass, the road wound down into another stretch of forest, this time punctuated not only by the road but also by a fast-flowing river. Not far in the distance, more great mountains reached their stony forms up to threaten the sky, clouds bumping against their height. Rémy urged her horse back into motion, and they trotted down the road, the magician following behind.

They hadn't gone far before a faint flash caught Rémy's attention. At first she thought it was merely the sun glinting off a menhir in the forest, but then she saw it again and stopped. It came again, a bright gleam that swelled into existence one moment, and was gone the next. Rémy squinted, but couldn't make out what was causing the flash. It was definitely something in the trees, reflecting the sun's rays.

"There's something up ahead, just off the road, by the look of it," Yannick observed, coming to a stop beside her as his horse puffed and stamped.

"Yes, but what?" Rémy muttered. "And how far away is that?"

Yannick shrugged. "A few hours' ride, I'd say, perhaps more. We'll be fine as long as it isn't bandits."

That was exactly what Rémy had been afraid of. Because it looked to her as if something was camped in the forest not far from the road, and who else but bandits would pitch camp in such a remote place? She glanced down at her ride. The animal was already showing signs of tiredness after the long climb out of the valley, and she knew that if they were attacked, they'd never escape – not on horseback, at least.

"Come on," Rémy decided, resigned. "There's no other way except back the way we came, so we have to carry on. We'll have to try and lose them in the trees, that's all."

They'd been riding for an hour when Rémy began to think that what they were seeing was something very different. They were close enough to see flashes of colour through the leaves – reds and yellows, bright blues and pinks. If these were bandits, they were unusually fond of standing out. Rémy's suspicions were further aroused when she spied a large grey mass meandering among the trees. At first, she thought that perhaps it was just the shadows playing tricks with her eyes, but then she saw it again, and knew exactly what it was.

"It's not a bandit camp! It's a circus – *our* circus!" Rémy cried. "That's old Marta the elephant! But what are they doing here? There can't be anyone nearby to come to a performance."

Yannick didn't answer as they spurred their tired horses on down the slope. The nearer they got, the clearer the circus became. There was old Anita's caravan, painted with all the flowers of her home valley in Andalusia. There was the lions' cage, with the two big cats lying sleepily in the leaf-dappled sunshine. There was, of course, no sign of Gustave's old home, but Rémy searched for

174

and saw Claudette and Amélie's caravan, nestling in the shade of a large oak tree. Relief flooded through her. At least they were here. At least they were safe.

She frowned, though, as they drew closer still. Something definitely wasn't right. The Big Top was nowhere to be seen. All the colours she had spied were folded tents, still stowed on their carts. By the sun, it was well after midday, but there was no sign of the kind of activity that should usually take place on a performance day, and if the tent wasn't up now, there was no way they'd get it up in time for that evening. And yet the circus must have been pitched here for at least a day, perhaps two – otherwise they wouldn't have caught up with it so quickly.

"Something's wrong," she muttered, more to herself than Yannick.

They drew close enough that they were spotted. A shout went up as one of the folk milling about the caravans recognised Rémy. It was the chief clown, Augustus, though he wasn't in costume and there was no trace of his usual absurd make-up. Rémy waved back, happy to see a familiar face, and soon a crowd had gathered by the road as she and Yannick approached.

"Little Bird!" exclaimed Augustus, clasping her in a bear hug as she dismounted. "We thought never to see you again! Grew bored of London, did you?"

Rémy grinned as she pulled away. "Just thought I'd better check on you all, Augustus. I know you can't do without me!"

Augustus chuckled, but Rémy could see anxiety beneath his jolly features. His eyes flicked to Yannick, but instead of offering a greeting, he merely nodded a curt welcome.

"Augustus–" Rémy began, but she was interrupted as something small and scruffy fastened itself to her leg.

175

"Little Bird, Little Bird!" It was Rolf, one of the small boys charged with looking after the circus' various animals.

"Rolf!" Rémy hugged the energetic bundle. "How are you? How is Marta? Is she behaving, or is she as grumpy as ever?"

"Still a grumpy old lady," said the boy, letting her go. "She'll be pleased to see you, though. And so will Dominique! She's missed you – doesn't like anyone else to ride her."

"Dominique!" Rémy thought of her pony, which had served her so well over the years. "I have missed her too, Rolf, so much. I'll visit soon. But first," she said, looking up at Augustus, "where is Claudette? And what are you all doing here? Why aren't you at the Jamboree – or at least in a village?"

A hush fell over the bubbling crowd. "Best ask Claudette that yourself, Rémy," Augustus said quietly, his gaze flickering once more towards the still-silent Yannick. "These have been strange days for us all, believe me."

A new murmur rippled through the crowd. It parted as Claudette appeared, as beautiful as ever, her long chestnut hair loose and drifting in the valley breeze. She held little Amélie by the hand.

"Claudette! Amélie!" said Rémy, embracing Claudette in a hug. "I've missed you both so much!"

Rémy pulled away, confused when Claudette did not hug her back. She was looking over Rémy's head at Yannick who, in turn, was studiously looking elsewhere. "Claudette?" Rémy asked. "What is it? Aren't you glad to see me?"

Amélie stepped forward and wrapped her little arms around Rémy's waist. Rémy hugged the girl back, so grateful that she could have cried, as Claudette finally looked at her. Her face was grave, and Rémy could see lines on her pale forehead.

"What are you doing here, Rémy?" she asked, her voice low and careful.

"What do you mean, what am I doing here? You didn't write for weeks. I was worried something had happened to you. And I missed you – all of you. So I decided to come home. Aren't you pleased to see me, *mes amies?*"

Claudette looked at her with tired eyes, as if she could not really comprehend Rémy's question. "You led him to us. Why would you do such a thing?"

"What do you mean?" Rémy asked, looking back to the magician, still standing silently behind her. "Don't you remember Yannick? He was a boy with the circus, many years ago. I bumped into him in London. He needs work, Claudette. He's a good magician. And doesn't every circus need a good magician?"

"He has lied to you, Little Bird," said her friend, "if he told you that was why he wanted to join you on the journey here."

"What?" Rémy asked, still more confused. "I don't understand, Claudette. What is happening here?"

Claudette looked into her face, as if trying to decide whether she was telling the truth or not. The realisation shocked Rémy. Claudette was her best friend, but right now it seemed she did not trust or believe her. The thought made Rémy sick.

"Do you want to tell her, Yannick? Or shall I?" Claudette said roughly.

"Claudette," Yannick said, his voice placatory, "listen, there is no need for this."

"Yannick was with *Le Cirque de la Lune* as a child, that is correct," interrupted Claudette, ignoring him. "But did he not tell you that he returned to us several months ago, as soon as *Le Cirque du Secrète* had set foot once more on French soil? He was waiting at the docks of Calais when we arrived, with a desperate story of hardship and saying that he needed a position."

"What?" Rémy asked, her head spinning. She turned to look at Yannick, who did not meet her eyes.

"He joined us then," Claudette went on, "and at first we were glad to have him. As you say, Rémy, a circus can always use a good magician, and Yannick is certainly that."

"You never told me this," Rémy said to Yannick. "Why didn't you tell me you had been with the circus again?"

"Because he left us… abruptly," said Claudette. "I told him I never wanted to see him again. And now you have brought him straight to us, Rémy."

"Aren't you going to tell her why, Claudette?" Yannick's voice was angry and he stood with his arms crossed defiantly. "What my great crime was? Go on – see if she can understand it. Why don't you tell Little Bird who the great Claudette Anjou *really* is?"

Twenty Five

Terror in the Forest

Claudette's face darkened further, fury alight in every clenched muscle of her face. There were a few moments of silence. Rémy stared at her friend, and suddenly it was like looking at a stranger.

"Very well," Claudette said, at last, her voice calm and very quiet. "My real name is Arriete, Comtesse de Cantal. I am what the children's tale calls 'the Lost Comtesse'. Until recently, this is the secret I have kept for many years, Little Bird."

Yannick surveyed the circus folk. "So you told them, but none of them saw sense, is that it?" He shook his head in disgust.

"Ahh, but we are none of us as clever as the great Yannick, eh?" Claudette spat angrily.

"You – you are the Lost Comtesse?" Rémy repeated, dazed.

Claudette offered a faint smile. "Believe me, Little Bird, I wish it were not true. I have done my best to hide all traces of that lost child. But Yannick here found out the truth. I don't know how, and I don't care to know."

"So that's why you were so interested in Claudette," Rémy said hoarsely. "I thought you were joking. But you knew all along."

"Whatever he told you, it's a lie, Rémy," Claudette said. "He is interested only in the reward he'll receive for turning me in."

Yannick made an exasperated sound and threw up his hands. "Listen to the woman! You make it sound as if you're some kind of wanted criminal. I don't understand you, Claudette. You're rich! You've been rich since you were born. You don't need to scratch a living in the dirt of French roads, reading the worthless fortunes of people who should be changing your chamber pot. All you need to do is make yourself known, and your life – Amélie's life – will change overnight. Why would you want to run from that?"

"You are a fool, Yannick. A damned, blasted fool," Claudette roared. "Who put up the reward? Tell me, who?"

Yannick blinked, taken aback by the strength of her outburst. "The Comte de Cantal."

Claudette nodded. "Cantal is the last of my birth family's line, the one clear inheritor of all its remaining wealth. Do you know the stipulation my parents placed on the inheritance of their fortune? The reason he might need to find me, instead of wanting to see me stay lost forever?"

Rémy saw a flicker of doubt pass through the magician's eyes, though his jaw remained stubbornly set and he said nothing.

"My parents' will stated," Claudette told them in a calm, cool voice, "that their wealth was to remain mine in perpetuity. The only way the money can be released from their vaults is if I make myself known and can incontrovertibly prove my identity. Or," here she paused, glancing down at her daughter as if not wanting her to hear, "if my death can be proved with the same certainty."

Silence followed Claudette's words. It weighed upon the gathered circus folk like a dark shroud.

Yannick shook his head. "The Comte would never harm you, or Amélie, or anyone. That's absurd."

"Is it?" Claudette's eyes glittered harshly. "You forget, magician, that I am a teller of fortunes. I have seen my own. It splits into two paths. One path is peaceful, happy. The other is full of death and destruction. I know which one I choose for myself, for my child. I don't want money. I want to be left alone to live my life in peace. I told you before I did not want to be found. I sent you away. And yet now here you are again, and I wonder what you have brought with you this time?"

Rémy spoke, her voice dry in her throat. "We are alone, Claudette. I swear. No one was with us, and no one followed us."

Her friend's face was grim. "Is that so? But surely you know by now that Yannick here does not always need to do his own bidding. He sent no messages?"

"No," said Rémy. "No, I don't—" Then she stopped, remembering the messaging device she discovered Yannick tinkering with on the road. Hadn't he been talking into it? He'd said not, but... the buzzing returned, filling her ears with distraction.

"You're wrong, Claudette," Yannick said, "about everything. All the Comte wants is his family. You're his last remaining relative, however distant the connection may be. I am here with Rémy because he and I thought she could talk sense into you. Because all the Comte is offering you is a better life. Tell her, Rémy. Tell her that she has nothing to fear."

Rémy shook her head. "If Claudette doesn't want to make herself known, who are we to force her? It's her life, not ours."

Yannick threw up his hands. "You're all fools! Give the money away if you want, Claudette. Look around you – there are plenty in need of it. But for goodness' sake, use it!"

Claudette laughed hollowly. "I would be free to do that, would I?" she asked scornfully. "What if I rode through Paris, throwing

181

handfuls of gold from my saddlebags? Would your Comte be as happy then? You are a rare fool, Yannick, if you believe he would stand by and let me do as I wish with that fortune."

The magician shook his head. "You should think better of people."

Claudette shook her head. "Every time I do that, magician, I meet a snake in the grass like you."

The magician barked a harsh laugh. "Well, it's too late, anyway. I've found you, and so the Comte has found you, too. Thank me or not, Claudette, you *will* inherit your money. Then we'll see who the fool is."

Before anyone could stop him, Yannick leapt onto his horse. The animal started, dancing forward on tired legs, but Yannick pulled it around and forced it into a flat gallop, heading back up the road the way they had come. Rémy went to follow, but Claudette's hand on her arm held her back.

"Let him go, Little Bird," she said, staring after the fleeing horse. "The damage is done."

"I think he... I think he hypnotized me," Rémy murmured, the buzz still filling her head. "I remember... telling him he shouldn't come, and then..."

Claudette grasped her shoulders. "He's a skilled hypnotist and you wanted to find me anyway, Rémy. It's no surprise he was able to use that."

"But I – I brought him here. I betrayed you, and now..."

"It is not your fault," her friend reassured her. "But I have to leave. The Comte's forces must be close."

"We are ready to move out, Claudette," said Augustus at her shoulder, "just as soon as you give the word."

"It's too late," Claudette told him, bending down to haul

Amélie into her arms and holding her daughter close. "I must take her and go on foot. The forest may slow them down."

"You can't," said Rémy. "There could be bandits in the forest, and it is almost dark!"

"Better that than what's waiting for me on that road," Claudette muttered. She held one hand to Rémy's face. "I am sorry to have spoken to you harshly, Little Bird. It is good to see you, but—"

A shout came from somewhere among the gathered performers. Rémy and Claudette looked up to see flickering tongues of flame pouring along the road from the valley pass in bobbing lines. From this distance it looked like a snake formed of fire, slipping quickly towards them.

"Horses, on the road," said Rémy. "They're coming fast!"

Augustus yelled for the circus to move out as Claudette ran for her caravan. Rémy followed, dodging the whinnying circus horses as they began to pull the caravans onto the road. Claudette ran up the steps of her home, setting Amélie down briefly and snatching up a bag waiting by the door. She thrust a fresh loaf in on top and pulled a heavy dark cloak from a hook.

Amélie, her eyes wide with fear, came to Rémy and reached for her throat, looking for the opal, the only thing that had ever allowed her to communicate in her own words. Rémy put her arms around the little girl. "It's gone, little one. I'm sorry. I can't hear you. But everything will be all right."

Claudette swept Amélie up again, pulling the cloak around her and slinging the bag over her shoulder. "We must go, now."

"I'll come with you," Rémy said.

"No, Little Bird," Claudette told her, pulling her close. "You must stay here. The circus will need you."

"But you need me, too!"

Claudette was already out of the door and down the steps. She turned back, briefly. "We'll find you, Rémy. I promise. We'll find you again – somehow."

And then she was gone, slipping through the darkest shadows and into the depths of the forest. Rémy felt sick, lost and alone. Around her, the circus was leaving, most of the caravans already on the road. Standing on the steps of Claudette's caravan, she felt it jerk forward as the panicked carthorse tried to follow its friends. Rémy jumped down and ran to the front, releasing the lock, leaping up onto the driver's ledge. The horse moved without urging as it followed the rest of the hurried procession.

Rémy stood on tiptoe to look over the roof and back along the road. The flaming torches were still bearing down on them, the thundering of hooves echoing through the valley.

"Rémy," Augustus shouted, and she looked down to see the clown running towards her. "We'll never escape them."

"We just have to hope they leave us alone when they see that Claudette is not here."

Augustus nodded, but Rémy could see the fear in his eyes. Suddenly she was angry. How dare these people hunt them? How dare they make them afraid?

"Augustus," she yelled, "tell everyone to get ready to fight if we have to. The circus is our home, yes? We have done nothing wrong. If they want a fight, we'll give them a fight."

The clown nodded, disappearing along the rows of caravans. Rémy heard shouts, echoing down the line, along with the odd cheer. She smiled to herself. *Yes, we'll be ready*.

The sound of a trumpet echoed so closely that her horse started. The snake of fire had caught up with them, and Rémy watched as two streams of riders slid past them on either side of the road. The circus horses screamed in fright, and Rémy heard the caged lions roaring as the smell of fear filled the air.

The column stopped as they were surrounded.

"We seek the woman you know as Claudette Anjou," shouted a voice, and Rémy saw it belonged to a straight-backed fellow atop a pure black horse. He was dressed in a dark blue uniform ribbed in gold, and wore a helmet, also tinged gold. Rémy held her breath and waited. Everyone was silent. "I'll say that again," said the rider. "We are looking for Claudette Anjou. She has nothing to fear, but we will not leave until we have found her."

"She's not here," Rémy shouted, into a thick silence punctuated only by the nervous snuffle of animals and the hiss of hungry flame. "She does not belong to this circus. You are mistaken."

The uniformed rider wheeled at the sound of her voice. He came closer, his horse prancing on elegant legs.

"And who are you?" the officer asked, staring up at her with shadowed eyes.

"I am no one," Rémy answered. "I look after the horses, that is all."

Another uniformed rider approached. He stopped beside the officer, passing him a piece of paper. As the officer unfolded it, Rémy realised with dismay that it was the poster Yannick had taken from the station in Calais – the wanted poster with her face clearly painted in its centre. The officer consulted it, and then looked up at her with a squint.

"You lie," he said, his voice smooth. "You are Rémy Brunel, the jewel thief also known as Little Bird. If this is your circus, then it is also the circus of Claudette Anjou. Where is she? I give you one chance to answer, thief, before I take you in."

Before Rémy even had time to think, she was in the air. She leapt at the officer as if she were jumping from Dominique to another horse, but this time she kept her lead leg straight and strong. It hit the rider in the chest, and with a shocked groan the Comte's officer fell in the dust. In another second she had his horse's reins and was wheeling it around, kicking and pawing at the rider behind. Rémy's only thought was to keep them occupied for as long as it would take for Claudette to escape.

She heard a cry behind her and looked back to see Jacques, the lead tumbler, leaping from the roof of his caravan onto the back of another of the Comte's horses. There was a great roar as, all down the line, the circus folk saw what was happening. They began to fight, using whatever skills they had to fend off the horsemen surrounding them.

The pandemonium was complete when Marta the elephant began to stamp her great feet, raising her trunk and trumpeting to the heavens. The unfamiliar sound of her cry sent the Comte's horses into a frenzy. They began to buck, their riders struggling to stay seated.

"Don't stop!" she called out to the circus folk, as she unseated another soldier. "We have them!"

She didn't see that the commanding officer had recovered until she heard his voice, hoarse but loud, rising over the melee.

"Burn them," he shouted to the soldiers still holding torches. "Raze the caravans! Set them alight!"

"No!" Rémy screamed as the men stepped forward. She saw one torch thrust through the open door of Claudette's home. In seconds the vicious flames were devouring it from within. She heard screams, and turned to see every caravan ablaze, glowing in the darkness. The inferno illuminated the road and the forest around it, the terrified screams of the still-tethered horses mixing with the children's wails of fear.

"The horses!" Rémy screamed, rushing towards Claudette's old carthorse, which was standing confused and fearful between the burning struts of its load. "Free the horses!"

The fire was too much for Marta, too. She reared up, her two hind legs still clamped in the irons that held her in train. The huge creature wrenched herself free and charged, scattering the reassembled line of soldiers and running into the night.

"Enough!" shouted the officer. "We have what we need. Leave them to their fates."

Rémy turned. The air was fugged with smoke, drifting from the burning caravans and obscuring the road. The Comte's men were riding back up the road. For a second, hope bloomed in Rémy's heart. They were leaving. They had destroyed the circus, but they were leaving – and without Claudette.

Then she heard a scream, rising above the others and dousing her with unnatural cold. Through the smoke, Rémy saw two soldiers leaving the treeline. With them they dragged a cloaked figure who struggled and fought, her chestnut hair flying wildly around her head. Claudette.

Now Rémy could see little Amélie, bound in the strong arms of another soldier, who laughed as she kicked at him. Rémy yelled with rage and ran headlong at their captors.

"Oh, for goodness' sake," she heard the officer shout. "Someone put that mongrel down."

There was the sound like a whip cracking. Something hit her in the shoulder with such force that Rémy found herself airborne. She was flung sideways, knocked from the road and into the solid trunk of a tree.

The sound of Claudette's screams faded as darkness overtook her.

Twenty Six

Reunion

It had taken Thaddeus and J almost all day to repair the tear in the airship's balloon. They had taken turns sewing while Dita looked on, nursing her damaged arm. J hadn't been exaggerating when he'd said that sewing oilcloth was hard work – by mid-afternoon, Thaddeus' fingers were bloodied and bruised from the effort of forcing the needle in and out of the thick fabric. Still, it was worth it when they were able to reinflate the balloon.

"We're back in business!" J cheered from the control desk. "Come on then, little miss and gent. Time's a-wasting, ain't it?"

They took off as twilight set around them. Thaddeus watched out of one of the portholes as the valley dropped away, the airship suddenly at a dizzying height as they headed for the pass directly opposite.

With the gathering darkness came a glow from the south that lit the sky like a bonfire. It rose over the mountains that edged the valley, and grew even greater as they neared.

"I don't like the look of that," said J uneasily. "It looks like the Thames on Guy Fawkes' night."

Thaddeus had to agree. "It can't be a forest fire," he said. "The trees are still dripping from the downpour."

"What do we do?" J asked.

"Carry on, J," the policeman decided. "Just don't get too close."

J patted the control panel. "Right then, old girl," he muttered. "Let's have a look-see, shall we?"

The airship bobbed, the propellers whirring quietly as J spurred the machine on towards the pass out of the valley. Inside the cabin, they all held their breath, waiting to see what would be revealed on the other side. Then something like the sound of thunder echoed down the road. They all strained to see through the darkness outside the airship's window, but a pall of smoke had spread with the glow, and they could see nothing but a smudge of burning orange.

"What is that?" Dita asked.

"No idea, little miss," J said, "but whatever it is, it's coming over that road with a vengeance!"

The smoke was suddenly split by the terrified whinnying of horses. They poured over the narrow pass in a panicked stream, sending up a storm of loose shale.

"Bleedin' 'eck!" J cried.

Dita ran to the back of the airship, looking through the rear porthole at the stampeding animals as they disappeared down the trail. "I count... five – no, six," she called. "No riders. Some look like... Zugpferd... horses that pull carts."

"Where the blazes did they come from?" J asked.

Thaddeus didn't answer for a moment, looking out of the window and down the road into the forest beyond. "I think blazes is exactly where they came from," he murmured.

J let out a gasp of shock. Below them, illuminating the edges of the wooded road like a thousand torches, was an inferno the like of which Thaddeus had never seen. It burned tens of feet high, and seemed to stretch out as if the road itself had been turned into a river of fire.

Dita came to stand beside them for a second, staring open-mouthed at the awful spectacle below. "What is it?" she asked. "What could burn so?"

"J," Thaddeus said, looking up at the airship's roof hatch. "Did you bring your night-glasses? I didn't pack mine."

"Yep," said J, as he reached for the bag he'd brought aboard and dug around inside. "Take 'em everywhere, don't I?"

Thaddeus caught the device that J threw him. Thaddeus put the strange arrangement of metal and glass on, feeling the familiar sense of dislocation as the world took on a weirdly unreal tint.

"What are they?" Dita asked in amazement, staring at Thaddeus.

"Night-glasses," J explained. "Rubbish in daylight – make you see as good as a cat at night."

Thaddeus climbed up until he could lean through the roof hatch, adjusting with the glasses. He knew what he was looking at as soon as he got the glasses to focus. What else could it be, with so many caravans in one place?

"J," he yelled, nausea and fear threatening to engulf him. "It's the circus! It's burning!"

He heard J curse as he scrambled back down into the cabin again, removing the night-glasses. "We've got to help them."

"Thaddeus," J said nervously, "remember what I said about the ruby's gas? If we get too close to that fire, we'll go up in smoke ourselves."

Thaddeus cursed. "We'll just have to get as close as we can."

"What if the fire spreads?" J asked. "What if—"

"We can't just leave them to it, J!" Thaddeus exclaimed. "There are people down there, a lot of them!"

"If we can help, we must try!" Dita interjected.

"All right, all right," J said, turning back to the control desk. "I ain't arguing about that bit…" He trailed off as the airship sailed down, over the smoke-clogged trees, towards a scrubby clearing about half a mile from the burning line of caravans.

Thaddeus was opening the cabin's hatch before the airship had even touched down. It landed with a bump, the gangplank slamming onto ground that was still wet. Even from this far away, the policeman could feel the heat of the fire.

"J," he said, "stay here, with the airship. You too, Dita. If it looks as if the rest of the forest is going to catch light, don't wait for me; take her back up. OK?"

"But Thaddeus—"

"I don't have time to argue, J," Thaddeus said firmly, jumping from the ship. "Just do it."

He ran down the road, which had been churned to mud by the rain and by what must have been hundreds of horses. Ahead of him, Thaddeus could see the circus folk, silhouetted in the darkness against the orange flames. Some had formed a line through the trees between the river and the road and were passing buckets of water, frantically trying to douse the flames. Others were rescuing what they could from the caravans that had already been put out, dragging from the wreckage scraps of clothes, cooking pans and other odds and ends.

He reached the first caravan, a smouldering wreck of wood and burned possessions. Thaddeus kept going until he reached the head of the water chain. Before he could speak, a bucket was thrust into his hands. He turned and threw the water at the flames licking around yet another of the wooden homes. Further down the line, the policeman saw a loose sheet of fabric flapping hopelessly as it was consumed by the fire. He recognised it as part of the Big Top. A flash of memory came to him, of the first time he had ever seen Rémy Brunel. She had been performing inside that very circus tent, flying through the air like a bird. Anxiety clutched at his gut. His eyes searched the line, trying to find her face, but he couldn't see her. Another bucket of water was pushed towards him, and then another.

There was a shout, and someone shook his shoulder. It was the big man behind him – the next in the line. He was yelling and pointing to the next caravan in the train, indicating that Thaddeus should move so they could try to extinguish it. More water was pushed into his hands, and he threw it as hard as he could, trying to reach the centre of the searing flames.

A scream of terror reached Thaddeus' ears. For one sickening moment he thought it was coming from inside the blazing caravan, but then he saw movement. It came from beneath the caravan, not inside it. Someone was trapped inside the ring of flames that circled the wooden cart wheels. He chucked the empty bucket back and threw himself flat to the ground to get a better look. There was another shout from behind him as the big man realised what was happening and did the same.

There was a child, trapped under the caravan. It was a little girl, cowering between the burning wheels. She was sitting in the mud with her knees pulled up to her chin, shaking and crying.

Beside him, Thaddeus heard the circus performer utter a curse. Thaddeus didn't need to know the translation to understand what he meant. The caravan was completely surrounded by fire. It was a miracle that the floor above hadn't yet caved in and fallen on top of the child.

There was no time to think. Thaddeus turned to the man beside him. "Give me your jacket," he yelled, over the noise of the raging flames, and then reached out to point at what he meant. "Give it to me, quickly!"

The man understood, hurriedly shrugging off his shabby coat and pushing it towards the policeman.

"Sorry," Thaddeus muttered before pushing it down into the wet mud under their feet. The garment was immediately soaked, coated with a thick slime of wet dirt. Thaddeus pulled it up from the sucking mud and threw it over his head and shoulders, the cold sludge a salve in the face of the fire's heat. He took a breath, staring at the flames, and suddenly his confidence crumbled. What on earth was he doing? Did he really want to throw himself into those flames? Thaddeus suddenly felt very young, and very scared, and very much as if he hadn't seen nearly enough of life in his eighteen years to throw it away so easily.

But then the trapped girl screamed again, pure terror lacing her voice. Thaddeus' heart clenched. He pushed the wave of fear and doubt away. What was the point of being a policeman if he didn't help people, whatever the cost? What else was he for?

He sucked in a breath and plunged into the flames, launching himself between the two front wheels. The little girl screamed again as he threw off the coat and pressed it into the mud at her feet, killing the first licks of fire that had danced across it.

"Come," he yelled to her, holding out his arms.

She screamed again, too terrified to move. A creak sounded above them as the caravan's floor threatened to give way. With no time to be gentle, Thaddeus grabbed the child by the forearms, pulling her to his chest and flinging the coat over her. He took one look at the ring of flames, then ducked his head beneath the sodden fabric and lurched forward. The girl screamed in his ear, her arms wrapped around his neck as they surged into the fire. Thaddeus felt the flames reaching for his legs, curling their heat around them like thousands of tiny, vicious whips. He tried to stagger forward a few more steps, but collapsed to his knees. The child screamed on, still clutched against him.

Thaddeus only realised they had escaped the fire when he heard shouting. The burning coat was ripped away and the child was pulled from his arms. Someone else grabbed him by the shoulders, shouting at him. That same someone pushed him to the ground and made him roll in the mud until the burning in his legs lessened. When Thaddeus stopped moving, he felt hands under his shoulders, helping him to sit. A hand tipped a cup of water to his lips and wiped the mud from his eyes. The policeman blinked and realised it was his companion from the water line. The big man patted his shoulder, nodding and smiling grimly.

"The girl," Thaddeus managed. "Is she—"

His new friend moved a little so that Thaddeus could see over his shoulder. The child was being cradled in a crying woman's arms. She was terrified, but seemed otherwise unhurt. Around them, the water line had broken up. The circus folk stood, looking at the burning hulks of their homes, resigned to the fact that there was no more they could do to save them.

"Mr Rec!" Thaddeus pushed his sodden hair back to see J and Dita rushing towards him. "We thought you was a goner, for sure!" said J, out of breath, as they came to a stop in front of him.

"You should be with the airship, J," Thaddeus said hoarsely.

"It's all right, don't you worry," said the boy. "It ain't reaching the treeline – look."

Thaddeus looked blearily to where J was pointing and saw that the boy was right. The big man who had pulled him out began to speak rapidly in French. Dita listened for a moment.

"His name is Augustus. He is calling you a hero," the girl told Thaddeus with a smile. "He says from now on, you are family."

Thaddeus nodded, too exhausted to smile and too overwhelmed to think. He struggled to his feet, scanning the crowd for one particular face. He saw no sign of Rémy, not even allowing for the covering of smuts that masked every face. His heart sank.

"Dita," he croaked, his voice still full of smoke. "Ask him what circus this is – was. What was it called?"

Augustus looked at him, and even Thaddeus could understand what he said next. *"Le Cirque du Secrète."*

"Do you – do you know of Rémy Brunel?" he asked, a sick feeling rising into his throat. "Little Bird, she's called."

"Ah *oui, oui,*" said Augustus. *"Petit Moineau!* – Rémy Brunel..." He continued in a gush of French.

Dita frowned as she translated. "She was here," the little girl said, her voice fraught. "With a magician called Yannick. It was he that brought the Comte's men."

"The Comte was here?" Thaddeus asked, a chill befalling him.

"Not the Comte de Cantal himself," Dita translated. "But his men came. For – for Claudette. They set the fire. Rémy..." The girl glanced up at Thaddeus with worried eyes. "He doesn't know what happened. There was chaos. They were trying to free the horses and move the lions. But..."

Thaddeus looked at her as she trailed off. "But what?"

"Perhaps nothing," said Dita hesitantly.

Thaddeus placed his aching hands on her shoulders and looked her in the eye. "But what, Dita? Tell me."

"Gunshots," said the girl reluctantly. "No one saw Rémy after that. And they were too busy..."

"…too busy to look," Thaddeus finished. He straightened up, ignoring the sting of the burns on his legs. "So now we look," he said, looking Augustus in the eye. "Yes?"

Augustus nodded, grim-faced. "*Oui.*"

* * *

In the end, it was Dominique who found her. Thaddeus recognised Rémy's circus pony. She stood quietly beside a tree, nosing at something on the ground. The little palomino had been let loose with all the other circus horses but, instead of running, she had found her long-lost mistress. Rémy was slumped, not moving, beside the tree.

Thaddeus spotted her a moment after he saw the horse. For a second, his legs turned to lead and he couldn't move. And then, almost without realising it, he was by her side, dropping to his knees. There was a nasty gash across her swollen brow and her shoulder was bloodied. "Rémy," he said, tipping her face towards him, taking in the strangeness of her short hair. "Rémy?"

The pulse beneath his fingers was weak, but it was there. Relief surged through him. Thaddeus ripped off his muddy shirt. Most of it was useless, but he tore the cleanest scraps into strips, wrapping the rags around her injured shoulder.

"I've found her," he shouted, his voice cracking as he lifted her into his arms. Oddly, he no longer felt pain. "I've found her!"

She stirred as they reached the airship, eyes fluttering open, bruised brow creasing into a frown as she tried to focus.

"T-Thaddeus?" she muttered. "What…"

"Rémy," he said, "it's all right. I found you. Everything's all right."

She remembered something then, and tried to struggle free. "C-Claudette," she grated, "I have to—"

196

Thaddeus held her fast against him. A moment later, she passed out again, her head against his chest.

* * *

No one slept much that night. For one thing, the circus folk had nowhere to sleep, and for another, they were busy trying to round up as many of the horses as they could. Some, like the ones seen from the airship, were far away and gone forever. But others had not fled so far, and these were the ones that were brought back, slowly, over the hours that stretched towards dawn. Marta the elephant came back, too, lumbering hesitantly towards her relieved keeper.

Dita and J went out to help in the search, but Thaddeus stayed with Rémy. He had placed her in his bunk in the airship. As far as he could make out, the wound to her head was worse than the wound to her shoulder. It seemed as if the bullet had only grazed her. Thaddeus bathed and wrapped the wound, and then did the same with the ugly gash on her forehead. Leaving her to sleep, he stepped outside into the gathering dawn.

The dead hulks of the caravans were still smouldering. To Thaddeus, they looked like the carcasses of a great herd of strange beasts. He stared at them for a while, and then went to help Augustus, who was trying to calm a still-terrified horse. They nodded at each other, smiling through the language barrier until Dita and J returned, another tired pony between them.

"Right, Dita," Thaddeus said. "I want to know everything that happened here."

Twenty Seven

A Plan

Rémy woke to pain and the sound of murmuring. She opened her eyes, and found herself looking at a curved wooden ceiling. Sunlight was streaming through an open hatch above her head. From somewhere above came the sounds of bumps and scraping. Twice shadows passed through the sunlight, as if someone was moving around up there.

Rémy tried to sit up, wincing at the pain in her shoulder. There was a blanket tucked carefully around her. She realised with alarm that, apart from her underclothes, it was all that covered her.

The murmuring stopped. Another shadow came nearer.

"Well," said a familiar voice, still speaking very quietly, "there you are."

Rémy squinted as she looked up, trying to focus. Her head was still fuzzy. The figure dropped into a crouch beside her.

"T-Thaddeus?" she croaked, her throat as dry as scorched earth.

The policeman smiled gently, picking something up from the floor beside the bed. He held it out to her – a glass full of water.

"Drink," he said, "but slowly. How are you feeling?"

Rémy took a few sips, then handed the glass back to him. "I – my head hurts. And my shoulder."

"I'm not surprised," Thaddeus told her. "It looks as if you had an argument with a bullet. And you hit your head."

Rémy blinked, still confused. She looked down at her bandaged shoulder, naked apart from the dressing. "Where is my shirt?"

"Ruined, I'm afraid. Your corset and trousers are all right, though." Thaddeus gestured to the end of the bed, where both lay. Her boots stood on the floor.

Rémy shifted, uncomfortable, and then saw Thaddeus glance away and offer a slightly abashed smile.

"Don't worry," he murmured. "We got Dita to undress you."

"Dita?" Rémy asked. "Who's—"

Thaddeus shook his head. "Never mind that right now. We'll introduce you in a little while. Right now, I think you need more rest. J and I are just there if you need us." He nodded to the light he had emerged from, and Rémy's eyes had cleared enough to see that it was some sort of doorway, with a ramp. She could just make out J's back and, beyond him, blue sky over green trees.

It was the trees that did it. The memory of the previous night flooded her aching head and she gasped.

"The fire! Claudette!" She tried to struggle up, forgetting for a moment about her damaged shoulder.

"Easy," said Thaddeus, holding her back. "You're not—"

"But – but they took her! They burned… everything!" Rémy said, almost in a sob. "I have to go after them!"

"Not yet," Thaddeus said, his voice firm as he tried to get her to settle. "Rémy, you're not well enough."

"Pass me my clothes, Thaddeus."

"Rémy—"

"My *clothes*."

Thaddeus looked at her and she looked back, summoning every ounce of defiance she had. After a moment he nodded, and reached for the garments.

"You need to take some time before you go rushing off," he said as he passed them to her.

"Turn around," she said curtly. He did, and she climbed gingerly out of bed. Standing upright was more difficult than she'd imagined. Her head swam and she blinked rapidly, trying to fend off the pain.

"Are you all right?" Thaddeus asked.

"Don't look!"

"I'm not!"

She managed to struggle into her trousers and fasten them, but the corset was another matter. Rémy succeeded in pulling it on, but the laces were hard enough to tighten at the best of times, let alone with blurred vision and a throbbing arm.

"Rémy?" Thaddeus asked after a few minutes. "I can call Dita…"

"No," Rémy said hoarsely. "I just need – can you–" She sighed. "You can turn around now. Can you do this up for me, please?"

She turned her back as he moved. There was a moment of silence, and then Rémy felt him step closer. Another moment passed and then she felt his fingers slide under the laces, pulling them in. He didn't say anything.

"As tight as you can," she said.

It was strange, feeling his fingers on her back. Thaddeus seemed reluctant to let them linger there, jumping slightly every time they came in contact with her skin. Rémy's mind was spinning, replaying not only the events of the night before, but also trying to work out what he was doing so far from home. She hadn't thought she'd ever see him again, but here he was.

"Did you come looking for me?" she asked, her throat still dry. "All the way from London?"

Thaddeus finished tying the corset. He said nothing for a moment, and then she felt his fingers brush against the cropped hair at the nape of her neck. The last time he had seen her, her hair had been far longer, though always tied up. For some reason she found herself holding her breath.

"Of course I did," he said finally, so quietly that she hardly heard it.

Rémy turned around and looked up at him. Maybe it was because her head still felt as if someone had hit it with a mace, or perhaps it was because she was so worried about Claudette, but she felt her lower lip trembling as she tried to stop her eyes filling with tears.

"You were right," she whispered.

"About what?"

"Yannick." Even saying his name made Rémy feel sick. "You knew he was the thief. You knew he was rotten. But I didn't listen."

Thaddeus shook his head with a faint smile. "I didn't know," he told her softly. "I just suspected. But even if he'd been the best man on Earth, don't you think I would have come after you anyway?"

"He's not the best man on Earth," Rémy said, almost choking on the words. "That's someone else entirely."

Thaddeus ran his fingers lightly up and down her bare arms, smiling down at her.

"I'm just so glad you're alive," he said. "There was a moment, when I found you, that I thought you weren't."

She laughed softly, and then shut her eyes, because laughing hurt. When she opened them again, Thaddeus was leaning forward and, for a second, Rémy thought he was going to kiss her.

Her heart jolted, and she realised that she wanted him to, more than anything she'd ever wanted before. She looked up at him, holding her breath.

Someone cleared his throat, cutting through the moment as surely as a knife passing through butter. The intruder was J, who stood in the doorway, looking at his feet.

"Sorry, lady and gent," he said. "But Augustus and the rest are about to head out. Thought you'd like to know."

"Augustus!" Rémy exclaimed, stepping away from Thaddeus fast enough to make her head spin.

"Whoa," said Thaddeus, putting an arm out to steady her. She leaned on him as they headed for the door.

Even though she'd remembered what had happened, it didn't prepare Rémy for the sight outside. The road was littered with the blackened hunks of ash and wood; the only signs left of *Le Cirque du Secrète*. Rémy blinked, eyes full of tears again as she took in the ugly mess that the Comte's men had made of her friends' homes. Milling between them were the circus folk, some with bandages and slings concealing injuries. At least no one had been killed in the inferno. Some people were on horseback, but most folk were on foot, leading horses or pulling handcarts loaded with whatever they had managed to salvage from the flames. Behind them, with her keeper, Marta the elephant stood calmly, waiting to be off. Further away was the lions' cage, its two occupants pacing within, still disturbed by the lingering smell of the fire.

Augustus dismounted when he saw Rémy, grinning. "Little Bird," he said in French, "how glad I am to see you up and about."

Rémy tottered down the gangplank and into the old clown's arms, sobbing. "I'm so sorry, Augustus. This was my fault. You've all lost everything, and it was my fault."

"Tsk, tsk," muttered Augustus, pulling back to look down at her. "There is enough badness in the world without you taking the blame for something you did not do. We are all whole, and that is something to be grateful for."

"But Claudette – and Amélie! They–"

Augustus ticked one finger beneath her chin and smiled, glancing up at Thaddeus. "Claudette and her chick will be back with us before you know it," he said. "This policeman of yours has a plan, *ma cherie*, and that is why we must be off at once. We have a long way to go on horseback if we are to accompany this wonderful machine."

Rémy sniffed, confused again. "Plan? Machine?"

Augustus smiled at her again, and then turned to remount his horse. "Thaddeus and J will explain everything," he said. "Meanwhile, we will take Dominique with us. She will be safe with the other horses."

"Dominique!" Rémy exclaimed, seeing her beloved pony among the gathered animals. Hearing her mistress's voice, the little palomino whinnied and stepped forward. Rémy petted the creature's soft nose. "I will see you soon, girl. I promise."

Dominique whickered gently into her hand as Augustus began to lead the homeless circus folk out into the road. They turned towards the southern end of the valley – the direction the Comte's men had taken. Rémy watched as Dominique joined them, trotting off in the dust.

Rémy turned around, putting her hand up to her bandaged head. "So, what's this plan Augustus says you have?" she said to Thaddeus. "And," she added, for the first time taking in the airship she'd slept inside, "what on the good green Earth is *that*?"

Into the Unknown

Thaddeus watched as J showed Rémy around the airship. Though the burns to his legs weren't nearly as bad as they could have been, they still caused him pain. Seeing Rémy, wounded but walking, made up for everything, though. He shouldn't have been surprised, of course. She was strong enough to weather anything – that was one of the things he loved so well about her. It was also one of the things that made her infuriating, but Thaddeus wasn't fool enough to believe that he could have one without the other.

He sat on a boulder a few metres away from the open gangplank, watching the circus procession as it disappeared up the long road out of the forest. He admired these people's resolve in the face of everything they had already lost and everything they still stood to lose. Around him loomed the silent shells of their lives and livelihoods, and yet still they were determined to save Claudette and Amélie.

"Penny for your thoughts? There, that's one English saying I learned in London."

Thaddeus looked up to see Rémy standing over him, a faint smile on her lips. Behind her, J was clambering up to join Dita on the roof, where she was checking to see how well their repairs had survived. Thaddeus made to stand up, but Rémy waved him back down and crouched beside him, wincing slightly.

"How are you feeling?" he asked.

"Not too terrible, considering," she said lightly, though the dark smudges under her eyes told him she should get more sleep. Then she nodded over her shoulder at the airship. "The ship is amazing. I can't believe you flew it all the way from England." She shook her head. "I don't know if you are crazy or brave."

Thaddeus smiled. "I know. It still seems like a bit of a dream to me. But without it – and J – we wouldn't be here now."

"It's good to see that the ruby finally found a good home, too," Rémy added dryly, no doubt thinking of their past argument.

Thaddeus gave her an awkward smile. "I like to think great things are often born out of difficult beginnings," he told her.

Rémy gazed out over the scene of ruin before them, her look of sadness more shocking to Thaddeus than the vivid gash and bruise still marring her forehead. He was used to seeing her angry and defiant, but he'd never seen her so readily near tears as he had over the past few hours.

"Augustus said you had a plan," she said quietly. "Please, Thaddeus, tell me it's a good one."

He sighed. "Augustus is an optimist. It's not really a plan. Well, unless you call 'let's go and get our people back' a plan."

Rémy smiled grimly. "If it means finding Claudette and Amélie, I'll take it."

Without thinking, Thaddeus took her hand. Rather than pulling away, as she may have done just days before, Rémy laced her fingers through his.

"While you were asleep, Augustus told me what he knew. Once Yannick had revealed that he knew who she was, Claudette realised it was only a matter of time before the Comte closed in on her. So she came clean to the whole circus, and told them that she and Amélie would leave alone if that's what they wanted. But they didn't."

"Of course they didn't," Rémy said. "She's family."

"They were trying to get over the mountains into Spain. Claudette thought she'd be safe there... as long as they got over the passes before the snow closed them. The only snag in the plan was that this area here, where we are now, is the Comte's territory. They travelled as quickly as possible, and they also stopped all communications with anyone outside the circus. That's why Claudette stopped writing to you."

Rémy nodded, tears filling her eyes again. "But it wasn't enough. Because of me."

"Not you," Thaddeus said firmly. "Because of Yannick. As Claudette expected, he went to the Comte and told him who she was. But the count must have refused to pay out the reward until he had Claudette in his clutches."

"So Yannick had to find her," Rémy concluded.

"Yes. News about what had happened to Gustave and *Le Cirque de la Lune* was common knowledge, including the fact that Little Bird had disappeared but had last been seen in London. Knowing how close you and Claudette were, he came looking for you."

Rémy shook her head. "*Mon Dieu*. He manipulated me so easily," she whispered. "I was just too pig-headed to see it."

"You weren't to know his real motives," Thaddeus soothed. "It does you credit that you would be so loyal to your friends, even ones you haven't seen for years."

Rémy looked up at him, the expression in her eyes so strange that Thaddeus couldn't understand it. "I should have been loyal to you," she said eventually. "I just let… stupid things… get in the way." Her fingers strayed to her throat as she spoke.

"You're not wearing your necklace," Thaddeus realised. He couldn't remember ever seeing her without it.

She smiled wanly. "It was stolen."

"By Yannick?" Thaddeus asked, in disgust. "I swear, when I find him—"

"I don't know if it was him or not," sighed Rémy. "He swore it wasn't. But then he hypnotised me to get me to do what he wanted, so…" She shrugged.

"I'm so sorry," Thaddeus said. "I know it was a gift from your mother."

Rémy looked out over the forest, a slight frown creasing her forehead. "You know," she said softly, "I'm not sure that I am sorry it's gone. Without it, we might not even have found ourselves in this mess." Then another flicker passed over her face, something like a mixture of realisation and fear.

"Rémy? What is it?"

"My pack!" she said. "I was wearing it when we were attacked. Where is it? Is it lost? Please say it isn't lost."

"Don't worry," he told her. "You had it when I found you. It's in the airship – I stowed it in one of the cupboards for safety."

She blinked, relief flooding her eyes. "Did you look inside?"

Thaddeus frowned. "No, of course not."

"No, I didn't mean – I didn't think you would have," Rémy rushed to say. "It's just… there's something I want to show you."

"Do you want me to get it for you, now?"

Rémy was silent for a moment. Then she shook her head. "No. I think I have to wait until all of this is done. But you're the one I want to show it to. I wanted you to know that."

Thaddeus had no idea what she meant, but her words touched him. It made him regret that he had to turn the conversation to more disturbing matters. "Rémy," he said, "there's something more I have to tell you. About the Comte de Cantal."

He watched her face darken with concern as he told her of Desai's list and the meeting he had witnessed in London.

"*Mon Dieu*," she whispered once he had finished. "And I thought all of that was done with."

"So did I," said Thaddeus grimly. "All we can do is hope that he doesn't have many of Abernathy's devices already. And if we can stop him buying the submarine, then…" Thaddeus trailed off, seeing Rémy's thoughtful face. "Rémy? What is it?"

She shook her head. "Maybe nothing."

"Tell me anyway."

Rémy pulled a face. "A couple of days ago, I found Yannick with one of those message-sending machines that the Professor made. He said he'd stolen it from the workshop, but what if he'd actually had it all along? What if the Comte gave it to him to communicate with? It would explain how those soldiers knew exactly where to find us."

Thaddeus sighed. "It would. I don't like the sound of that at all. If the Comte has devices like that, what else does he have?"

Rémy rubbed a hand over her face. "And this is the man who wants Claudette – dead or alive," she said. "What – what if we're already too late? What if he's done something to her? What if…"

Thaddeus shook his head. "He put out posters, didn't he? He made his search public. Which means he wants her return to be public. He couldn't just produce her body and use it to claim the inheritance – it'd be too obvious that he killed her."

Rémy shivered. "Those soldiers that attacked the circus. Thaddeus, we're no match for them. And what if he has more?"

"I know," Thaddeus said grimly. "I know."

* * *

They waited until the skies had faded to the violet of dusk before taking the airship skyward. Thaddeus was at the controls, Rémy leaning beside him to see the Earth drifting away beneath them as they rose. The sensation was like nothing she'd ever felt before – the pit of her stomach rising and dipping with excitement and a tiny lick of fear. The trees below looked like children's toys, the river and road like strips of discarded ribbon.

"Strange, isn't it?" Thaddeus said, watching her face. Rémy nodded, wordless, eyes fixed on the horizon.

Thaddeus turned them south-east and in the distance, she saw an outline of a mountain that, in the darkness, seemed like a prism reaching for the stars. It was immense and intricate, a network of yellow stars that seemed to be harnessed to the Earth, as if some great power had pulled them out of the sky. She couldn't imagine what they were – how they burned so brightly or what had created them. She wasn't sure she wanted to find out.

"What's that?" she asked, nonetheless, her voice hushed as if they'd wandered into a cathedral by mistake.

"That," Thaddeus said, his voice unusually harsh, "is Mont Cantal, and it's where we're going."

Twenty Nine

The Devil's Lair

They flew on through the night, the darkness hardening around them like obsidian. Overhead, the stars battled to outshine the ones that grew ever larger in the airship's sights. The city of Mont Cantal loomed out of the landscape like a huge monolith to an unknown god. The lights, which Thaddeus could now see were great torches of yellow flame, had burned all night, and that achievement alone made him take a breath. *What kind of mind could have constructed this place?* he wondered. *What was the architect afraid of, that he made it look so spectacular, and yet so forbidding?* He thought of the underground empire that Abernathy had built beneath London. Here, the wonder wasn't hidden away: it was on the surface for all to see. The policeman couldn't decide if that worried him less or more.

Augustus had been right to describe Mont Cantal as impenetrable. Thaddeus himself could not imagine how anyone could enter its vast walls unbidden, let alone reach the castle itself. The city was such a part of the mountain that in some places it was difficult to tell where the rock ended and the buildings began.

A great wall had been built at the base, between two huge

natural cliffs that formed permanent stone sentries. Behind this wall, the city was divided into three distinct sections. The largest was at the foot of the mountain, directly behind the wall and between the two cliffs, a higgledy-piggledy collection of buildings that alone would look like any city. This one, though, was set around a deep, clear lake, filled from a fast-flowing river fed by a great waterfall that cascaded from above.

A winding path had been hewn out of the rock itself, just wide enough for two carts to pass, leading to the city's second level. Here there were fewer buildings, constructed so closely against the mountain that Thaddeus had no doubt that part of them must be made of caves that led deep inside the rock. The houses were whitewashed and neat, clearly owned by more affluent citizens than the ones below. This part of the town had an elegant square with a clock tower circled by cobbles.

Yet another road, narrower and more winding than the first, led to the great castle that oversaw it all. High above his people, the Comte had constructed a forest of gleaming white towers and spires. These were so tightly packed and bound so closely by another great wall that it seemed impossible for anything but a shaft of light to penetrate beyond the narrow windows that peppered their sides.

Flowing down from an outcrop jutting out above the highest of these spires was the waterfall. It splashed and thundered, running beside the castle and down a chasm cut by centuries of snowmelt and rainfall. It bypassed the second tier and flowed into the lake. From the lake flowed a river that shot, deep and fast, through a grilled archway that had been constructed in the lower wall. On either side burned another two of those great torches, the smoke from which smudged the night air with ash.

"*Mon Dieu*," Rémy whispered, standing beside him as she took in the immense sight. "Whoever built this place is either a genius or a madman."

Thaddeus felt a shadow pass across his mind. "I've known men that were both," he said.

"What we going to do?" J asked, leaning over his seat and staring out at the sight before them. "I didn't fink they'd see us coming in the airship at night, like – but with those torches, now I ain't so sure. They could see a fly comin' at fifty paces."

"Go around," Dita suggested, with a twirl of her finger to indicate what she meant.

Thaddeus nodded. "I think Dita's got the right idea. Let's keep our distance for the moment, and do a circuit of the mountain before the sun comes up. See what's on the opposite side."

There was a general murmur of agreement, hushed as if those sleeping below in that fearsome city might somehow hear and look up, despite the distance. Thaddeus flew the silent airship in a wide circle, keeping Mont Cantal on his right. It soon became clear that the huge torches they had seen burned only on the south side of the mountain, where the city stood. Once the ship had drawn level with the north face, it became clear why – here Cantal was nothing but a sheer rock cliff, almost entirely smooth from the tip of its height to where it met the plain at its base. There was no path, nor any way of climbing the expanse of stone by hand. It was as if, some time in prehistory, the mountain had been smitten in two, leaving one side smooth and featureless.

"Cripes," muttered J. "There ain't no army going to make it up and over that way, that's for sure."

"Not unless they've got an airship," said Thaddeus with a hint of grim triumph. He flew them closer and then rose up the sheer rock until they crested the very top of Mont Cantal. Doing so made it evident that the great line of torches did not actually reach the mountain's highest point, but began burning beneath a small plateau that jutted out just below the summit.

"Well, well, well," said Thaddeus, looking down at the narrow space. "I believe we've just found one advantage we have over the Comte de Cantal."

No one spoke during the landing. For all that the little plateau seemed flat, in reality it was as stony and uneven as any other part of the south face. Audible sighs of relief echoed through the cabin as the airship touched down safely. Everyone inside sat quietly for a moment afterwards, looking out at the orange glow that rose over the edge of the plateau and hinted at what was waiting below.

"We have to try and climb down, into the city," Rémy said.

Thaddeus nodded. "We'll have to do it now, before the sun comes up. Anything moving during daylight risks being seen. Rémy and I will go. J and Dita should stay here, with the airship."

"Wait a mo," said J. "You'll never get down there, find the lady, and get back up here before sunrise. The sky's already getting pink over yonder."

"We'll have to stay in the city all day, until the sun sets again," said Rémy. "It'll probably take us that long to work out where Claudette is, anyway."

"If they see you, you'll be trapped," Dita exclaimed.

"We'll be fine," Thaddeus reassured her. "They don't know who we are. We'll blend in with the locals. Don't worry. As soon as it gets dark again, we'll head back."

"What about the ship?" J asked. "What 'appens if someone comes lookin' up 'ere in the meantime? I dunno – a patrol, or sumfin'? We'll be sitting 'ere in broad daylight for hours!"

"You'll have to keep a sharp eye out, J. But why would they send a patrol this high? If they were worried, the torches would be burning all the way up here, too, but they're not. They've no reason to think anyone would be up here. This is probably the safest place you could be."

"But what if–"

Thaddeus cut the boy off, laying a hand on his shoulder. "If you're worried, at all, for any reason, then you take off."

"We can't just leave you two behind!"

"We can look after ourselves, J," Rémy said. "Anyway, it's not going to come to that. Trust us."

J looked doubtful, but eventually he nodded. "You'd best get going then, ain't yer? No sense hanging about waiting for trouble."

* * *

Outside the airship, the night air was cold. Rémy and Thaddeus made their way towards the plateau's edge, stepping carefully. Several times stones skittered away from their feet, the noise seeming to clatter as loudly as thunder in the silence. But there were no shouts; no stampede of booted feet. Up here, near the roof of the world, they were as invisible as ghosts.

The most difficult part of the passage down was getting over the plateau without any ropes or safety net. Pausing at the edge, they looked over at the drop below. The ground disappeared, curving in below the outcrop's lip and only jutting out again many feet lower. Here was where the line of ever-burning torches stood, perpetual sentries standing testament to Mont Cantal's might.

Thaddeus leaned close to Rémy until his lips were almost brushing her ear. "Are you ready?" he asked, his voice barely louder than a breath. "What about your shoulder?"

"Let's go," she whispered back, ignoring the question just as she was ignoring the pain from her injury.

He nodded, and a moment later they were on the rock face, searching for handholds and scrambling down as quietly as they could. Rémy was faster, of course, but Thaddeus impressed her. He was different, she realised, to the 'little policeman' she had met all those months ago. He was more confident, stronger. She was glad he was there. Rémy couldn't imagine wanting to take on this monstrous mountain with anyone else.

By the time they reached the line of torches, the sky at the distant horizon was a deep rose colour as the sun edged towards it. They were running out of time, but neither of them could stop themselves pausing beside one of the burning plumes, staring at it in amazement. The base was a metal cylinder as thick and as tall as a tree trunk. It had been plunged directly into the rock face, as if some giant tool had gouged a hole in the mountain itself. The fire that burned atop was so fierce that it shot several feet into the air like a fountain. Just one of these would be a wonder, but Mont Cantal had too many to count.

"What fuels them?" Thaddeus murmured, holding out his hand to the metal cylinder. Even from a foot away he could feel the intense heat.

"I don't think I want to know." Rémy shuddered.

Sound rose up from below them, echoing from the narrow track that connected each of the torches. Rémy grabbed Thaddeus' arm and pulled him behind a boulder. Two men were making their way up the track, their heavy boots scattering dust and stones from the path as they walked. Both wore the uniform and helmets of the Comte de Cantal.

"A patrol," Thaddeus mouthed silently.

Rémy nodded. They held their breath as the men drew ever nearer. Neither soldier spoke. Apart from the heavy tread of their feet, they were utterly silent. They must have climbed all the way from the city itself – a long trek, even for the fittest of folk. Yet there was no hint of them puffing breath into the cool dawn air.

Rémy looked at Thaddeus with a frown, and knew from his expression that he was feeling the same anxiety. There was something off about these two, something strange. She risked peeking out from their hiding place long enough to see that they had solid visors beneath their helmets. Their faces were completely covered by a rounded gold plate. Looking at one of these soldiers was like looking at the blank curve of a goblet. Despite herself, Rémy shivered. Thaddeus gripped her arm, silently reminding her to keep quiet.

They stayed huddled behind the rock until the soldiers' footfalls had faded.

"How do they see?" Rémy whispered, disturbed by the sight of the blank faces. "Why are they covered so?"

Thaddeus shook his head. "I don't know. We've got to hurry, though – there may be more of them."

Rémy nodded. "We'll stay off the path. Come on."

They slipped from boulder to boulder, pausing every time they heard a sound. Another patrol passed, as silent and as strange as the first, but they were not detected. As Rémy and Thaddeus got lower down the mountain, they began to pass caves. There seemed to be hundreds of them – some were tiny, little more than mouse holes in the rock, but others were larger, snaking away into the unknown. Rémy was relieved to see them – they would make excellent hiding places, a useful thing in such a hostile place.

The roar of the waterfall reached them long before they got to its source. The path passed directly beside where it gushed from the mountain, but Rémy and Thaddeus detoured around it, still anxious to avoid any patrols coming the other way. There was no way across the river until it reached the second tier, though, so they gave up on the idea of trying to get directly into the castle. As they stared at its turrets, Rémy wondered which one of them, if any, held Claudette.

The sun was up by the time they reached the middle city. They hid outside the main wall, waiting for a gaggle of market traders and their carts to pass, before slipping inside behind them. Once there, they both breathed a little more easily.

"So far, so good," said Thaddeus with a slight smile.

"What do you English say about famous last words?"

Thaddeus nodded, acknowledging the point. He was about to say something else when a bell began to ring.

"Ah, there we go," said one of the market traders to another. "It's time for the Comte's proclamation. Better get up there before all the best places are taken, eh?"

There was a general murmuring as everyone around them left their carts and began to head for the road that led up to the castle. One by one, the doors of the whitewashed houses opened and people poured out onto the street. Young and old, rich and poor, servant and master – it seemed that all were destined for the same place.

"Come on," said Thaddeus. "We'd better find out what's going on."

Thirty

The Comtesse's Return

Thaddeus looked around uneasily as they slowly followed the crowds. It seemed as if every road, path and stairway around them was now clogged with people. There were soldiers everywhere, too, though these ones had their faces uncovered as they scanned the throng with cold eyes for signs of trouble. Thaddeus felt hemmed in. He kept trying to calculate how swiftly they'd be able to get out if they needed a quick escape. The answer did nothing to quell his anxiety.

They had finally reached the wall of the castle when a fanfare sounded. Thaddeus looked up, shielding his eyes from the morning sun, to see four trumpeters, dressed in what he had come to recognise as the count's colours – royal blue, gold and white – standing in a tight line above the castle's gates. The crowd surged forward. Thaddeus passed through the gates, carried along by the press of eager bodies around him. Together, they all spilled into the courtyard beyond, and found themselves standing beneath a stone tower that dominated all the rest. Huge white steps led to a great wooden door at its base, but what drew the crowd's attention was the balcony halfway up its crowning spire. On it, two more trumpeters stood at attention, and from its balustrade hung another large flag, fluttering slightly in the wind. The fanfare sounded again, shorter this time, and a soldier stepped forward onto the balcony from within. He wore an elaborate helmet, plumed with white feathers to mark him out as more than a common soldier.

Thaddeus felt Rémy grip his hand, her angry gaze fixed on the balcony. "That's the one," she whispered in his ear. "He's the one who led the attack on the circus. *He* took Claudette."

"People of this great city," boomed the officer. "Pray silence for Comte de Cantal de Saint-Cernin."

The soldier retreated as another, longer, fanfare played out across the castle keep. Despite the numbers of those gathered in the courtyard, there was absolute silence.

The fanfare went on as a new figure stepped onto the balcony. Thaddeus felt his breath leave him. There stood the Comte de Cantal, the man who had mocked him across Sir Henry's dinner table, the man he'd seen negotiating for the purchase of one of Abernathy's infernal submarines. The man who had been convinced that in just one month, he would have enough money to buy the wretched war machine outright. And why?

Because he knew, Thaddeus told himself. *He knew, thanks to Yannick, that it was only a matter of time before he found Claudette and her fortune.*

Rémy pulled on his hand. He bent down so that she could whisper in his ear.

"I've seen him before," she said. "On the train from Calais. He spoke to Yannick."

The Comte wore a well-cut suit over his broad shoulders, and stood with an air of assurance that radiated from the balcony like heat. He stepped to the balustrade and regarded the subjects below with a smile, but, even from this distance, Thaddeus could see this genial look was deliberate and calculated.

When at last the fanfare died away, the count raised his hands.

"Valued subjects," he began. "We all know that this, our beloved city, is the greatest in all the land."

The silence shattered in a cheering roar that threatened to shake the very foundations of Mont Cantal. Around them, the gathered crowd exploded in applause and yelled in whoops of delight. After taking a few moments to soak up the adoration, the Comte raised his hands for silence. The applause echoed away.

"As you know," the count went on, "I have made it my mission to locate the lost daughter of my great family, my second cousin who has been known since she was a child as the Lost Comtesse. For too many years, we have been bereft of her presence. It was a difficult task, for we knew not where to look, or even if she still lived. But I would not be deterred."

There came more adoring cheers. Thaddeus looked at Rémy to see her jaw clenched, her eyes hard.

"And so," the Comte continued, as the sound of the crowd subsided, "it is my very great delight today to announce that the Lost Comtesse is found." The rest of his words had to carry over a storm of clapping and whooping that not even the count could quell, and nor did he seem to want to. With a broad grin on his handsome face, he announced, "My lords and ladies, people of France, I present Comtesse Arriete de Mont Cantal."

Thaddeus felt Rémy grip his hand tighter as the Comte turned back to someone further inside the tower. Rémy's lips were moving, as if she were trying to tell him something, but the words were lost beneath the thunder of the crowd. The noise reached a crescendo as a new figure stepped out onto the balcony, reaching for the proffered hand of the Comte.

Thaddeus had only seen Claudette Anjou twice before. The first time was a fleeting encounter when he had been in pursuit of Rémy as the thief of the Ocean of Light. The second had been when Rémy had brought her friend to see her new lodgings at the Professor's workshop before Claudette and the circus had returned to France. He remembered her as beautiful, yes, but even so the woman he saw now was as far removed from the one he recalled as a peacock was from a sparrow.

Her chestnut hair had been swept up into a complicated knot that glittered as if studded with jewels. She wore a dress of light blue silk, patterned with flowers and leaves in pale green and pink and edged with intricate lace, both at the open neck and at the sleeves, which tapered at her elbows. It was her face, though, that etched itself into Thaddeus' memory and made his heart clench in sympathy. Claudette's eyes were blank, as if they had been hollowed out. Her mouth was set in a line so emotionless that it seemed impossible she would ever smile again. She stared ahead, expressionless as a porcelain sculpture, as if entirely ignorant of everything that was happening around her.

"Arriete!" shouted someone in the crowd, and then another shouted, and another, and another, until the entire multitude was chanting a name the woman herself appeared not to recognise – *"Arriete! Arriete! Arriete!"*

The count stepped towards Claudette, who was as motionless as stone. He touched one hand to her back, and leaned to whisper something in her ear. She blinked, once, as if waking from a deep sleep, and then raised an arm to wave at the crowd, smiling widely and nodding. Her eyes, though, remained as blank as a painter's primed canvas.

"Show us!" someone else yelled. "The birthmark! Show us!"

"Yes," shouted another voice, "the birthmark!"

The count leaned towards Claudette once more, whispering something else in her ear. She hesitated for a moment, dropping her arm. And then she turned around.

Claudette's gown had been cut to leave her back bare to the mid-point, her pale skin almost translucent beneath the power of the sun. There, curling between her shoulder blades like a serpent lost from the sea, was a birthmark, several shades darker than the skin around it. The Comte held out his arms to the crowd, as if to say, "See? It really is her," and the multitude cheered once more. Claudette turned around, her face settling back into a blank mask.

"My people," the Comte boomed, once the noise had died down once more. "I have more joyous news to impart. For I called you here not only to celebrate the return of the Lost Comtesse, but also for another reason. I am to be married."

There was a sudden hush, and in it Thaddeus heard Rémy draw in a harsh breath.

"Yes," went on the count, "the Comtesse and I are to be wed, joining the two great wings of our families once and for all. Rejoice with us, for the next three days will be ones of great celebration!"

The crowd exploded once more as Thaddeus looked down at Rémy. She was staring up at her friend with huge, shocked eyes.

Cantal seized Claudette's hand and held it aloft as the crowd cheered. Then, turning, the Comte swept back into the tower, pulling Claudette behind him. The crowd began to filter away, excited chatter filling the air.

"That was his plan," Thaddeus said. "He's not going to kill her. Once they're married, he won't need to. Her money will be his. And the people love him because of it."

Rémy shook her head. "I don't understand. Why would she agree? She can't!"

Thaddeus touched her shoulder. "Rémy, I imagine she doesn't have a choice."

Rémy blinked, her eyes focusing on his. "We have to get her out of here. Now – tonight."

He nodded. "I agree. Which means we need to know exactly where she's being held." Around them, the square was emptying quickly. "Come on, we need to leave."

Thaddeus wove his way through the remaining crowds, keeping close to the high walls. They had to conceal themselves away from the watchful gazes of the Comte's men, who were herding the townsfolk out of the castle's main gate and back down to the city's two lower tiers. They had almost reached the gate when Rémy grabbed his wrist suddenly and pulled him into a narrow alleyway.

"Wait," she hissed.

"What is it?"

"Look!" She pointed back towards the main gate to a small knot of soldiers who were conferring beside it. They seemed to be paying attention to one in particular, a tall, thin young man in a plumed helmet that denoted a higher rank. "It's him," Rémy hissed. "It's Yannick!"

Rémy was right. Her old school friend seemed to be a magician no more. Instead he had taken on the garb of the Comte de Cantal's army.

Thaddeus grabbed Rémy before she could run at him. "Let me go!" she growled, her face a perfect mask of fury. "Let me go, Thaddeus! *Mon Dieu*, I will kill him, I will–"

"Rémy!" Thaddeus continued to hold her as she struggled,

pulling her deeper into the shelter of the alley. "Go after him now and we're all dead! Think of where we are, for God's sake!"

His words seemed to bring Rémy to her senses. She stopped struggling and nodded. Thaddeus let her go, and they watched from their hiding place as Yannick and his group of men marched away.

"*Mon Dieu*, I will kill him – he's joined them," Rémy said, her voice laced with sadness now, as well as anger. "How could he do such a thing? If he had just been tricked by the Comte, misled somehow... But he knows the truth now, and still..." She trailed off, shaking her head.

Thaddeus let the silence between them float for a moment, before touching a hand to her back. "Come on," he said. "The sooner we work out where Claudette is and get out of here, the better."

Rémy nodded, though the fury did not leave her eyes. Together, they rejoined the last of the people and slipped out through the castle gates before they were shut and bolted at last.

It wasn't hard to get the people of Mont Cantal to talk about the Lost Comtesse, or their city. In fact, it was the only topic of conversation that seemed to be of any interest to anyone in the bars and cafés that threw out their colourful awnings as soon as the sun touched the yardarm. The talk bubbled with the news of the Comte's coming nuptials.

"How lucky that woman is," said one smiling woman to Rémy, over lunchtime coffee. "Just think! To be plucked from the gutter to live in such a place."

"Yes," said Rémy through gritted teeth. "She is indeed the luckiest woman alive. How I envy her the chance to see inside the castle itself!"

"Oh, I know! And to live there, too. I've heard," said the woman, leaning closer with the glint of conspiracy in her eyes, "that the Comte's given his betrothed his own room. Isn't that marvellous?"

"Really?" whispered Rémy. "That must be the grandest room in all of Mont Cantal, no?"

"Oh, I should think so," agreed the woman. "They say it's the highest, too, with the greatest view of all." She sighed, and sank into a reverie as she finished her coffee.

And that was how Rémy and Thaddeus filled their day – with many cups of coffee, a few glasses of beer, much gossip, and a slow understanding of the design of the Comte's castle. By the time they began to make their way back up to the airship, it felt almost as if they'd lived there themselves.

Thirty One

In an Ivory Tower

When the sun had fully set, the ruby airship rose into the air as silently as a bird on the wing. J was at the controls, Dita leaning beside him as they left the relative safety of the plateau and sailed out over the city of Mont Cantal. The atmosphere in the cabin was tense. They all knew what was at stake – it would only take a single shot from one of the Comte's riflemen to down the airship and all who sailed in her.

Thaddeus had made a rough sketch of the castle and where they thought Claudette was being held, to help J navigate the airship. Rémy sat on the cabin floor and looked at it by the light of a candle stub. She didn't even move as Thaddeus sat down next to her and crowded in close, looking over her shoulder.

"How are you, Little Bird?" he asked softly.

She looked up then, watching the candle cast a festival of shadows across his serious face. "You haven't called me that for a long time. In fact, I'm not certain you have ever called me that."

He smiled, though the look in his eyes was still serious. "Tonight you need to be Little Bird more than you need to be Rémy. Will your shoulder hold up? Are you healed enough?"

Rémy flexed her arm to prove that it was healed. In truth, the wound was still sore, but it was no worse an ache than some of the bruises she had sustained during practice on the wire, and they had never prevented her from performing. She was determined that this one would not stop her now.

"It's fine," she said, looking once more at the picture he had drawn. It showed four imposing towers, smooth but for the single, guarded door at the bottom and several narrow windows. For all its gleaming white paint, in Thaddeus' drawing the towers looked more a prison than a home.

"Tonight I will fly as surely as this ship," she murmured, tracing a finger lightly over the paper. "Don't worry, my policeman."

Thaddeus sighed. "Your policeman," he repeated quietly. "Am I never to be anything else to you than that, Rémy Brunel?"

Rémy looked up at him, her heart thumping a little in surprise. He wasn't looking at her, instead studying the paper in her hands. For a moment she wasn't even sure he'd said anything at all. Her fingers fluttered to her throat, before she remembered her opal wasn't there.

"You're not," she began, and then swallowed, "I don't..."

Thaddeus cut her off with a gentle shake of his head and a brief smile. "Don't think of it now. Now we have to focus on the task at hand," he said. "But when this is over – one way or another – we must talk."

Thaddeus stared at her then, as if he could read her mind through her eyes. He moved his hand towards her, and for a moment Rémy thought he was going to touch her cheek. But instead he stood and held his hand out to help her up. She blew out the candle, throwing the cabin into near darkness. They didn't want a sentry spotting a strange light floating towards them through the night.

Thaddeus let go of her hand and they stood either side of J and Dita, looking out over the looming city. The torchlights were burning still, and in their yellow flicker the castle looked sickly, its white walls flushed as if with jaundice. Rémy shivered.

They sank towards the castle from directly overhead. As they dropped towards the central tower, J let the ruby's gas out slowly enough for the hiss to be almost silent, even inside the cabin.

"Better get ready," Thaddeus said in a low voice, as they sank lower.

Rémy checked the rope that she had already coiled on the cabin floor beside the airship's main hatch. One end was tied securely to a metal ring that J had driven straight through the ship's hull. They had tested how much weight both the rope and the ring could take, and Rémy was confident it would be enough for what they had planned. While she gave the rope another tug, Thaddeus went to stand by the lever that would open the hatch, waiting for the signal.

"OK," J said a few minutes later, taking a deep breath. "Open the hatch... now."

Thaddeus pulled the lever. The hatch opened, jerking a little at first, but then swinging down silently on its recently greased hinges. J had made some swift adjustments so that the gangplank would fold all the way down and away. Rémy leaned out, watching it disappear from view as the night breeze ruffled her short hair. She looked back over her shoulder.

"A little to the left, J," she whispered. She looked out again as the ship drifted in the right direction. "More... more... stop."

J threw the rudder and the airship stopped moving, hanging in the air. Rémy tossed out the rope, and watched as it uncoiled to its full length, hanging exactly as they had planned, outside the highest window of the tower they hoped was Claudette's.

"*Bon*," Rémy nodded, and glanced at Thaddeus. He was breathing quickly, his gaze intense and fixed on her. She smiled at him and then dropped silently out of the airship, slipping down the rope.

Far below, she could see the ring of soldiers encircling the base of the tower. From the lower town levels there drifted the faint hubbub of evening – occasional notes of music, the rise and fall of chatter as someone entered or left a bar. Around her came the haunting caw of gulls, wheeling to and from their nests in the rock of the mountain. Rémy hoped these accumulated noises would be enough to mask any she made herself.

The end of the rope came suddenly. Rémy looked up, seeing Thaddeus' pale face looming in the dark hole of the airship's hatch. She glanced down once more, but the soldiers were oblivious, too intent on keeping a watchful eye front and centre to realise what was going on over their heads.

Despite her careful directions to J, now that Rémy was level with the window, she realised it was further away than she'd thought. She reached out, but her fingers were still inches short of the diamond-patterned window panes. She glanced up at Thaddeus, but he'd vanished. Thinking quickly, Rémy hooked one foot and twisted it around the rope to make a hold and then reached out with her free leg. The motion swung her just near enough to get a toe to the narrow ledge. She pulled herself closer, until she was flush against the window.

Rémy tried to see inside, but though embers smouldered in a hearth, the rest of the room was in darkness. She made out the vague shapes of a bed, and a mirror, but there was nothing to convince her that this was the right room. What if the rumours they had heard had been wrong? What if she woke the occupant, only to discover it was the Comte rather than Claudette?

She swallowed, her heart thumping against her ribcage. Looking down to check that there was no movement from the guards, Rémy put two fingers in her mouth and produced a soft whistle, a little like a bird call. It was like none she heard in the air around her, and she feared that one of the guards would immediately realise that something was amiss, but there was no shout of warning, no sudden clatter of footsteps. She took a breath and made the call again. It was a tune she hadn't called to her lips for a long time, and she could only hope that if Claudette was inside this room, her friend would recognise it.

A face appeared at the window, large eyes full of shock. Rémy could have whooped with happiness, for it was Claudette herself, dressed in a long white nightgown. Her friend fumbled with the window, lifting it open quietly. Rémy slipped inside, pulling the rope with her.

"Rémy," hissed Claudette, a horrified look on her face. "How did you get here? What are you doing?"

"No time to explain," said Rémy, looking towards the rumpled bed, expecting a sleepy Amélie to appear at any moment. "We're here to get you out. Quick, get Amélie and come – Thaddeus will pull you up on the rope."

Claudette looked mystified, going to the window and looking up. "What–?"

"It's a ship that floats in the air," Rémy whispered, glancing towards the door of the room. A light flickered from beneath it, and she guessed that there was at least one guard outside. "Please, Claudette, we have to leave!"

Claudette turned to her. "No. *You* have to go, Rémy. Go now."

"What are you talking about?" Rémy asked. "Claudette, we can get you out. Both of you. Come on, we have to go!"

"No, Rémy. I cannot." Claudette stepped towards her, gripping her shoulders. "Amélie is not here with me. *He* has her. The Comte de Cantal has my little girl."

A sick feeling gripped Rémy. "Where?"

Claudette shut her eyes against the tears that had sprung into them. "He has dungeons. They are in the caves, deep in the mountain, between the castle and the middle city – level after level of cells to imprison his enemies. He spends hours there, doing God knows what to those poor souls. He has her somewhere there, but I don't know exactly where, or how to get there. He won't let me go to her. He won't let me leave this room unless it is to see him."

Rémy shook herself. "We'll find her, Claudette," she said, pulling her friend to the window. "I promise. But we have to get you out now – we won't have another chance."

"You don't understand," Claudette hissed. "The Comte has a messenger standing by. If I do anything to make him angry, he'll send word that she must be killed. There won't be any time to find her."

Rémy stared at her friend. "But I can't just leave you here! Not with him!"

"You can – you must! All he cares about is the money. Once we're married, he'll have it, and he'll let me have Amélie."

Rémy shook her head. "But what then? What kind of life will the two of you have? He won't let you leave, Claudette. He'll keep you prisoner here. Forever."

Claudette closed her eyes. "But Amélie will be safe. What else can I do?"

The rope twisted suddenly, and then disappeared from the window. Rémy ran to it, looking out to see Thaddeus making his way down the rope. Reaching out, she grabbed his hand and quickly pulled him to the window.

"I was worried," Thaddeus said, once he was inside the room. "We have to go, now. Every second we stay risks us being seen."

"Claudette won't come," Rémy told him. "The Comte is holding Amélie hostage."

Thaddeus narrowed his eyes in anger. "Miss Anjou," he said, "I know what you must be feeling, but…"

Claudette cut him off with a shake of her head. "But nothing, Mr Rec. I appreciate the efforts you have made, but I must do what I must do. This you understand, I think?"

Rémy watched them stare at each other for a moment. Then Thaddeus nodded sharply. "I do. Rémy, we have to go."

"What! We can't just—"

He gripped her arm with enough firmness to add urgency to his whispered words. "We'll find another way. But there will be no other way if we are caught. Understand? We must—"

A shout echoed from outside. Rémy and Thaddeus both fled to the window. Below, more shouts broke the quiet. Beside her, Thaddeus swore.

"They've seen the ship," he said, but before there was time to do any more, the door to Claudette's room burst open.

"Well, well," said the cool voice of the Comte de Cantal. He stood in the open doorway in black trousers and a white shirt that was open at the neck. Beneath his shoulder was a holstered pistol and at his hip hung a sheathed sword. Behind him was Yannick, still in full uniform. "What do we have here?"

Thirty Two

Escape

"Comte de Cantal," Claudette said, her voice full of fear. "It's nothing. These – my friends believed I needed help, but I have told them I do not. They – they're going now. Please – please, Monsieur – please, let them go."

Cantal stepped into the room, entirely unmoved by Claudette's pleas. The scar on his cruel face seemed like a vein of cold silver in the flickering torchlight that lit the room. He looked at Thaddeus with a slow frown that gave way to lazy amusement.

"Don't I know you from somewhere?" he asked. "Wait a minute… aren't you the little London gutter rat that became a policeman – or should I say police*boy*? What on earth are you doing here?"

"Rémy, go," Thaddeus said tensely, stepping in front of her. "Go now!"

"Oh, no," said the Comte. "I really don't think so…"

He went for the holstered gun, his eyes fixed on Thaddeus. The policeman didn't hesitate – he lunged for the poker leaning beside the hearth, slashing it hard across the nobleman's forearm. The Comte roared with pain, dropping the gun, and Thaddeus spun back towards the fireplace, grabbing the silver sword that

233

hung in a bracket above it. It was decorative, and had probably never once been fought with, but it was all there was.

"Why are you just standing there?" the Comte yelled to Yannick as he drew his sword. He nodded his head at Rémy. "Kill her!"

Claudette uttered a short scream as Yannick belatedly drew his own sword, but he was too slow. Rémy leapt onto a small table that stood between them, rocking it forward and using the momentum as it tipped to propel her towards him. She moved so fast that he didn't even see her coming. Rémy landed her foot at the centre of his chest, his ribs cracking beneath the force of her kick. He crumpled back out through the doorway, landing in a heap as Rémy ran to the door, slamming it shut and dragging the table she'd upended across it.

Shouts and footsteps echoed from below as more soldiers began to climb the tower stairs.

"Thaddeus," Rémy shouted. "We'll be outnumbered in seconds!"

She ran to the window. The airship was still waiting for them, but, below, she saw soldiers running this way and that, pointing up at the flying vessel.

The Comte and Thaddeus, meanwhile, were in the midst of a full-bore sword fight. Thaddeus knew enough to keep him at bay, but the Comte was by far the better swordsman. He slashed towards the policeman with a series of lightning blows. Thaddeus grunted, pulling low and slicing wildly at the count's thigh, but he was easily parried with a clang that made the policeman's teeth clatter. Thaddeus fought on, clenching his teeth harder and driving in again as the Comte curved in another slash.

"Stop!" Claudette shouted, as the two men fought. "Stop it! I am not going with them – I'm staying! Do you hear me? I'm staying!"

The sound of running came ever closer as more soldiers made their way up the stairs. The Comte lunged forward as Thaddeus deflected another blow that sent him crashing backwards against the bed. Thaddeus jumped onto it, his feet tangling in the bedclothes as he backed away. The Comte grinned, sensing a victory, but Thaddeus found his balance again, jumping to the floor as he brought his sword down in a sweep that almost caught the nobleman unawares. The Comte yelled in fury, slashing so wildly that he dislodged one of the flaming torches that lit the room. It crashed to the ground amid another scream from Claudette.

The flame bloomed against the bedclothes, which caught light with alarming speed. In a second, the hungry fire had shot up to engulf the ceiling in a fury of heat and acrid black smoke.

Rémy grabbed Claudette's hands and dragged her to the window. "Now," she screamed, over the sound of the inferno and the clanging of the men's swords. "We have to go *now!*"

Rémy scrambled onto the windowsill. "J," she yelled, hoping against hope that he would hear her over the melee. "J!"

The boy's face appeared at the open hatch, pale and worried.

"You have to bring it down," she shouted, her eyes full of smoke. "The airship – you have to bring it level with the window."

"I can't," he shouted back, pointing to the flames. "One spark and she'll go up in flames herself! And look!"

Rémy followed the direction of his finger as he pointed down into the castle courtyard. To her horror several of the soldiers were preparing bows and arrows. Even worse, one of them held a burning torch. If one of those hit the airship…

Rémy grabbed Claudette, dragging the end of the rope around them both. "Thaddeus!" she yelled, as she tied it off, but the furious fight went on. "J," she shouted, "lift us up!"

235

Rémy felt the rope tighten against her stomach as the airship rose. Claudette screamed as she was pulled from the window and into the air, but Rémy held her fast. She blinked the smoke from her eyes as the room disappeared from view, shocked to see that the flames had already bitten into the roof.

"What about Thaddeus?" Claudette yelled, looking down in horror.

"He'll get out," said Rémy. "He has to. He'll get out…"

A whistling sound shot past them and the airship jerked, bouncing them on the rope like fish on a line. Rémy looked up to see a flaming arrow just miss its target thanks to J's lightning reaction. He tried to right them again, but the sudden course changes sent the rope – and the two women hanging from it – on a wild swing, straight towards one of the other towers.

"Hang on," said Rémy through gritted teeth, as she saw a stone balcony coming fast towards them. She lifted her feet, planting them against the balustrade, crashing against it hard enough to judder her teeth. Claudette screamed, the rope around them loosening as the hurried knot slipped undone.

"Claudette!" Rémy yelled, as both her friend and the rope threatened to slip from her grasp. She grabbed the slithering rope with one hand, wrapping her legs around Claudette to prevent her falling to her death. Claudette reached for the safety of the balcony, just as the doors inside were flung open with a crash.

Yannick staggered onto the balcony, clutching his injured ribs.

"I can't let you get away!" he shouted, a mad fury in his eyes. "He'll kill me! Do you understand? You have to stay. You must *stay*!" He grasped Claudette and pulled her, struggling, over the balcony's edge.

Rémy felt the airship jerk again and looked up to see another fiery arrow shoot past, even closer this time. If J didn't take her up and out of reach soon, one of them would find its target. A strike from one of those flaming arrows and the ruby airship would explode. Rémy swung herself towards the balcony again as Yannick wrestled Claudette inside the tower, kicking the door shut behind him. Rémy's feet touched the balcony wall and she teetered there for a second before righting herself and letting go of the rope.

"J," she screamed, as loudly as she could. "Go! Go!"

He must have heard her because, as another arrow grazed the balloon, the airship lifted up and away into the night. There was a shout of fury from below as the archers realised their quarry was escaping, but by that time it was too late. As Rémy rushed to the balcony doors, the airship was already out of reach.

Thirty Three

Fire and Brimstone

Thaddeus stumbled, crashing against the wall, coughing as the smoke filled his eyes and lungs. There seemed to be no air anywhere in the room, and the heat from the fire was even worse. Still the Comte seemed unwilling to give up, lunging at the policeman like a demon, almost goring him with his blade. Twice Thaddeus tried to reach the Comte's discarded gun, and twice it was kicked further out of reach.

"Comte," Thaddeus yelled over the roar of the flames. "This is insane! We have to get out of here!"

"Only one of us is leaving, English rat," the Comte yelled. "And I swear to you it'll be me!"

"I don't want to fight," Thaddeus said, coughing again, almost blind as he parried another blow. "Neither of us needs to die, but both of us will if we don't get out of here!"

"You don't want to fight," Comte repeated, sneering. "So, a coward as well as a fool. I should have known!" He drove right quickly enough to nick Thaddeus' thigh. He cackled with glee as the policeman yelped in pain and stumbled backwards. The nobleman lunged again, cursing with annoyance as Thaddeus parried. "Enough of this," he hissed.

The Comte drove forward with added fury, forcing Thaddeus back towards the flames. Thaddeus bluffed a falter, drawing the nobleman to him. The Comte sensed victory and overstretched himself in a lunge. It was enough to give the policeman the upper hand. With a grunt of effort, he pushed the nobleman against the wall, hard enough to stun him. They both dropped to the floor, Thaddeus' left leg pinning the Comte's left arm, his sword against his throat.

The Comte de Cantal spat in his face. Thaddeus flinched, which was just enough for his opponent to get one elbow free, crashing it into the policeman's temple. Stunned, Thaddeus almost blacked out, and the Comte was on his feet again in a trice. He grabbed his sword, took one step backwards, ready to go for the killing stroke.

There was a deep, creaking groan. The wooden floor beneath them shook, and then gave way. One minute it was there, the next it had collapsed, crashing to the level below in a flurry of sparks and flame. The Comte disappeared through the ragged hole, crying out. Thaddeus lurched forward, still on his hands and knees, catching hold of his enemy's arm and slithering to a halt against the ragged edge of wood. He scrambled to his knees, clenching his teeth as he braced his feet against the uneven floor, trying to keep hold of the nobleman. The Comte was still holding on to the sword with his other hand.

"Drop the sword," Thaddeus yelled, as the flames blazed around them. "I can't hold you!"

The Comte swung himself towards the edge, but wouldn't let go of his weapon, trying to use his elbow to gain purchase, instead. Thaddeus reached out with one arm to grasp his shoulder, but he still couldn't drag the man over the edge.

"Comte!" Thaddeus shouted. "You need both hands! Let it go, before–" There was another crash as the fire ate away a second part of the floor. Thaddeus felt it threatening to give way beneath him, but still it held. "Comte," he tried again, his throat sore with the effort, "I can't–"

The Comte de Cantal screamed as he fell. Thaddeus tried to grip his shoulder, but the nobleman slipped away. A second later, he had vanished into the inferno below. Thaddeus rolled backwards just as a tongue of flame burst through the hole, threatening to swallow him, too. He staggered to his feet, searching for a way out. But the door was too far away and the floor had disappeared. Thaddeus felt the rest of the planks buckle beneath him, rising and falling like an ocean wave. Then they collapsed, sucking him into the black void below.

One Last Chance

Yannick grabbed Claudette by the hair with one hand, holding a knife to her throat with the other.

"Yannick, stop," Rémy begged. "You don't need to do this. Please, just let her go."

"I can't, don't you understand?" the magician hissed. "He'll blame me for everything."

"Then – then come with us," Rémy said, thinking fast. Outside, the soldiers were still shouting, and the sounds of the fire were growing ever louder. "We can all escape together. Come on, Yannick – right now, let's go."

Yannick laughed, but the sound echoed hollowly off the chamber's stone walls. "And then what, Little Bird? There's no place for the likes of me in your new circus, is there? You told me that already, remember?"

Rémy shook her head. "I changed: you can, too. All you have to do is help us now, and we'll help you. Isn't that what family does? And that's what we are, isn't it, despite everything – family?"

Yannick squeezed the knife tighter to Claudette's throat. A bright bead of blood appeared against her skin.

"This isn't you," Rémy whispered. "I know it isn't, not really."

The magician shook his head, but a look of uncertainty crossed his face. He hesitated, loosening his grip just for a moment, and that was all Rémy needed. She glanced up to where the servants' bell rope hung through a small metal ring that fastened it to the ceiling. Once a bird, always a bird...

She jumped, taking off as easily as if she were taking a step. Rémy hooked one finger through the ring and at the same time raised her legs into a split position, moving so quickly that Yannick had no time to react. Claudette, though, saw what was coming and slammed her hand into her captor's wrist, jerking the knife away from her throat. Rémy twisted in the air, turning her finger around the ring as easily as if she'd been holding onto a trapeze. Her other hand grasped the scarlet bell rope, sending it ringing wildly as she dragged it tightly through its mooring. A second later it was looped around Yannick's neck and she was in the air once more, dragging him to the ground. His knife clattered to the floor beside him as he lay, gasping and coughing.

"Run!" Rémy shouted. She and Claudette reached the door together, flinging it open and crashing into the corridor beyond. Yannick roared with anger as he scrambled back to his feet and came after them, lurching into the corridor like a drunk.

Rémy and Claudette ran, searching for an escape.

"We can't go down," Rémy shouted as soldiers' yells echoed up the stairs.

"Over the roof?" Claudette asked.

"Can you make it?"

"If the fire hasn't taken it already," Claudette said, raising a hand to wipe away the blood at her neck.

They crashed through a door at the end of the corridor to find another bedroom, with no balcony this time. Their only option was the narrow, diamond-leaded window. Rémy rushed to it, flinging it open as her friend slammed the door shut and searched for something to block it with. Looking out, Rémy was dismayed at the lack of handholds she saw. She could make it, but could Claudette?

"We don't have a choice," said her friend, reading her mind as she joined her at the window. "You go first, Little Bird – show me how." She bent down, grasping the skirt of her long nightdress and tearing it off at the knees.

There came the sound of splintering wood as Yannick hammered at the door behind them.

"Go," Claudette urged. "I'll follow right behind you."

Rémy did as she was bid, first standing on the ledge and then turning sharply. She gripped the lintel above, pulling herself up, finding purchase difficult against the smooth, whitewashed walls. She braced herself, relieved that the tiles of the spired roof were close. Hauling herself up, she turned and sat on the edge, looking over at the tower that had been Claudette's prison. The fire had bitten hard and was flaming hungrily over the roof, sending up a plume of smoke thick enough to obscure the stars.

Don't think about Thaddeus, she told herself. *He's probably already out. Maybe J came back. Maybe...*

There came crash after crash from below as Yannick rained blows against the door. Claudette was perching on the windowsill just as she had done, but Rémy's heart quailed at the sight beyond her friend. The archers were gone; everyone was concentrating on fighting the fire. But if Claudette fell, there would be nothing but a hundred feet of air and then a harsh stone courtyard to break her fall, and Yannick could be behind her in moments.

"OK," she told Claudette, more calmly than she felt. "First rule is, don't look down…"

Rémy felt something loom over her and looked up. The ruby airship sailed over the rocky outcrop, cabin lights blazing like the sun rising in the dead of night. She stood up, waving her arms as J brought the ship in lower.

"Claudette," she yelled, as Dita appeared in the hatch, throwing out the rope. "Get Claudette!"

Yannick appeared at the window, screaming with rage as Claudette grabbed the dangling rope and was whisked away. Rémy waited until her friend was climbing the rope to safety, then glanced back over her shoulder at the opposite tower. If she dropped over the right side of the roof, Rémy calculated quickly, she could reach the narrow wall that connected the two closest towers. Once she was across that, all she needed to do to reach Thaddeus was—

A groan swelled into the night: strange, inhuman and terrifying in its magnitude. A fresh billow of flame exploded up through the tiles of the tower's roof, splintering them as if they were matchsticks. The sound of a hundred glass panels shattering filled the air, and a wave of heat rolled over Rémy, so powerful it stole her breath right out of her lungs. There were hoarse screams from below. The count's men ran as cracks appeared in the tower's walls, ripping through the bricks as if they were paper, huge belches of flames erupting from the tears.

Then, the tower crumbled. It seemed to hang there in the flame for a moment, before toppling like a child's toy, collapsing in on itself with a rumble as deep as thunder.

Rémy stared at the space where it had been, and could think of just one word.

Thaddeus.

Shock rolled over her like a cold wave. The world turned silent as Rémy stared at where the tower had been.

"Oh dear," Yannick's voice sneered in her ear. "Not even your beloved policeman could get out of that, eh, Little Bird?"

The fury was like a white-hot pain. She spun so quickly that Yannick's knife didn't even have chance to cut her. Blind with rage, Rémy struck out, slamming her fist into his throat. Yannick gulped like a fish, eyes bulging in shock, and she kicked him hard in the ribs. His knife clattered to the tiles and slid down the roof. The magician slumped to his knees, gasping for breath.

"You tricked me," he whined. "You lied. You said–"

She spotted something hanging around the magician's neck. Leaning forward, she hooked her fingers under it and wrenched it free. It was a small opal pendant, hanging from a slim gold chain.

The rope tapped her shoulder. Above her, Claudette leaned out of the airship, urging her to climb. Rémy grasped the rope, shaking off Yannick's hands as they pawed at her legs.

The ruby airship lifted away and down the mountainside.

Thirty Five

Thaddeus

The tower crumbled around Thaddeus, level after level giving way. Flames licked at him as he plummeted through the ruin of wood and stone. He grabbed at some of the remaining floor as he fell. The plank broke under his grip, but it was enough to slow his descent. His feet hit solid ground, hard. He collapsed, rolling on cold stone, winded, aching and with fresh burns.

Thaddeus lay, staring up at the flaming innards of the tower, stark voids where the fire had eaten through floors. More rafters began to fall towards him as the fire tore them from their couplings. He scrambled to his knees, flinging himself out of the way as hellfire rained down. Thaddeus screamed in pain as a burn on his left arm connected with rock.

Crouching against the rough wall, Thaddeus blinked as his eyes adjusted to the uneven light. There were passages around him, leading in all directions. He remembered the caves he and Rémy had seen during their climb down from the airship. *Perhaps the entire mountain is riddled with them*, he thought: a honeycomb of passageways beneath the surface. If that was the case, there must be a way out. Struggling to his feet, Thaddeus picked up a shard of burning plank to use as a torch and chose a direction.

He'd only gone a few paces when he heard something behind him. The sound echoed against the walls just a second before he felt something sharp touch his neck.

"I should have known," said the cold voice of the Comte de Cantal. "Only a peasant boy would abandon his sword."

Thaddeus turned slowly, feeling the steel of the Comte's sword bite at his neck. The nobleman stood silhouetted against the burning rubble of his castle. He was bloodied and bruised, his hair unkempt, his clothing singed and tattered. But he still clutched his sword, and his scarred face still bore an air of infuriated arrogance.

"Comte–" Thaddeus began, but was cut off.

"Look what you have done," hissed the Comte. "You will pay for this, all of you, I swear. Where is Arriete?"

"Her name is Claudette," Thaddeus corrected him, finding it hard to draw breath with the Comte's blade still pressed against his neck.

"She can call herself what she likes," said the Comte dismissively. "As long as she hands over her fortune."

"She's not going to marry you, Comte," Thaddeus told him. "She's miles away by now."

The Comte laughed. "Either you think I am an idiot, or you are actually one. She won't go anywhere without her little whelp."

"She doesn't need to," Thaddeus said, with as much conviction as he could muster. "We rescued Amélie earlier. They've already been reunited."

The Comte laughed again. "Impossible. Come, we must go. I suspect we will find the Comtesse at the girl's cell. She will do as I say when she sees a knife at her baby's throat." He wiggled the sword, scraping at Thaddeus' neck. "Go on – move."

Thaddeus stumbled as the Comte pushed him down one of the stone passageways. "Not even you would really harm a child."

The Comte made a sound of disgust in his throat. "She's a mute wretch conceived in some miserable circus hovel. Even if the Comtesse does as she's told to keep her alive, do you think I'd have that brat living as my own kin? No, I'll get rid of it one way or another."

Thaddeus swallowed the sick anger in his throat. "I saw you," he said, his words echoing off the tunnel walls as they passed swiftly through them. "In London – or should I say, under London. I know about Abernathy and what he tried – and failed – to do. It's what you need the Comtesse's inheritance for, isn't it? To buy his war machines. You're trying to make them work for yourself. You'll fail, Comte. Just as he did."

"Abernathy?" the Comte repeated with disdain. "Abernathy was nothing but a fool, a stuffed shirt who thought he could defy the cause and follow his own agenda. His achievements were nothing – a storm in a teacup, as you English say."

Thaddeus frowned. "The 'cause'? What cause? What do you mean?"

The Comte laughed, the sound unpleasant against the stony backdrop of the passageway. "Ahh. So, you do not know everything after all. Of course you do not. A child like you cannot possibly understand any of what you stumbled upon in London – how big it is, how important. How laughable it is that you, a mere London street boy, could dare to think you understand anything."

Thaddeus' head was spinning. What was the Comte talking about? How could anything be bigger than what he and Rémy had battled in Abernathy's lair?

"If Abernathy was such a failure, why did you want his machines?" he asked, as they turned down another stone corridor.

"So that some other deluded idiot like him doesn't try to use them. That would only risk more failure. I told them," de Cantal went on, "I warned them that Abernathy was greedy and weak, but they wanted someone in position in England. I must admit though, Abernathy's engineer had a certain genius. That airship of yours, for example; I look forward to adding that to my army."

"A-army?" Thaddeus stuttered, stopping. The policeman had the sudden sense that he was standing at the edge of an abyss. "What—"

The Comte shoved him forward roughly. He stumbled, steadying himself against the stone wall. The policeman coughed, his lungs stinging. There was now an acrid tang in the air, stronger than the stench of burning rubble they had left behind. It smelled like rotting eggs. He almost gagged as another wave of the noxious fumes rolled down the passageway towards them. Thaddeus heard a tearing sound and saw that the Comte was ripping off the front of his shirt, using the strip of fabric to cover his mouth and nose.

Thaddeus stared at de Cantal's bare chest. Over the honed muscle was an ornate tattoo of a short, curved sword – a cutlass. The hilt was shown with a cupped guard that crossed directly over the Comte's nipple, which had been pierced with a pale blue, faceted stone.

"Aha," said the nobleman, with an amused nod at Thaddeus' shocked expression. "Indeed, I imagine this is different from anything you have ever seen before, yes?"

"A – a sapphire?" Thaddeus asked, his voice hoarse with fumes.

"Well done," said de Cantal, pushing Thaddeus in front of him again. "Now move!"

Thaddeus coughed again, staggering forward. It was becoming harder and harder to breathe. He held one hand up against his nose, trying to filter out some of the stench. Ahead of them, a bright glow lit the sides of the rocky walls. There were sounds, too, pounding loudly out of the semi-dark.

"Is that sulphur?" he asked, his eyes watering so badly that he could hardly see.

"Again, you impress me, Englishman," the Comte said.

He forced Thaddeus forward faster as the policeman coughed and spluttered. Thaddeus stumbled around a corner and found that the passageway ended on a lip of stone that jutted out over an open space. Half-blind, he almost walked straight over the drop, catching himself just in time.

Heart pounding, Thaddeus threw himself back against the wall and then slid down it, his legs buckling beneath him as the fumes proved too powerful for his lungs. He could hear the Comte coughing too, the fumes defeating his makeshift mask. Thaddeus shut his eyes, gasping in vain for air. He was surrounded by noise of all description – banging, hissing, creaking, whining, whistling – a conglomeration of sound that was too great to separate. Then there came another sound, much closer – the tinkling of glass as something smashed it.

Something tapped him on the shoulder. He struggled to lift his head, and saw the Comte holding something out to him. Thaddeus blinked at it blearily. It was a leather mask, with two circles of glass to see out of and a metal disk peppered with tiny holes over the nose and mouth. There was a pipe leading from it, connected to a small cylinder that the Comte held in his other hand.

"Put it on," the Comte ordered. He passed Thaddeus the contraption and then pulled an identical mask over his own head.

Thaddeus did as he was told – anything would be better than breathing more sulphur. He pulled the leather straps on around his ears so that the visor fitted into place over his face. It was tight, and his fingers fumbled around the edge of the mask, touching a cog he found there. Turning it, he heard a faint hiss, and cool air brushed against his skin. It was immediately easier to breathe, and Thaddeus gratefully sucked in a lungful of oxygen.

He struggled to his feet, clutching the canister. His vision was clouded despite the viewing glasses. The Comte moved to stand beside him, still holding on to his sword. Over the man's shoulder, he could see what had caused the sound of smashing glass – a cabinet, screwed into the wall. The Comte must have punched through its doors in his hurry to retrieve the masks.

"You see, boy?" shouted the nobleman, lifting his arm and swinging it out in an arc over the drop beneath them. "You see how foolish your friends have been to cross me?"

Thaddeus looked down. He saw, in the base of the cavern in which they stood, a great hole cut into the rock of the mountain itself. In it bubbled molten fire, a furnace so hot it could never be quenched.

"It's a – a volcano," Thaddeus managed, staring at the sight below with horrified eyes.

"Many mountains have the potential to be a volcano," the Comte said, his voice muffled but the glint of insane pride in his eyes visible even through his mask. "It just depends how deep you drill into its belly. Get a move on, would you? These masks are so tedious."

Thirty Six

Amélie

Claudette, Rémy, J and Dita watched the pandemonium below through the airship's windows. The townsfolk were trying to flee the city as the castle burned above them. Clods of flaming brick and mortar were scudding down the mountainside, threatening to set their homes alight. All they could do was run.

"I have to get to Amélie," Claudette whispered tearfully, watching the continuing destruction below. "I have to at least try."

Rémy blinked dry eyes, trying to focus on what could be done instead of what couldn't. Thaddeus was gone, she told herself, but Amélie could still be alive.

"We have to go down again, J," she said quietly.

"What?" J asked, aghast. "Rémy, I can't!!"

"You don't have to go near the flames," she said tiredly. "Take us down to the middle section of the city and get low enough for us to use the rope. We have to do this, J. We *have* to. *D'accord?*"

J looked at Rémy, his young face grim in the shadows. For a second it seemed as if he would argue. Then he changed his mind and, with a brusque nod, began to bank the ship. None of the soldiers on the ground took any notice – they were too intent on fighting the fires that were destroying the Comte's fortress.

Rémy peered out of the window as they sank lower. Already, two or three of the tall townhouses on this level were smouldering. Soon the flames would take hold in earnest.

"This is close enough," she said, as the airship floated level with one of the houses. She looked at Claudette. "Ready?"

Her friend nodded, her face still streaked with tears.

"OK, then," she said, and lowered the hatch. "Let's go."

The air outside was thick with heat, the stench of burning, and the screams of the desperate townsfolk. The dungeons were not hard to find. As Claudette had said, they were carved straight out of the rock, and thus stood behind the last of the once-proud townhouses now cowering in the face of the fire. Two huge solid iron gates proclaimed the entrance. There were sentry boxes on either side, but they had been abandoned by their soldiers. The gates, though, were locked fast. Claudette shook them, but they would not budge.

"We'll have to climb," Rémy told her. She pointed to the top, where there was a small gap between the gate and its rock housing.

"I don't know if I can," Claudette muttered, her face pale in the soot-smogged air.

"You can," Rémy told her. "You must."

The gates were as simple as a ladder for Rémy. She was up to the top in seconds, but Claudette took longer. The trapeze artist paused to help her friend, easing her through the gap, untangling her long hair when it became caught. By the time they had made it to the ground on the other side, one of the houses they had passed on their way in was fully aflame.

Inside, sound echoed like unsettled ghosts. Screams and shouts thrown up from outside ricocheted around the enclosed space. There were torches burning on the walls, which seemed almost sedate in view of the inferno raging above them. They lit the way, but that didn't help much. A dozen caves led from the entrance into the rock.

"Which way?" Claudette asked, her voice nearing a sob. "I don't know which way! Amélie!" she shouted. "Amélie!"

The sound of footsteps clattered towards them from the passage on their left. A flustered soldier, wild-eyed and sweating, appeared. He hesitated when he saw them, as if wondering whether to go for his weapon. Then another of the castle's towers crumbled, a distant *whump* overhead that made the mountain shiver. Fragments of the cave's roof rained down on them in a flurry of choking dust. The soldier forgot about his duty and hurried past them instead.

"Not so fast," said Claudette. Together, they grabbed him, hauling him up against the wall.

"Hey," the soldier cried, puffing and sweating even more now. "I weren't going to stop you. Let me go!"

"Tell us where Amélie Anjou is," Claudette growled.

"Eh? Who?"

"The little girl!" Rémy shouted. "The little girl you monsters locked up in this unholy place! Where is she, or I'll—"

"Oh," interrupted the soldier, with a shrill laugh. "Her! She's down there." He pointed to the furthest cave mouth. Unlike the others, it was dark, with no torches burning to alleviate the gloom.

Claudette and Rémy looked at each other. As one they let him go, the soldier almost stumbling to his knees as they moved away.

"You don't want to go down there," the soldier called, his voice fading behind them as they ran deeper into the passage. "It's the

Comte's orders! Not even us guards are allowed. No one who goes down there ever comes out..."

"Amélie!" Claudette shouted, her voice echoing along the dank stone corridor and dying in its depths. "Amélie!"

There was no sound, no indication at all that there was anything alive in the tunnel. Rémy hated to think of Claudette's little girl being kept in such a place. Surely not even a man as cruel as the Comte de Cantal would do such a thing to a child?

It was impossible to hurry. There was no light to see by, only a dim, grey glow. No, it was not even a glow – it was merely a sign that somewhere far ahead, the darkness was not as deep as here. Rémy and Claudette edged their way along, their hands against the uneven walls. At least, Rémy thought to herself, everything here seemed dry. She didn't like being underground again, but it would have been far worse if it had been dank, as the tunnels of Abernathy's lair had been. Here, at least, there seemed no chance of a flood – no sign of any water at all.

"Amélie!" Claudette shouted again, making Rémy jump. "Please answer, baby. We can't find you. Please!"

Rémy's heart went out to her friend. She had never given up hope that one day Amélie would speak to her – that one day, she would be able to talk to her little girl. Amélie's silence was perplexing and, at times, frustrating. Here, it could also be the difference between her life and death.

Rémy's hand struck something other than stone. She stopped, and reached out again to touch whatever it was. She found metal, rough and old, a thin bar. "Claudette," she said, "wait a moment."

In the gloom she saw the murky figure of her friend pause and turn back. Rémy reached out with her other hand and found another bar. Crouching, she ran her hand down to where it met the stone floor, and then, standing again, reached up to where it disappeared above her head.

"What is it?" Claudette asked with anxiety.

"A cell," Rémy told her. "I don't know how big."

"Amélie!" Claudette shouted again. "Are you here? Please tell us! Please!"

They listened for any hint of an answer, but there was nothing.

"What if she's not here at all?" Claudette asked tearfully. "What if the soldier was lying and we're just wasting time?"

Rémy couldn't answer that question – it was one she'd been asking herself, too. But what if the soldier had been telling the truth? Turning around and abandoning Amélie to this terrible place was too awful to think about.

"We'll go a little further," Rémy decided. "See how many cells there are, yes?"

She saw a slight movement in the darkness – Claudette nodding. They carried on, arms outstretched, hands brushing against cell after cell. The further they went, the harder it became to breathe, and Rémy became aware of a strange smell in the air. The faint reek of old eggs mixed with musty air.

Thirty Seven

Metal Men

The Comte hustled Thaddeus towards the edge, the point of his sword jabbing viciously at the policeman's back. For a moment Thaddeus thought he was about to be thrown from the ledge, but then, through the dusty eyeglasses, he saw steps hewn into the rock. Thaddeus lurched down them, putting one hand out to steady himself while the other clutched his oxygen tank. It was difficult to see properly in the mask, but the terrible power of what he managed to catch sight of sank deep into his bones.

From the lake of liquid fire flowed small, carved channels, directing the lava into passages that vanished from view. Vast slabs of rock kept these smaller lava flows in check, redirecting and restricting their flow as required. Each of these was connected to a huge metal arm that was in turn connected to a massive metal chamber built into the roof of the cavern. As Thaddeus looked up at a square metal cabin with glass windows at one end of the chamber, he saw movement. There were men inside. In fact, he realised, there were men everywhere, dressed in strange golden armour and with the same blank visors worn by the mountain patrol.

"How do they breathe without oxygen containers?" he yelled.

The Comte laughed. "Look again. Why would they need air when they have no noses, no mouths?"

The policeman frowned. "But – but they must need..." he began. "Unless..."

"Ahh," said the Comte. "Now the truth of my brilliance occurs to you. Why employ human soldiers when you can build ones that will never tire, never disobey, never wear out?"

His heart pounding, Thaddeus thought back to the Professor's illustrations of mechanical soldiers. "This is your army?" he asked.

The Comte laughed again. "This? No, this is not my army, peasant. These are merely the workers. I will show you my *army*."

He bundled Thaddeus forward, following one of the smaller lava channels, its heat bathing Thaddeus in a thick sheen of sweat. The policeman flinched as the giant machine overhead reached down to grasp an impossibly huge slab of rock. It lifted the stone, swinging it around and placing it into the path of one of the smaller lava flows. The burning stream bubbled against it for a moment before turning to flow into a different channel.

"Lava," the Comte shouted, over the clamour of industry that seemed to emanate from every corner, "is the most extraordinary natural resource in the world. It is a fire that never goes out, yes? With its power, I heat my people's homes and warm their water, for which they love me. And," he added, pushing Thaddeus through the cave's mouth, "it allowed me to build... this."

Thaddeus found himself, not in a stone corridor, but in another, adjoining cavern. The stream of lava they had followed cascaded down a short drop into a small pool that then fed into another channel like the ones in the first cavern. At the other end was a great door, built into the wall, leading who knew where. What he saw below him, though, made Thaddeus sick with fear.

"You see?" said the Comte. "*That* is my army, Englishman."

The Comte pointed to rows upon rows of silent men. Their bodies were formed of metal, smooth, lean and indestructible – because what Thaddeus had taken to be armour was in fact their skin. Each of their faces was golden and as blank as a new sheet of paper. And there were hundreds of them. Perhaps it was because they were so silent and so very still, but the sight of so many automatons in one place was even more terrifying to the policeman than Abernathy's human army had been all those months ago.

"Your silence does you credit," yelled the Comte. "For truly, there is nothing to say in the face of this wonder."

Thaddeus swallowed, pulling himself together. "How do they work?" he asked. "How did you even build them?"

The Comte pointed again, this time to the lava flow they had followed from the first cavern. It flowed towards a large metal chamber that sat over the boiling stream. The chamber was curved and set with a chimney in its roof. For the first time, Thaddeus also realised that he could hear water – a lot of water, crashing and rolling as its thunder added yet another sound to the riot of noise. He looked up, his vision still obscured by the mask, and saw that the noise came from a waterfall that splashed through the wall of the cavern, close to the ceiling. This, too, flowed towards the metal chamber. What Thaddeus had first assumed was smoke smudging the air was actually steam.

"It's a steam engine," he said aloud, in utter amazement. "You're using lava to heat the water instead of coal!"

"Well done," said the Comte, as if he were talking to a promising student. "This engine is the most powerful ever built. It drives both the machine you have already seen and that one over there."

He pointed to another large contraption that stood silently behind his gathered army. "When that is running, it can press out one of my soldiers every thirty minutes. Their armour is formed from a single sheet of metal, heated and moulded into form. They are then assembled, insides and all, by other soldiers who have been designed specifically for such work."

"And what about the men?" Thaddeus asked, his mouth dry. "How do they work?"

"A combination of miniature friction engines and clockwork," said the Comte. "They have taken a long time – and my entire fortune – to perfect."

"I don't understand," said Thaddeus. "Surely, all you need to do is sell one of these mechanical men and you will be the richest man on the planet! Why do you need Claudette?"

The Comte narrowed his eyes inside his mask. "I will never part with a single one of these soldiers," he hissed. "I can't risk lesser men getting their hands on my mechanical marvels. All my soldiers are needed, all are necessary for what is to come."

"And what's that?" Thaddeus asked, his heart thumping. "Comte? What is to come?"

"We are wasting time," said his captor. "I begin to think you are delaying me deliberately. Move."

The Comte pushed him up a flight of steps and towards a wooden door. Thaddeus stumbled through it and found himself in darkness.

"Take off the mask," the Comte ordered, pulling off his own and dropping it to the ground. "No sense in wasting oxygen when it's not absolutely necessary, eh?"

Thaddeus did as he was told. The Comte's sword pricked his spine, forcing him forward once again.

Thirty Eight

A Chink of Light

"Amélie," Claudette shouted again, and Rémy could hear the fading hope in her friend's voice as they continued along the passage. "Little one, if you can make a sound – any sound – please tell us where you are!"

There was more silence. Then, a loud but distant clanging started up somewhere ahead, the sound of metal hitting metal. Echoing around them, it stopped as quickly as it had begun.

"Amélie!" Claudette cried. "Is that you? We're coming!"

The clanging started up again as Claudette and Rémy hurried towards the sound. They passed cell after cell, and as they did so, Rémy realised that the light ahead was getting brighter. It was easier to see what was around them – how small these chambers were, how miserably bare. The chemical smell in the air was also stronger now, making them both cough.

Ahead of her, Claudette disappeared around a corner and cried out, skidding to a halt. Rémy reached her and saw what had caused the cry. They had indeed found Amélie – but she was not alone.

The Comte de Cantal lounged lazily against the bars of her cell, a metal cup dangling from one elegant hand. His other held a sword, which was crooked around the neck of someone he had forced to kneel on the floor before him – someone Rémy had never expected to see again.

"Thaddeus!" Rémy couldn't believe her eyes. "But how did you…? Where did you…?"

The policeman looked up at her with a faint smile. "Don't ask."

"You're alive," she said, still trying to take it in. "I thought… I thought…"

"Yes, yes, yes," barked the Comte impatiently. "We're all very touched, I'm sure. Now do shut up, or I may be sick. You," he said, standing up straighter and jabbing the metal cup towards Claudette. "You're the one I want."

Claudette's tearful gaze was fastened on her daughter, who sat at the back of her cell with her arms wrapped around her thin knees. Amélie's face was streaked with dirt, her hair was matted, and her eyes were large with fear.

"It's all right," her mother told her quietly. "Amélie, I'm so sorry. But everything's going to be all right, I promise."

"Oh, really?" said the Comte. "I'm not sure you're in a position to promise anything of the sort. Ah, ah, ah," he said, to Rémy, who had taken a step towards Thaddeus. "I don't think so. Stay right there."

"I told you," Claudette said tiredly. "I never had any intention of leaving you, Comte. My friends were mistaken."

"They destroyed my castle," said de Cantal coldly. "I think that's rather more than a mistake."

"Take my money," Claudette told him. "Once you have that, you can rebuild it. You can make it twice, three times as big, if you want to. Just let my daughter and my friends go, and you can have it all."

"What makes you think I need to bargain with you?" the Comte barked. "I will take exactly what I want, when I want it."

Rémy was staring at Thaddeus. He was looking directly back at her, his eyes alight with a fierce internal fire, and she had a feeling he was silently trying to tell her something. The problem was, they had spent so much time actively avoiding looking each other in the eye that she wasn't sure what it was. It made her tense, though, that fierce look. Thaddeus still had the Comte's sword at his neck – if he tried to move, de Cantal would slit his throat. But Rémy had the feeling that Thaddeus was poised, preparing to act.

She glanced around. The walls were uneven but otherwise featureless – there were no handholds, nothing to cling to. The bars of Amélie's cage were rusted, but firm. The curved ceiling of the roof offered no suggestions, either.

Claudette stepped forward and dropped to her knees on the cold floor. "Sir," she begged the Comte, "dear sir, I know you have a wise heart in your noble body. Please – please – let these two take my daughter far away from here."

The Comte merely laughed, apparently amused by the sight of the pleading woman. "Oh?" he said. "And why on earth would I do that, when I already have you all within my power?" He twisted the sword against Thaddeus' neck. Rémy winced as she saw the policeman flinch.

"You have no need to show us mercy, I know that," said Claudette in the same beseeching tone, scrambling closer on her knees. She was close enough now that her pleading hands could reach the Comte's legs. She scrabbled at them feebly, her dusty fingers brushing at his thighs, at his naked waist. "We are indeed in your power," Claudette went on, "which will only go to prove how great you truly are should you honour this one request. I will do anything you so wish, my lord, anything – but please, let my child and my friends go. This wish only you can grant and, in your great mercy, I beg you will do so."

Rémy watched her friend uncomfortably. She was about to tell her to stop, that this was accomplishing nothing but humiliation, when she realised what Claudette was doing. Her heart leapt. *Once a pickpocket, always a pickpocket.* Rémy saw the movement, as quick and as light as it was – with one hand, Claudette continued to paw pleadingly at the Comte's body. With her other, her fingers slipped into the pocket of his tattered trousers. There was a flash of silver in the dim passageway as she deftly pulled the keys from his pocket.

"Enough," said the Comte, still laughing, "get back, woman, before I lose my patience."

"But Comte–" Claudette reached for his arm – the one that held the sword against Thaddeus' neck.

It was all the intervention Rémy and Thaddeus needed. In the fraction of a second that Claudette pushed against the Comte's hand, the policeman lifted his own to intercept the sword. Rémy ran forward, aiming a kick high at the man's arm, while Claudette flung the keys into the cell.

"Amélie," she shouted, back on her feet in an instant. "Quickly!"

The little girl knew exactly what to do. She scooped up the keys and in the next moment was fitting each key to her cell's lock in turn, trying to find the one that would release her.

"Treacherous imbeciles," the Comte screamed in rage, realising that he was no match for a combined attack from the three of them. "You will all die for this! You will *die!*"

He lashed out at Thaddeus with the sword, almost scoring the policeman a nasty gash across his stomach. Rémy responded with a kick to his sternum while Thaddeus went for the blade. The weapon tumbled to the ground as the man wrenched himself free, stumbling backwards.

Claudette turned at the sound of the cell door squeaking open – Amélie had freed herself. She threw herself at her mother, who picked her up and hugged the little girl tightly.

"Go!" Thaddeus shouted. "Claudette, take Amélie out now!"

Claudette hesitated, looking at Rémy.

"Yes, do it!" Rémy nodded. "Go, quickly!" She watched as her friend fled back down the passageway towards the prison's entrance as she and Thaddeus blocked the Comte's way.

"Fools!" the thwarted nobleman screamed, backing away into the darkness behind him. "You imagine you can defy me? You will rue the day you even tried!" He turned from them and ran, disappearing along the darkened passageway.

"Rémy, we have to stop him," Thaddeus told her. "What he's got back there – it's worse than Abernathy. A hundred – a thousand times worse."

Rémy was out of breath, but nodded. *"D'accord,"* she said. He was alive and Claudette and Amélie were free. Right then, she felt as if anything were possible. "Show me."

Achilles' Heel

When they reached the engine room, Rémy could do nothing but stare at the scene before them with a horrified look on her face, ignoring the hideous fumes that swirled all around them.

"What are they?" she asked, regarding the rows and rows of silent soldiers.

"Mechanical soldiers. The most fearful fighting men ever created," Thaddeus said. He looked around as the sulphur began to burn his lungs. He'd left the masks the Comte had discarded where they lay in the passageway, hoping to find new ones with fresh stores of oxygen. "Where are they?" he muttered, and then spied a glass cabinet riveted into the rough stone a few feet away. Thaddeus smashed it, pulling out two of the breathing masks and canisters. He held one out to Rémy. "The fumes – you don't want to breathe them for long. This will help."

Rémy pulled it on. Thaddeus reached over and twisted the valve cog so that she could breathe. "I can't see him," she said, her voice muffled. "The Comte, where did he go?"

As if in answer, there came a loud, booming screech that almost deafened them despite the leather covering their ears. Then they saw him, standing among his golden army.

The Comte de Cantal was wearing one of the breathing masks. He was also holding a silver box beset with switches and antennae.

"That looks like one of the Professor's transmission boxes," said Thaddeus tensely.

The Comte flicked a single switch, and it was as if the mechanical army had been woken from a deep sleep. As one, each figure lifted its head. The eerie silence that accompanied the movement was almost dreamlike. Then the Comte flipped another switch and they instantly came to attention, lifeless hands stiffening at their sides, feet sturdily stepping apart to stamp loudly on the stone. A second later, they began to march. The relentlessly even tread of their boots echoed around the chamber as each line stepped forward and then turned sharply in tight formation. The great doors opened in the rock wall. The men disappeared from view, four abreast, until the cavern was almost empty.

Below them, the Comte spread his arms in triumph. "They are programmed to protect Mont Cantal," he bellowed up at them. "No one will exit. No one will enter. No one will be able to defeat them. Welcome to your graveyard!" The Comte began to laugh, the sound echoing eerily around the great chamber.

"What can we do?" Rémy asked Thaddeus, looking around frantically. "How do we defeat them?"

Thaddeus grasped her by the shoulders, spinning her around to face him. "I was wrong. We can't. Maybe if we'd got to him before, but not now he's activated them. You have to run. Go now, and you can make it before the metal men reach the main gates. Get out of here."

"What about you?" Rémy asked. "Why aren't you coming?"

"There is something I must do," Thaddeus told her. "Go, Rémy. Save yourself. Please."

"No," Rémy said, her voice rasping inside the mask. "No, whatever you are going to do – I'm coming too."

"Rémy–"

"Thaddeus," Rémy answered. "Whatever it is, I can help."

"It's extremely dangerous," Thaddeus warned. "If it works, I don't think there's a lot of chance of me making it out of here."

"Good," she said stoutly. "Anything other than extremely dangerous has a habit of being boring. Now come on, little policeman, get on with it. We're wasting time."

Thaddeus stared at her for a moment, and then grabbed her hand and pulled her down the short flight of rough stone steps. He hauled Rémy under the stone arch and into the connecting cavern where the stench of sulphur was at its strongest, even with their masks.

"*Mon Dieu!*" Rémy exclaimed, when she saw the lava pool.

"Up there," Thaddeus said, pointing to the huge machine in the ceiling. Its arms were still moving, and inside the metal cabin some of the mechanical men were still at work. "It controls the lava flow. It's what keeps it in check."

Rémy looked at him. "You want to destroy it?"

"I can't think of anything else we can do," he said. "If we can make the lava overflow–"

She nodded without him having to finish. "Well," she said, with a sharp grin, "it's better than drowning again, eh?"

If she hadn't been wearing that damn mask and if there had been time, he would have kissed her then. But she was, and there wasn't. There never seemed to be enough time, or at least not for them.

"You take the stairs," she told him, pointing to the metal rungs set into the wall for the soldiers to climb.

"What are you going to do?" he asked.

Rémy was already running. "What do you think?" she shouted back, over her shoulder.

Thaddeus didn't have time to watch her. He ran to the ladder and began to climb. It was difficult to see in the mask, and he had to wedge the oxygen canister into what was left of his trousers in order to use his hands, but he struggled on.

Halfway up he turned to see what Rémy was doing. He paused for a moment in amazement. She'd climbed onto one of the huge slabs of rock. The machine had started to lift it, but that didn't deter Little Bird. Instead, Thaddeus watched as she began to climb the mechanical arm itself.

He reached the top of the ladder and found himself on a narrow ledge that led to the machine's control room. For one jubilant moment he thought the way forward was clear, but then he heard a shout from below. It was the Comte, still wielding the controls to his fearful army. He yelled something Thaddeus couldn't make out, and then flicked another switch. Inside the control room, one of the metal men began to move. It stepped out onto the ledge and headed for Thaddeus.

The metal soldier was shockingly fast, and on him in a moment, moving fluidly as it tried to grab for his neck. The policeman ducked, feigning a left and then moving right before launching a kick at the machine's leg. It was like attacking solid rock – Thaddeus' foot simply slipped off the polished metal. The move unbalanced him, and the mechanical soldier launched another attack, punching at his shoulder with enough force to hurl Thaddeus against the wall, jarring his spine and winding him.

Through his pain, the policeman saw the soldier reach for something at his hip. It was a cruel-looking knife, with a long, hooked blade of the sort he had seen down on the docks in the hands of shipmen arriving from the Orient. The soldier pulled it from a scabbard built into its metal flesh, and plunged the weapon towards him.

Thaddeus' only advantage was the narrow ledge on which he and his apparently impervious foe fought. If only he could find some way to make the monster miss a step – to stray too close to the edge…

He quickly looked the machine over, searching for some weakness, however small. The metal of its torso was forged from one smooth piece, and each joint in the arm and neck overlapped so that its inner workings were hidden. The legs, though, were slightly different – one hip housed the evil-looking knife, and so bore no such smooth overlap. When its knife was in use, that could be a weakness. Besides this, the ankle joints were exposed to show an assembly of cogs and gears, constantly turning as the monster moved forward.

Thaddeus lashed out, aiming a stout kick at the unprotected hip, but to no avail. The soldier anticipated his move a fraction of a second before the blow connected, and turned slightly before slashing the knife at Thaddeus' shoulder blade, missing by a hair's breadth. Instead of pulling back, though, the policeman forged forward, ducking under the soldier's arm and slipping behind it.

Just as the contraption started to twist its featureless face around, Thaddeus slammed his heel into the gears at the soldier's ankle, unbalancing it slightly. The soldier lifted its arms and splayed its metal fingers to steady itself, which was all the hesitation Thaddeus needed. Gathering his strength, he brought up one leg and propelled it into the soldier's torso. The kick hit with enough force to make the metal man step back – straight over the lip of the ledge. Thaddeus lunged forward as it fell, grasping for the knife. He grabbed it by the hilt and wrenched it out of the soldier's hand, and then watched as the contraption plummeted to its end in total silence, without even a hint of emotion.

A bellow of fury echoed off the walls. It was the Comte, watching from the floor of the lava room. The soldier crashed to the floor, half in and half out of the molten inferno. It lay there, torso, arms and head still operational, but it was too late. Its legs and innards melted into the river of fire, disappearing like ice melting into a pond on a sunny morning.

The Comte bellowed his rage again, but the policeman was already on the move. He could see that Rémy was ahead of him – she'd made it all the way up the metal arm.

"Rémy," he shouted at her, "their ankles are their weakness!"

She turned at the sound of her name and nodded once before launching an attack on the glass windows of the control cabin. Thaddeus saw another metal man coming for him. It charged through the door of the cabin as the glass behind it shattered under Rémy's attack, falling like sharp rain to the floor below.

"No!" the Comte screamed again. He threw another switch on the control box, and the soldier running towards Thaddeus stopped abruptly. It turned and started back to the control cabin, where Rémy had plunged through the broken window and launched an attack on the two machines left within.

Not even these inhuman contraptions were fast enough to catch Little Bird, who leapt and pirouetted around the cabin as they thumped and bashed their way after her, damaging the controls with far more efficiency than they did their prey.

"This place is the heart of his entire operation," Thaddeus shouted, as he stepped into the cabin. "If we can destroy it…"

Rémy didn't reply, too busy evading the reach of one of the metal men. She threw herself back against one of the control panels and then slammed her foot against the soldier's arm. At the same time, Thaddeus used his knife to incapacitate it, black oil spurting everywhere as he slid the knife under the armour at the back of its neck and wrenched upwards, hard.

With Rémy keeping the other two occupied, Thaddeus looked around. The cabin was a dense forest of controls, none of which were labelled.

"Can you turn it off?" Rémy yelled, as she rammed one of her opponents back against a large pulley that hung down through a hole in the ceiling. It flailed its arms uselessly, entangled in the chains, unable to free itself.

"That won't be enough," Thaddeus shouted over the sound of crashing metal. "We've got to make the lava overflow somehow…"

He looked up, seeing through the dirty glass circles of his mask the clamps that held the cabin to the rock ceiling. He realised now that the whole structure was hanging on two huge rails that crossed the cavern's roof. The machine must have been designed to slide so that the stone slabs could reach different areas when needed.

Thaddeus leaned through the smashed glass window and looked down – they were almost directly over the main lava pool. If the machine were to fall, not only would every one of the stone slabs be unable to operate, the weight of the cabin might just be enough to crack the edge of the lava pool.

"I could really use some help here!" Rémy shouted.

Thaddeus turned to see that the final mechanical soldier had managed to corner her. It caught one of Rémy's legs in mid-air, making her overbalance. She crashed back against the control panel, crying out in pain as the switches and levers smashed into her back. Thaddeus leapt forward, slamming his knife up and into the soldier's left knee joint. It staggered, giving Rémy a chance to get up, but righted itself almost immediately. It swung around, smashing one clenched fist at Thaddeus' face and catching his jaw with a crunching blow. He heard Rémy yell and the soldier slid sideways, off-balance enough that its next punch connected with one of the glass panels. It shattered, showering them all in glass.

"Tip it out!" Rémy screamed. Together they each grabbed one of the soldier's legs and lifted it up and out through the broken window. It made no sound as it fell.

"Look," Rémy said, breathing hard.

Below, a fresh column of gleaming metal soldiers were marching into the cavern. The Comte was directing them towards the cabin in which Rémy and Thaddeus stood, his ranting and raving visible even from where they stood watching.

"What do we do?" Rémy asked. "Tell me you've got a plan, Thaddeus, because I don't think we can delay that many for long!"

Consumed

Thaddeus looked around, suddenly feeling helpless in the face of so many unknowns. "Start pulling levers," he said. "It's all we can do. Quickly!"

Together, he and Rémy began wrenching levers and throwing switches. Some did nothing; others caused audible whines from the machine. He threw one switch to the upright position and felt the cabin move slightly. Looking out, he saw one of the huge metal arms move. It lifted, taking its massive load of stone slab with it. Thaddeus flicked the switch next to it and another arm did the same thing.

"Rémy," he said, "quickly! Help me with these."

Together they moved all of the switches into the upright position, lifting all of the metal arms and the huge slabs. The cabin shook with the immense strain of lifting so much weight at the same time.

Below them, the small lava channels – the ones that had been blocked or controlled by the movable rocks – began to overflow. Thaddeus looked down to see the Comte stepping backwards warily as one river of fire burst its hewn banks and crept across the floor towards him.

There was a creaking sound from above them as the clamps holding the cabin began to buckle under the strain. The creak turned into a squeal as one of the four pinion points gave way. A second later, another broke, and one side of the cabin dropped completely, hanging down towards the pool of lava. Rémy lost her footing and was thrown against Thaddeus.

"We have to get out of here," she gasped, pushing away from him as he held her steady. They fought their way to the doorway and scrambled out onto the ledge.

From outside the cabin, they could see the Comte yelling frantically, waving his transmitter and trying to direct his column of metal soldiers. One of the lava flows had already cut off their route to the ladder. The soldiers were now clawing their way directly up the rock face on the other side of the cavern, making for the opposite end of the narrow walkway on which Thaddeus and Rémy stood.

Another of the cabin's clamps began to give way, the huge metal screws holding it in place scraping loudly free of the rock. Dust and chunks of stone began to pepper the ledge, falling on Thaddeus and Rémy.

"We've got to get to the engine cavern before they cut us off," Thaddeus yelled over the violent creaking of the cabin. "We can get out through the cells."

"I'm running out of air," Rémy shouted back. She pulled the canister of oxygen from her belt and shook it.

"I know – me too," Thaddeus told her. "Go!"

The metal ladder that the policeman had used to get to the upper walkway was useless, the lower rungs eaten away by the flood of lava. To get to the second cavern, they'd have to make it to another ladder that reached from the walkway to the arch that connected the two stone rooms.

"It's too far!" Rémy shouted over her shoulder. "We won't make it before they do!"

Thaddeus looked to where she pointed and saw the first of the Comte's golden men complete its scramble up the wall. In seconds the machine was on its feet and coming for them.

"We'll make it!" he promised. *We have to*, he added silently.

Below them, more and more lava was flooding out of the pool, creeping across the floor. It moved faster as the flow deepened. The heat radiating upwards was phenomenal – Thaddeus felt as if his hair might begin to smoulder at any moment.

Then, with a final deafening scream of metal, the last clamp holding up the machine behind them failed. Thaddeus spun around to see the great machine crash to the floor of the cavern. It thundered into the pool of lava, sending the boiling hot liquid splashing over the side. There was a cracking sound as the machine crushed the edge of the pool, opening further the hole the Comte had drilled. Waves of molten fire washed out in an unstoppable flood, engulfing the carcass of the machine, which had already melted into a weird, twisted version of itself.

A blood-curdling screech echoed around the cavern. Thaddeus looked down to see that the Comte had been cut off. His precious lava had surrounded him, leaving him one tiny, shrinking island of untouched stone that was disappearing fast.

Thaddeus paused, watching in horror as the Comte fumbled with his control box. Obeying their commands, some of his soldiers turned back. They tried to return to the Comte, some stepping from the rock on which they clung, some striking out directly into the molten fire. None of them could reach him – their metal bodies, so impervious in the face of human attack, melted in seconds when they came into contact with the lava. More and more of the mechanical men sank into the burning flood, until all that could be seen of them was their golden hands, reaching hopelessly for their master. Then they too were swallowed up by the lake of fire.

The Comte's island swiftly disappeared. The lava's appetite was as unquenchable as its heat, and it consumed him as he screamed, still frantically fiddling with his useless control box. He vanished, burned up by the fires of his insane ambition.

"Thaddeus!" Rémy shouted at him. "Don't stop! Hurry!"

He looked back to see that she had made it to the ladder and was climbing down. The lava below was rushing towards the archway, threatening to cut them off. Thaddeus ran to the ladder, slipping down it as quickly as he could. He narrowly avoided jumping into the river of lava as it snaked its way past the bottom rung, landing just inches from its burning flow. Rémy pulled him to safety.

"We're too late," she said, sounding breathless as she used up the last of her oxygen. "Look!"

Thaddeus saw what she meant – the lava was already sucking hotly at the stairs that led to the cells. Their escape route was cut off. They were trapped.

Out of the Mountain

"There!" Thaddeus shouted. Rémy looked up to see that he was pointing at the only high point the lava couldn't possibly reach – the ledge below the waterfall that gushed down the wall.

"Go!" she shouted, glancing down and dancing forward to avoid the lava's reach.

They clawed their way up the rough wall to reach the water. It cascaded through the ceiling and then split in two. Some of it flowed down into the man-made riverbed below, to provide the steam for the Comte's huge engine. The rest, though, disappeared back into the rock through a void, down into the pitch-black belly of the mountain.

Standing close to the dark passageway, Rémy was filled with a dread she hadn't felt even when she saw the lava break its banks. She was rarely afraid, least of all for herself. She had spent so much of her short life risking it that to put herself in peril was almost second nature to her. But here and now, when there was no option but to plunge into the icy waters before them, she felt afraid. A memory surfaced, of trying to breathe but being unable. Of darkness, and cold, cold water.

"We have to go through there," Thaddeus yelled.

"Where does it come out?" Rémy asked. "Do you even know if it does? Maybe it just disappears down into the earth. Maybe—"

"What other choice do we have?" Thaddeus shouted to her over the quaking rumble all around them. "Look!"

Rémy turned to see where he was pointing. The lava had completely filled the archway and was pouring into the lower level. They were utterly cut off – soon the only thing not burning would be the ledge on which they stood.

The last of the oxygen in her canister gave out. Rémy pulled off her mask and tossed it into the raging lava. Thaddeus did the same. They stood together, coughing as the sulphur choked them.

"We're out of time!" Thaddeus yelled. "We have to go now."

"D'accord," Rémy said, as her heart pounded in her chest. *It's only water*, she told herself silently. *You can do this. You've done it before.*

Thaddeus stepped close to her, putting his hands either side of her face and forcing her to look him in the eye instead of at the water. "It won't be like last time," he promised, as if he'd read her mind. "This isn't Abernathy's flood. I'll be right with you."

Rémy didn't push him away as she might once have done. She tried to smile instead. "You're lucky you're not stuck here with J," she shouted. "You know how he hates to take a bath."

Thaddeus smiled warmly at her. "I'll go first," he told her.

"No," she said, taking his hand. "No, we go together."

The water was icy cold after the intense heat of the cavern, but it was shallower than Rémy had expected it to be. It pulled at their feet as they clambered into the tunnel's opening. Ahead, the passageway sloped downwards into darkness, the water gushing past them with terrifying speed.

They tried to stay upright as they picked their way towards the abyss below, but it was impossible. Thaddeus was the first to slip, his drenched shoe striking slick stone. He let go of Rémy's hand and flung his arms out to steady himself, but to no avail.

"Thaddeus!" Rémy yelled as he vanished from sight. She froze for a second, shivering in the cold dark, and then took another tentative step forward.

A sudden surge of water knocked Rémy on her back, the wet stone scraping at her spine as the waterfall rushed over her. She tried to push herself up out of the torrent, but only succeeded in taking a single gasp of air before being dragged under again. The water was so cold it had numbed her instantly, and she tumbled over and over as the water cascaded down, down, down. Time and again she thought she had taken her last breath and then the water lifted her up just long enough to take another before dragging her back down again.

Then, suddenly, there was daylight. Rémy was spat out of the mountain like a mouthful of cold coffee and found herself slaloming down the great waterfall that cascaded through the three tiers of Mont Cantal. Struggling to right herself, she saw Thaddeus ahead of her. He clung to a rock, soaked, his hair plastered against his head as his eyes searched the water for her. She threw up an arm and he saw her. Their hands reached out and found each other, their fingers grasping each other tightly.

Thaddeus pulled her to the rock and she clung to it beside him, one of his arms around her as they both gulped in air. Rémy blinked the river water from her eyes and saw that Thaddeus was as bruised as she felt – one welt covered his left eye, and blood trickled from his wet hair. Worried, she reached frozen fingers up to his cheek, but he shook his head with a shaky smile.

"I'm fine," he managed, through heaving gasps. "We made it. We made it!"

Forty Two

Yannick's Remorse

They struggled out of the water. The waterfall had carried them all the way down into the deep pool at the lowest tier of the city. Overhead, the night air was smudged with smoke and the orange glow of flames. The fire from the Comte's castle had spread all the way down the mountainside, burning the city in its entirety. The place seemed completely empty – there were no screams or shouts, no sound of running feet. Mont Cantal had been abandoned, its people fleeing their burning homes and crumbling city.

Thaddeus helped Rémy to her feet. The path on which they stood led from the pool to join the main thoroughfare in and out of the mountain fortress. Here, the houses were alight, but the road was wide enough for them to walk between them unscathed. They soon realised that the fire was not their biggest problem.

"Look," said Thaddeus, nodding ahead at the great wall that encompassed the mountain's split.

The Comte's golden army stood sentry along the walls and in front of the main gates. They were in pairs, one facing in, one facing out, so there was no way to approach them without having to confront their blank faces and fierce strength.

"I hoped that the Comte's death would mean they'd stand down," said Thaddeus. "But it doesn't look that way."

Rémy scanned the wall, looking for a way out, but there was none. The grille that shut off the river was intact and, other than the main gate, there was no other exit except over the walls. "What about Claudette?" she asked. "Could she and Amélie have got out before they blocked the gate?"

Thaddeus shook his head, still catching his breath. "I don't know."

"Claudette!" Rémy shouted. "Amélie!"

None of the mechanical soldiers made any sign that they had heard. Then there came the sound of scrabbling. It echoed around the empty houses, above the crackling flames, finally resolving into footsteps.

"Claudette?" Rémy shouted again. "Is that you?"

There was no answer. Rémy glanced at Thaddeus, and for once they could both tell what the other was thinking. They began to look around, searching for something to use as a weapon. Thaddeus picked up a large rock, while Rémy grasped a chunk of fallen roof beam. The sound grew nearer. They braced themselves as it became apparent that the sound was hurrying human footsteps.

"Claudette?" Rémy shouted again.

A ragged figure appeared from between two charred houses. It most definitely was not Claudette.

"Yannick?" Rémy cried in disbelief.

He was a pitiful sight. He had lost his military jacket and the rest of his uniform was blackened and torn. His face and arms were smudged with soot and he looked exhausted.

"Please," he said in French, "please, don't hurt me, Little Bird. You're the only other two people I have seen! You must help

283

me get out. Those things… those things!" He pointed a wavering finger at the soldiers on the wall.

"What did he say?" Thaddeus asked suspiciously. "What does he want?"

"He just wants help. Speak English, Yannick," Rémy snapped at him. "Do you know any other way out of here?"

The wretched magician shook his head. "No. There is no other way. We are trapped! Either the fire will get us, or those monsters will." He brightened for a moment. "Unless you can call your airship back? Then we can escape the same way as Claudette and Amélie?"

"Wait," said Rémy. "You saw them? They got out?"

Yannick nodded. "Will it come back? For you – for us?"

Thaddeus shook his head, looking at the flames around them. "They'd be mad to. The flames are too high, too much of a risk."

Yannick sagged. "Then we're done for. It's hopeless!"

"Ach, be a man for once in your life," Rémy said scornfully. Turning to Thaddeus, she said, "We don't have to fight the whole of the Comte's army. All we need to do is get through their lines – make them leave a gap so we can get over the wall."

Thaddeus nodded. "What's your idea?"

Rémy pointed to where the stones of the arch across the river created the only features in the great wall. "We aim for those. They will be easier to climb. I will create a diversion – draw some of them away. Then you climb. Once you are high enough, I'll lose them and double back."

"No," Thaddeus said. "I can't let you use yourself as bait!"

"It's the only way," Rémy insisted. "I'm the fastest of us all – I have a chance. You two have none. You know it's true."

From his grimace, she could see that Thaddeus did know, even if he didn't like to admit it. "I don't think–"

She cut him off. "We don't have time to argue, little policeman," Rémy told him. "The lava we let loose is not going to stop. It is coming."

Thaddeus rubbed one hand over his eyes, and she knew she'd won. "All right," he said unhappily. "What do we do?"

Rémy led the way as they ran swiftly down towards the wall. The soldiers took no notice of them at first. Rémy split off from Yannick and Thaddeus, waving with her hand to indicate they should hold back. She picked up a stone and skimmed it through the air so that it glanced off the shoulder of one of the golden men. It turned, primed and ready for attack, as she quickly began to scale the archway. She got three quarters of the way up before the soldier above sensed what was happening. It reached for her in one strong movement and she started back down the wall again, scrambling quickly backwards, though careful not to go so quickly that it abandoned the chase. It followed her, and so did the second in the pair. The two mechanical sentries came down the wall, leaving a small gap in its defence.

"Go!" she shouted to Thaddeus, as she drew the two soldiers away. "I'll follow! Quickly!" They were faster now that they were on flat ground, but she was faster still. Rémy headed for the streets of burning houses, hoping to lose her metal pursuers in the tangled, smoky alleyways.

She glanced back over her shoulder to see Thaddeus and Yannick on the wall, making for the gap. For a moment her heart leapt – it looked as if they were going to make it! Then the two soldiers pursuing her stopped dead. Rémy paused, too, out of breath and wary, but they didn't attempt to catch her. Abruptly, they turned and started back to the wall, heading for their posts.

"Thaddeus," she screamed. "Yannick – look out!"

Thaddeus had gone up first and was almost at the top. Yannick was several steps below him. They both hesitated, wondering if they could reach the top and begin the scramble down the other side. The answer was no. The two golden men were back at the wall in an instant. Yannick froze where he was, fear stilling him against the wall, blocking Thaddeus' path back to the ground.

"Yannick, jump!" Rémy shouted, scared.

It was too late. One of the soldiers started climbing up the way Thaddeus and Yannick had used, cutting off their escape. The other leapt directly at the wall, launching itself several feet into the air and landing beside Yannick, clinging to the stone like a spider. Yannick screamed and tried to get away, but the soldier clamped its hand around his leg, pulling at him. The second soldier reached Yannick and began to pull at him, too.

Rémy saw Thaddeus start back down towards the fray, intending to help the magician, who was screaming fit to wake the dead. She looked around and grabbed a hunk of fallen wood, hauling it up and running forward.

"Thaddeus!" she shouted. He looked up and saw her coming. She used all her might to throw the wooden beam towards him. He caught it and swung it at Yannick's inhuman captors as Rémy searched for another weapon. Then she, too, joined the attack.

The soldiers showed absolutely no reaction to their blows. Yannick struggled feebly in their grip as Thaddeus tried again and again to free him. Then Rémy saw one of them reach for a small panel on its side. It flipped it open and pressed a button on the plate within.

Instantly, four more of the soldiers on the wall turned and began to walk towards the scuffle.

"Thaddeus," Rémy screamed. "Look! Get out of there!"

But in the act of turning to see what she meant, Thaddeus lost concentration. He wobbled, dropping the beam to catch his balance. In that moment, one of the soldiers reached out and caught hold of his leg.

"No!" Rémy shouted, as Thaddeus yelled in pain at the heavy grip on his burned skin. The sight of Thaddeus trapped and in pain opened up a well of strength she didn't know she had. Rémy hurled the chunk of wood she was holding. It hit the soldier square in the back hard enough to knock it forward against the wall. The policeman yanked his leg free.

"Jump," Rémy screamed up at him. "Don't think, just jump!"

Thaddeus did as he was told, letting go of the wall and throwing himself down towards her. He sailed over the heads of the soldiers, and landed hard in the dust below. Rémy darted forward, dragging him up before they could react. Together they stumbled away as swiftly as they could.

"Yannick," Thaddeus managed, winded.

Rémy turned back to see her childhood friend surrounded by the Comte's mechanical men. Each of them seemed to be pulling him in a different direction, like a pride of lions with a carcass. She drew her lips into a straight line and kept moving.

Friends in Need

The soldiers didn't seem interested in following them. They'd been ordered to protect the wall, and that's what they were doing. *No one in; no one out.* Thaddeus' body was smarting, both from his hard landing and from the soldier's frighteningly powerful grip. He leaned heavily on Rémy as they ran to the shelter of the smouldering houses of Mont Cantal.

"Rémy, it's no good," Thaddeus said, doubling over to catch his breath. "There's nothing more we can do."

She settled beside him against the wall, breathing hard. "So we just give up?"

"I can't see any way over that wall, can you?" he asked, as he straightened up. "Not alive, anyway."

She hesitated, and then shook her head. "*Non.* I just hate to let them – him – win."

Thaddeus smiled, and then moved to put his arm around her, pulling her close against him. "He hasn't won," the policeman reminded her. "Claudette and Amélie got away. We destroyed that awful place of his. I count that as a win."

She smiled, and then pressed her face into his shoulder, wrapping her arms around him. "You English. So easily pleased."

Thaddeus pushed his nose into her short hair as he stared at the wall of flame licking steadily towards them. "Yes, well. It looks as if I got the girl in the end. So there's nothing for me not to be pleased about, really, is there?"

Rémy lifted her head, her lips parting as if to come back with some smart answer. Thaddeus took the opportunity to kiss her instead, firmly and as if it was the only thing that mattered at that moment. Which it was.

The ground began to shake. It was only slight at first, but the tremors quickly grew until the burning houses around them began to crumble. The stones on the road shook and bounced, cracks beginning to appear in the ground as the quaking grew worse.

"What is it?" Rémy shouted over the noise.

Thaddeus looked up at the mountain. The waterfall had slowed to a trickle, exposing the mouth of the cave through which they had escaped. Steam and gouts of yellow smoke were gushing from the depths in great roiling belches. The smell of sulphur began to reach them.

He looked down at Rémy, holding her even closer even as they both trembled in the quake. "The lava," he said. "It's coming."

Another sound rose into the air. This one came from the wall, not from the mountain. At first it was indistinct, a raucous hubbub that bubbled under the grating of the quake and the roar of the flames. Thaddeus and Rémy looked out from their shelter just as a volley of large rocks shot over the wall, raining down on the golden soldiers. Most missed their targets, but some found them. One of the larger rocks even dislodged a mechanical man, hitting it so hard that it lost its footing and fell off the wall completely. There was a cheer as it disappeared from sight.

"People," Rémy said, in amazement. "It's people! But what—"

A trumpeting noise filled the air, a harsh shriek of anger that would be enough to scare the unwary into the grave.

"Marta!" Rémy shouted, astonished. "That's an elephant! It's the circus! Augustus must have made it!"

As if on cue, more people began to appear on the wall. One was pushed up by the elephant's trunk, others looked as if they had climbed, but all were ready to fight. And, as Rémy and Thaddeus watched, fight they did – but not in the way of any usual army. Silhouetted against the wall, facing off against the Comte's army, was the most unlikely fighting force Rémy had ever seen.

She saw Erik, the great Danish strongman who rarely spoke to anyone. As Rémy watched, he swung his huge barbells, left and right, yelling obscenities as he marched along the wall, crushing the Comte's soldiers. There was Augustus, yelling as he barged at one of the mechanical men, and there was Marcus, the fire-breather, belching in the blank faces of the soldiers. There were the Tumble Twins, using each other as catapults so as to rain blows on the men from above with their acrobatics. There was Angelique, the square-jawed Spanish knife-thrower, pelting one of the mechanical men with her blades hard enough to pierce it until it slumped to its knees.

It was the circus, in full attack. And it was winning.

"Come on," Thaddeus shouted, grabbing her hand. "They're giving us one more chance!"

They ran for the wall as the lava exploded out of the mountain behind them. It came like a torrent, a storm of liquid fire that devoured everything in its path. It ate up the dead waterfall, boiling the last of the water into steam and burning the riverbed to dry black ash. The heat was phenomenal, and it hit the people below like a wall. The mechanical soldiers, however, did not pause, even as the mountain itself began to split in two.

Rémy glanced back over her shoulder as she ran. Everything was collapsing, vanishing into the great and terrible crack that tore towards them like a rip in paper. There was lava everywhere. It wasn't just flowing out of the waterfall, it was bubbling up from the rents left by the quake, sucking the houses down into the mountain's crumbling, burning guts.

Still the Comte's soldiers fought on, senseless, careless for nothing but their orders. There were gaps along the wall now, but none that were breachable, or at least not for Thaddeus.

"If you can climb it, climb," Thaddeus shouted to Rémy.

"I'm not going without you," she yelled back.

"I can find another way out!"

"No!" she shouted. "I'm not going without you!"

There was a ringing thump as something struck the great gates. The blow came again and again – the circus folk were trying to force the gates open from outside. The huge wooden doors shook on their hinges, but wouldn't budge and didn't splinter.

The lava was gushing towards them now, crushing everything in its path. The sulphur in the air was choking, blinding.

"There's got to be a way out!" Rémy screamed, in sheer frustration. "There must be!"

"There is – for you!" Thaddeus told her. "Climb the wall, Rémy. Do it!"

She shook her head, the tears in her eyes caused by more than the sulphur. "No," she said, her voice dropping to a whisper. "I will not go without you. I won't."

Thaddeus pulled her towards him, wrapping himself around

her so that her head was under his chin and she was snug against him. Rémy shut her eyes and pressed her face into his chest, hearing the roar of lava roll closer and closer. She heard Thaddeus raise his voice to shout up to the circus folk on the wall.

"Go," he bellowed. "Run – the wall won't stop the lava. Get as far away as you can!"

There was a pause, and then a shout came back. It was a voice Rémy recognised. It was J.

She pushed away from Thaddeus and turned to see the airship rise above the wall as the circus folk scattered and disappeared. The policeman swore hard and waved his arms, trying to send them back.

"What are they doing?" he said. "The heat—"

"Come on," urged Rémy. The airship was hovering over the wall, letting down a rope just long enough to graze the ground.

They ran towards it. Thaddeus forced Rémy to go up first, and she did, faster than she'd ever climbed before. J and Dita stood in the open hatch, white-faced, to haul her in.

"Climb!" she yelled down to Thaddeus. "For God's sake, climb!"

J lifted away before Thaddeus had even got halfway up the rope. Rémy wrung her hands in fear as the policeman was scraped harshly against the stone, but he held on. The lava reached the last line of houses as Thaddeus' feet were dragged over the top of the wall. He had stopped climbing and was merely clinging on for dear life.

A Pause for Breath

The fear was that the lava would devour the walls of Mont Cantal and set fire to the forest outside, turning it into an inferno that would be impossible to escape. But in the end, the mountain that had appeared so impenetrable from the outside had been weakened from within by the Comte's own folly. It collapsed, folding in on itself like a house of cards and taking the remains of the city down with it. The lava reached the walls, chewing on their stones and picking off the golden men with its hot tongue, but then it, too, was sucked down into the great sinkhole of what once had been the Comte de Cantal's fearsome home.

The airship fled the flames, flying far enough to touch the edge of the forest where it met a river. Thaddeus jumped from the rope, his arms aching with the effort of holding on, his leg painful from his earlier burns. It was dawn, the pink tinge of a new day spreading out like a brilliant flag of peace.

"J," said Thaddeus, once the ship was safely down, "that was insane. But thank you. We'd be dead now, if not for you."

The boy grinned, as he and Dita stood close together on the gangplank. "Well, I wasn't just going to let you two roast now, was I? But I'm not keen to have that kind of lark again in a hurry."

Thaddeus nodded, the exertion of the past day settling on him like a shroud. He felt more tired than he ever had in his life. "You and me both, J. You and me both."

He and Rémy looked at each other, and J cleared his throat.

"Ahem," said the boy, "well, I reckon we'll go and see where the rest of the folk 'ave got to, eh, Dita?"

"Yes," said Dita, flashing them a bright grin. "We will... leave you two. Back soon, yes?"

J and Dita headed off down the path they had followed from above the trees, soon disappearing into the greenery.

"They were holding hands," Rémy murmured. "Did you notice?"

Thaddeus reached for one of hers, lifting it to his lips and kissing her fingers gently. "I suppose an experience like that makes people think about what's important," he said.

Rémy smiled, and they sat side by side, both utterly exhausted. She frowned suddenly, and dug into the pocket of her breeches. She pulled something out and dangled it from her hand – it was a thin gold chain with a pendant hanging from it.

"Your opal," Thaddeus exclaimed. "You found it!"

Rémy nodded. "Yannick did have it. He knew what it meant to me, but he took it anyway." She looked up at Thaddeus. "How could I ever have trusted him over you?"

Thaddeus smiled. "None of that matters now. Do you want me to put it on for you?"

Rémy hesitated, staring at the jewel in her palm. "What's the matter?" Thaddeus asked. "Don't you want to wear it?"

Rémy grimaced. "I do, but..."

"But what?" Thaddeus asked.

She took a breath. "It's just... the opal. I never told you, but after I nearly died – back in London, with Abernathy..."

Thaddeus took her hand, holding it tightly. "Whatever it is," he told her, "you can tell me. You know that, don't you?"

"I hear other people's thoughts," she said simply, before she lost courage, willing him to believe her. "I don't know how, or why, but... since that day, when I'm wearing it, I can tell what people are thinking."

He stared at her for another moment, and then looked down at the stone. She watched his face as he frowned in silence.

"I'm so sorry," he said.

"You're sorry?" blurted Rémy, surprised. "What have you to be sorry for?"

Thaddeus sighed. "The robberies, back in London. That night you got the ruby ring, and I came to see you – you were upset because you thought I suspected you. But you didn't just think it, did you? *I* thought it, and you heard me. And I'm sorry. I'm sorry that it ever crossed my mind."

Rémy shook her head. "I don't blame you. I don't. I didn't even then, I just..." She sighed. "Why wouldn't you have suspected me? But it made me think... it made me think that we just don't... that we just can't... that we'll never be able to..."

"Rémy, look at me," Thaddeus said, interrupting her. She did, and he smiled. "I don't think you need a mystical stone to tell what I'm thinking right now."

She didn't. He kissed her softly. Rémy reached for him, and Thaddeus pulled her against his chest. When they finally broke apart, they stayed like that, as entwined as a stone in its clasp.

"I love you," she said. "I don't know why I find that so difficult to say. But I do. I just don't know how we're ever going to work."

Thaddeus kissed her again. "We already do," he said. "We just have to remember that. No matter how complicated things seem."

There was a rustle in the woods beside the caravan. Rémy sprang out of Thaddeus' arms, spinning around, imagining an attack. But it was Amélie who stepped from the leaves, followed by Claudette. Rémy rushed to her friends, pulling them close.

"Thank you, Little Bird," Claudette said huskily. "Thanks to you, the Lost Comtesse is finally gone for good. She's dead, and I can go back to being nothing but a fortune-teller. And a pickpocket, if need be." She glanced at Thaddeus. "Sorry, Monsieur. I am too tired for anything but the truth, and I do not know how else we will make a living with the circus gone."

Thaddeus shook his head. "No need. We are a long way from England, and my desk. If I even have one any more, of course."

"What do you mean?" Rémy asked, looking up at him. "Why wouldn't you?"

"It's not important now," he said. "But I left without taking proper leave. And with Yannick... gone, I'll never recover the jewels he took. I can't imagine my name will be anything but mud back home. Not that I care," Thaddeus added. "I would have come whatever the cost."

Claudette looked from Rémy to Thaddeus, smiling. "What a good pair you make. Odd, but then who among us is not?"

Amélie left her mother's side and surprised them all by wrapping her arms around Thaddeus' waist. He crouched so that he was her height.

"Hello," he said to the little girl. "I don't think we've ever been introduced, Amélie. But I am very glad to know you."

The little girl looked at Rémy expectantly, then pointed to her neck. She wanted her to wear the opal, it was clear. Rémy opened her hand, looking at the jewel with misgiving. She had missed it, and the love that her mother had given with it, all

296

those years ago before Rémy had even had a chance to know her. But she didn't want to wear it – she didn't feel she could. Not any more.

"Claudette," she said. "I want you to have this. I think it will change your life. And Amélie's."

"What?" said Claudette, startled, as Rémy moved forward and began to fasten it around her friend's neck. "No, Rémy – I can't! I know how precious it is to you. Why would you…"

"I was told once that the opal is a talisman when given in love," Rémy said, taking Claudette's hand. "I think this will work. Shut your eyes and think of Amélie. No," she said, before Claudette had a chance to say anything. "Please, just do as I say. If it works, you'll understand."

Claudette shut her eyes. For another moment or so, the confused frown stayed on her face. Rémy watched and waited. A moment later, Claudette's eyes flew open, shocked, as she stared at her daughter. She looked at Rémy.

"What is it?" she asked. "I don't understand. How–"

Rémy shook her head. "Just listen. Amélie is talking to you."

Claudette's eyes filled with tears. "She says she wants you to know she is grateful, Thaddeus Rec," she said, smiling. "And that you are family now, just like Rémy. She's right, of course," the woman added, wiping her eyes, before taking Amélie's hand.

The little girl hugged her mother fiercely. The pair stepped away, talking properly for the first time ever. Thaddeus walked to Rémy, watching them.

"Won't you miss it? Talismans must be a rare thing," he said, taking her hand.

She smiled, squeezing his hand. "It's fine," she said. "I have a new one."

An Impossible Parting

By mid-afternoon, the circus folk were all assembled again. Thaddeus made a point to find Augustus among the crowd of performers, taking Dita along with him to translate his gratefulness. If the Circus of Secrets had not come, if they had not displayed such bravery… Thaddeus shivered at the memory of the city crumbling all around them and the blistering lava coming ever closer.

Augustus accepted Thaddeus' thanks with a warm smile and a hearty hug and began replying in French. "When one of us is in trouble," Dita translated for the clown, "we are all in trouble. He says we are all family."

Thaddeus nodded. That became even clearer as he watched them all milling about, laughing and chatting, the relief of their victory – and that they were all alive – clear on their faces. Someone started to play a guitar, then someone else began to sing, and before anyone knew what was happening, there was a party taking place right there in the forest beside the river.

Thaddeus watched Rémy, talking to Claudette, hugging Augustus, dancing with the circus children. She seemed so at home here – she *was* at home here. She had even retrieved her pack from the airship and seemed determined not to be parted from it. The sight sank something painful into the pit of his stomach: a lump of stone that was as cold as it was heavy. He had a feeling that the next time the airship took off, it would be without Rémy Brunel. For how could she leave these people, who had risked so much and lost everything but their lives?

The thought made Thaddeus feel ill because, as much as he might want to, he couldn't stay here. Neither could he return to London, at least not straight away. He knew, somehow, that for him this unexpected journey was not yet over. An image of the Comte's tattoo floated into his mind – a cutlass set with a sapphire stone.

What was it that Desai had said as he'd left? That he had to return home to India... to deal with the Sapphire Cutlass. What had the Comte meant when he'd boasted about a plan in his terrifying cavern? Whatever it was, whatever the truth that lay at the heart of the madness that had taken over both Lord Abernathy and the Comte de Cantal, Thaddeus knew he couldn't simply return to London and forget about it.

J appeared at his elbow, rosy-cheeked and cheerful. "They sure know how to party, these circus types, eh?"

Thaddeus smiled. "You could say that." He was still watching Rémy who, feeling the scrutiny of his gaze, disentangled herself from the dance and walked towards him, smiling.

J clapped his hands against his thighs as she approached. "Right then," he announced, with an air of decision. "I says we get some grub inside us, then sees about saying our goodbyes. If we take it in turns at the controls so I can get some shut-eye, we could be back at the Professor's warehouse before sun-up tomorrow. How does that sound?"

Rémy frowned, glancing at him and then away again, and this time Thaddeus' heart sank fully to his shoes. He knew then that she wasn't going to come with them. Of course she wasn't – her friends had an entire circus to rebuild, and they needed all the help they could get.

"J," he said, quietly, "slow down a little. There's no rush. Let's – let's just stay here for tonight, eh? Get our strength back."

"Yes," said Dita, "and what about me?"

J looked at her. "What about you?"

"You aren't even going to offer to take me with you? After everything I've done for you?"

"What you've done for me?" J repeated, in his best 'offended' voice. "After everything I've done for *you*, you mean! Anyway, what makes you think you'd be welcome in London?"

"Agh," Dita shouted, her hands on her hips. "After all those stories you've told me about your amazing warehouse! There's room enough for a hundred people, so it sounds! You can fit me in! Me, who has no home, and has risked her life over and over for this stupid contraption!" She nodded violently at the airship, her dark curls bobbing furiously.

"It ain't stupid!" J yelled back, incensed. "And anyway–"

"Thaddeus?" He jumped a little as Rémy spoke at his elbow. She was frowning up at him. "Can I talk to you for a moment?"

"Of course," he said, though he'd rather cut off his own ears than hear her say goodbye. He left Dita and J to thrash it out between them, and followed Rémy into the woods.

"So much has happened," she said, walking ahead of him, pulling the pack from her shoulder. "And there's something I need to show you."

Rémy turned, and Thaddeus saw that she had unwrapped the object she'd taken from her bag. It was a golden cube, carved with intricate patterns. She traced her thumb over it before looking up at him and holding it out.

"What is it?" he asked, fascinated, taking the cube and turning it over in his hands.

"It's a puzzle box. I have to solve it," she said. "And when I do... I think it will tell me how to find my brother."

Thaddeus looked up at her in surprise. "I didn't know you had a brother!"

"I didn't... I don't," Rémy said, her face a confusion of emotions. "I might not. But on the other hand, I might, and if I do, then I've got to find him, haven't I?" She bit her lip. "What if I asked you not to go back to London, Thaddeus? What if I asked you to come with me?"

"Come with you where?" Thaddeus asked. "Rémy – what do you mean? Where are you going?"

She didn't answer. Instead she stared out through the dappled forest leaves to where the airship's balloon drifted gently in the breeze.

"How far do you think the airship can fly?" she asked.

About the Author

Sharon Gosling always wanted to be a writer. She started as an entertainment journalist, writing about television series such as *Stargate* and *Battlestar Galactica*. Her first novel was published under a pen name in 2010. Sharon and her husband live in a very small cottage in a very remote village in the north of England, surrounded by sheep-dotted fells. The village has its own vampire, although Sharon hasn't met it yet. The cat might have, but he seems to have been sworn to secrecy and won't say a thing.

* * *

The author would like to thank Laura Knowles, Julie Gassman, Penny West and Abby Huff for being such great editors. Thanks also to Julia Deppe for help with Dita's German speech and to Adam for unerring support. Most of all, though, thanks to the readers!

For more exciting books from
brilliant authors, follow the fox!

www.curious-fox.com